Bello

hidden talent rediscovered

Bello is a digital-only imprint of Pan Macmillan,
established to breathe new life into previously
published, classic books.

At Bello we believe in the timeless power
of the imagination, of a good story, narrative
and entertainment, and we want to use digital
technology to ensure that many more readers
can enjoy these books into the future.

We publish in ebook and print-on-demand formats
to bring these wonderful books to new audiences.

www.panmacmillan.com/imprint-publishers/bello

Noel Streatfeild

Mary Noel Streatfeild was born in Sussex in 1895. She was one of five children born to the Anglican Bishop of Lewes and found vicarage life very restricting. During World War One, Noel and her siblings volunteered in hospital kitchens and put on plays to support war charities, which is where she discovered her talent on stage. She studied at RADA to pursue a career in the theatre and after ten years as an actress turned her attention to writing adult and children's fiction. Her experiences in the arts heavily influenced her writing, most notably her famous children's story *Ballet Shoes* which won a Carnegie Medal and was awarded an OBE in 1983. Noel Streatfeild died in 1986.

Noel Streatfeild

AUNT CLARA

First published 1952 by Collins

This edition first published 2018 by Bello
an imprint of Pan Macmillan
20 New Wharf Road, London N1 9RR
Associated companies throughout the world

www.panmacmillan.com

ISBN 978-1-5098-7679-2 PB
ISBN 978-1-5098-7680-8 EBOOK

A CIP catalogue record for this book is available from the British Library.

Typeset by Ellipsis, Glasgow

Visit www.panmacmillan.com to read more about all our books
and to buy them. You will also find features, author interviews and
news of any author events, and you can sign up for e-newsletters
so that you're always first to hear about our new releases.

AUNT CLARA

SIMON HILTON lay in bed. He felt in good humour. It was a pleasant day. It was June, his favourite month. He had done well recently on the horses. He gave a mental satisfied nod. Done remarkably well especially at Ascot. There was something to be said for being too old to attend race meetings. Taking the round he had done better since he had betted off the course. That was partly due to Henry, the fellow had a wonderful nose for smelling out winners. Thinking of Henry made Simon turn his head to look at the clock. Eight ten! No breakfast! No papers! Damn the fellow, he was late. He put a finger on the bell and held it there.

* * * * *

It was nearing eleven years since Henry, in the course of his duty as an air-raid warden, had broken into a house he believed to be empty, to look for an unexploded bomb, and had met Simon. Simon, wrapped in a brown check dressing-gown which once had fitted but, as he had aged, had become several sizes too large, was blazing with indignation. What the devil did Henry think he was doin' breakin' into a gentleman's house in the middle of the night! Henry's explanation did nothing to soothe. Wasn't there a bell? Simon didn't know what things were comin' to when a feller could break into a house on a trumped-up excuse of an unexploded bomb.

Back at his post, describing the scene to his fellow wardens, Henry had said, "Nice old gentleman though. You couldn't 'elp likin' 'im, p'or old geezer." Later he had repeated the same remarks to his post-warden and had thereupon been detailed to visit in the morning to try and discover what was happening. The house was scheduled as empty, what was the old gentleman doing there? Was he alone? Who was looking after him? Could he be persuaded to sleep in a shelter?

Henry had visited Simon, this time ringing the door-bell in a proper manner. Simon, still wearing his dressing-gown, had been grumpy and suspicious, but the genuine warmth and friendliness shining from Henry's cockney soul won him over, and with a gesture of his head he had beckoned him to follow him upstairs.

Simon rented the first and second floor of a five-story house, but all Henry saw on that first visit was the bedroom and bathroom. Henry was not tidy himself but he did think the bedroom a shocking mess. The bed was unmade but he thought nothing of that, it was more the mixture of things on the floor which bothered him. There were several dustsheets, many packing cases, some half prised open, some shut, a pile of sheets and towels, a quantity of books, some dirty plates and glasses, and oddments of clothing. Simon seemed unmoved by the muddle in which he lived. He rummaged in a cupboard, and brought out a bottle of whisky and a siphon.

"Sit down." He looked round. "Push whatever's on that chair off it. Can you see any clean glasses anywhere?"

There were no clean glasses, but Henry took the used ones to the bathroom and washed them, and while drinking whisky heard something of Simon's history.

"My man Peterson, naval reservist, wonderful fellow, did everythin' for me, gettin' on or he would have been called up before. Pity."

Later, as a second whisky mellowed him, Simon told Henry why he was inhabiting a house scheduled as evacuated.

"My eldest nephew George got me out of here. Dirty business. I hate crooked dealin's. He said to me, 'I'll run you down to stay with Father for a day or two while I look round for someone to replace Peterson.' His father, my only brother William, lives in Somerset, damn wet barrack of a place. Nothin' to do, nowhere to go, nothin' to drink, no race meetin's within miles. My brother William's failin', been failin' for years. I soon got on to George's little game, and I smelt his wife Vera's hand in the business. Thought his father needed company, been lonely since his wife died. God knows why, fussy type of woman Constance was. My niece Clara's there, of course, but she's a proper old maid, no company for William. George thought he'd landed me there for the duration. Silly chump, can't catch an old 'un that way. Two days ago I upped and came back here."

Over a third whisky Simon's original feeling of liking for Henry ripened. He liked the look of him. The sparrow-like eyes. The sturdy, though rather stunted body. The heavy thatch of nondescript hair.

"Tell me about yourself. What you doin' in that comic uniform? Why aren't you soldierin'?"

It took some time to drag Henry's story out of him, and much of it Simon only picked up in later years. The childhood in which enough to eat was a rarity, Dad's wages as a casual dock labourer being uncertain, and made more uncertain by strikes, lock-outs and patches when he tried to make easy money and was caught and sent "inside." Henry, at the age of ten had been found to suffer from a rheumatic heart, a complaint all too common amongst the children in the low-lying, damp area in which he lived. He had enjoyed the next years, first in hospital, then in a convalescent home, finally at an open-air school, and at fourteen he came out into the world with reasonable health, provided he chose a career which would not mean weight-lifting. Simon learned that in Henry's family you did not choose careers, you took on whatever was going at the time, the word "lad wanted" being the pointer. Henry did not tell Simon all the jobs he had held, it was likely he had forgotten half of them; he had worked in a tea factory, "but they was water machines and the damp was chronic." He had spent some months rag sorting, but it had made him cough; he had been errand boy to various firms. Finally he had worked as a van boy. That, Henry said, had been a smashin' job. Apart from his work on the van he had helped look after the two horses. Bit of all right that had been. Then the slump came. The firm for which Henry worked was small, so Henry was laid off. For a time he had joined the other men and boys, loafing outside the labour exchange, but it had "given him the sick," so he had "done jobs" for a chap he knew who was in the street betting line.

It was when he came to this part of his history that the friendship between Henry and old Simon began to bud. Simon had never made a bet at a street corner in his life, but as Henry told him in his flat, under-stated way, of the men and lads whose days were dead of hope, who hung about outside the labour exchange, and shoved pence squeezed out of their dole, wrapped in a scrap of paper, surreptitiously into his hand, he grew angry.

"Why shouldn't the poor devils have a bet if they wanted to? Lot of nonsense the police interferin'."

Henry, after years of police-dodging, was surprised and a little shocked.

"It's not legal, see, doin' it that way. You got to put it on proper with a bookie what knows you, or one on the course."

"But the fellers you're talkin' of wouldn't be on a book-maker's books."

"Too right they wouldn't, nor 'ave the coppers to tele-phone 'im, that's where we come in, see; but it's not legal, we'd 'ave been for it if we'd been caught."

Simon was unaccustomed to whisky for breakfast, and Henry, who was a beer drinker, unaccustomed to it at all. The effect was therefore potent. It was not long before Simon was holding out an unsteady hand, saying:

"Like you, Henry me boy. Dir' shame 'bout the bettin'. Ought to do somethin' 'bout it."

And Henry, who was almost incapable of replying at all, was murmuring:

"Said strai' away, like the p'or ole geezer."

By mid-morning both Simon and Henry were asleep, Simon sprawled on the bed, Henry in his chair, and they did not wake until the wail of the siren at sunset. Almost nothing else would have woken Henry, but by then his life was built round what he called the sireen, and its note practically would have called him back from the dead. He looked round and recalled where he was. He went to the bathroom for a quick wash and brush up, then he was fit for duty. As he was leaving the bedroom Simon sat up. He turned inflamed, angry eyes on Henry.

"You here again?"

Henry beat up the pillows; it was no good bothering with the bed, which by that time needed very considerable attention.

"Can't stop now, sir, the guns is starting up, but I'll be back later with a bit of supper for you. Where's the key?"

The next day Henry moved in. He had been working for a Kensington bookmaker when war was declared, and had lodged with a married brother in North Kensington. Turned down for the Services because of his heart he had signed on as a warden at the post nearest to his work. Officially he was still lodging with his relatives in North Kensington, actually the distance from his post made that impossible, so he boxed and coxed with a day worker, a system which even his not very fastidious code found unpleasant.

Henry came into Simon's life at a crucial moment. He had never married, but his brother William had not only married but produced five children, all of whom save one had married, and the marriages had resulted in progeny. In time most of the progeny had married and had produced between them eight great-great-nieces and nephews for Simon. As far as Simon was concerned his family could do what they liked so long as they left him alone, but that was not how his family viewed the situation. Simon was old and Simon was believed to be rich; times were hard and children expensive; Simon must be watched, guarded, cherished. When his escape from Somerset became known, and it was discovered he had returned to London, his nephew George with his wife Vera came up to London prepared to take Simon back to Somerset, if necessary by force.

Both George and Vera were busy, they had already once packed and despatched old Simon. It was asking a good deal of nephews and nieces to pack and despatch an aged uncle twice. On the journey up they reminded each other how good they were being, with the result that the nearer they got to London the more they inwardly swelled. By the time they reached London the inward swelling was coming out in expressed self-satisfaction. They were being wonderfully tolerant and splendid . . . no harm in knowing it.

"Poor old thing," said Vera, pressing Simon's doorbell, "alone in this place without a soul to look after him, and air-raids and all. He may pretend he's not glad to see us, that's his way, but really he'll be thankful."

It is annoying when you arrive bursting with good intentions to rescue one in dire straits to find the straits non-existent. George and Vera's visit was in the morning; Henry was home from night duty but not yet in bed. The previous night's raid had not affected the area looked after by Henry's post, so his uniform was free of dust and rubble, in fact, for him, Henry looked spruce. He had never seen either George or Vera before, and had no idea who they were. He behaved as he would have behaved in his own home. He opened the door about a foot, and used the resentful, upward inflected "Yes?" of his world, designed to give nothing away, discourage salesmen, and prevent those demanding money from learning there was money in the house.

George and Vera took an immediate dislike to Henry. Who was this daring to stand in that possessive manner on their uncle's doorstep? Who was daring to be there at all, upsetting their plans for rescuing a lonely, frightened old man? George explained who they were, then he pushed the door, intending that he and Vera, without discussion, should go up to Simon. Henry had been trained since birth to keep a foot behind a door when opening it, so the door did not move, but Henry's eyes had grown thoughtful. This must be the eldest nephew George, the one who had got the poor old gentleman down to that nasty damp Somerset by a trick, just to keep his old father company. Still, he was a relative and as such had a right to be let in. Unwillingly he drew away his foot and held the door open.

Henry was in no sense a valet, but he had strong views on how the elderly should be treated. You did what you could to make them comfortable. Gave them a share of anything that was going, and when possible let them have their little comforts. Simon was different in many ways from the other old persons Henry had met, but in one way he acted as he expected. Simon might talk in as independent a manner as he liked, he might have money and need no one to earn for him, but he was lonely and counted on Henry's company. He tried to disguise it but Henry was not fooled. When he came home in the mornings he might be greeted with "Damn noisy feller you are. Must you slam the front door?" But he knew from the look on Simon's face that he had been listening for the front door, and had thought up something "sarky" to say to hide his real feelings. From the day Henry moved in he had taken charge, not obtrusively, Simon would have resented that, but casually. "Don't see what we want with all this on the floor. What say I take it down the apples and pears and put it in the front room?" "One of our wardens has a trouble and strife does washin'. Reckon I'll take a bundle along to 'er when I go on duty to-night." "Where d'you keep your shavin' things? If you don't 'ave a shave soon I'll 'ire you out for Father Christmas when the time comes." "Give me the sick seein' you in that old dressin'-gown; seems a bit off wearin' that with a 'ouse full of posh suits."

Simon's bedroom, bathroom and what had been Peterson's room and had now become Henry's, were on the second floor. What Henry called the front room, the enormous stuccoed Victorian drawing-room, and the kitchen, were on the first floor. Henry never had thought much of front rooms, and Simon's shuttered, dust-sheeted sample was, he felt, no concern of his, except that it made a fine dumping ground for everything not wanted elsewhere. Henry, after night duty, had more than enough to do tidying Simon's room and the kitchen, and it seemed to him, seeing Simon appeared to be in good health, ridiculous that he did nothing to help.

"Can't peel a potato, the p'or old B," he told his fellow

wardens, "and if you ask 'im to do somethin' he doesn't 'alf give you a funny look, as if 'e was wonderin' if you'd a brick loose suggestin' such a thin'."

On the day of George's and Vera's visit, Simon, thanks to Henry, had eaten a good breakfast, and was shaved and dressed. Henry had made the bed, slightly tidied the room and lit the electric fire, and Simon was sitting beside it reading *The Times*. That there had been stormy words between himself and Henry, and that he was still bristling with annoyance, was not apparent. Henry was glad of a roof and Peterson's room, but there were limits to what he would do to pay for them. He was willing to cook breakfast, for he was fond of a good breakfast. He was willing to cook a meal about five, for he needed something to eat before he went on night duty, and he was willing to tidy up the place, but he was not willing to do the shopping. Simon must do that. Before he went to bed he gave Simon the shopping list.

"You put on your tit-for, it'll do you good to get out."

Simon, although he paid him no wages, considered Henry had taken the place of Peterson. He forgot that Peterson had used the help of a daily woman, and that in the days before the war shopping was done over the telephone, and goods delivered, so he was bitterly resentful of what he considered "damned impertinence." "Funny thing," he told himself, "when your man sends you out to do the shoppin' for him."

It was by accident that Henry discovered the way to force Simon into the shops. The newsagent that Simon had dealt with had been called up, so Simon, who loved reading the papers over his breakfast, was dependent on Henry buying them on his return from night work. He took *The Winner*,

The Sporting Life, *The Greyhound Express* and *The Times*. On Henry's third morning in the house he was early leaving his warden's post, and Simon's newsagent was not open, and the only paper on Simon's list he could buy was *The Times*. Simon was furious.

"I don't read this thing till the afternoon and you know it. How d'you think I'm goin' to lay me bets?"

Henry saw the answer in a flash.

"If I find you done the shoppin' when I get up, I'll fix it so you 'ave your papers breakfast time."

It took two more days without sporting papers before Simon gave in, and the second morning without them was the morning when George and Vera called. Simon looked at them, his eyes flinty with bad temper.

"What d'you want?"

George and Vera did not know what to answer. Their carefully-planned arguments faded as they looked at him. They could not say you can't stay here with no one to look after you when clearly someone was looking after him. George had heard before how little Simon bothered about air-raids, and knew his words on that subject included asp-like remarks on the impossibility of everyone living in safe spots, by which he meant George's cottage on the Sussex Downs, so George was unwilling to re-open that subject. He could not say the truth, which was that if he could know for certain that his uncle had made a will, leaving, as was surely right, everything of which he died possessed to his eldest nephew George, and later to George's children, he could stay in London risking death from a bomb, or indeed risk dying anywhere he fancied for all he

cared. Rather winded by the sudden transition from guard-
ian angels of the old to interfering relatives, which was what
Simon obviously considered them, George and Vera, after
making attempts to start a conversation, slunk out of the
room. Slunk was not the word either would have used, but
both knew it described their departure. But then who
wouldn't slink when, after a tiring journey, you had to try
and talk to somebody who refused to answer, in fact never
took their eyes from *The Times*.

To raise their lowered morale George and Vera looked for
Henry.

Henry was washing the breakfast things in the kitchen,
his ears alert for sounds from overhead. "Bet he wroughts
'em," he thought. "No papers and on top of that they turns
up. Can't 'elp bein' sorry for the poor old B."

George was a partner in a firm of solicitors. They were
an old firm and had a large number of elderly clients, whose
small incomes had been left in their charge. When it was
necessary to see these clients it was usually George who
saw them, with the result that he had acquired a manner
which could shift easily from gently paternal to aloof
severity, with a hint that the power of the law could, under
certain circumstances, be invoked. He used the latter tone
to Henry.

"My Uncle seems to prefer to stay in this house. It's not
wise, nor what we wish, but he is getting on and it is understandable. You have undertaken a great responsibility,
and as a family we will of course keep in constant contact
with you."

Henry might have said a great deal, but he did not

because he thought George a joke, and as he often said, he would put up with a lot for a good laugh.

"I'll do what I can for the old gen'leman, but as I s'pose 'e told you, I'm on night duty . . ."

George had a well-controlled face, but Vera's let her down. It was clear she was surprised. Henry began to enjoy himself. He thought of Simon staring sulkily at *The Times* and gave him in imagination an admiring pat on the back. "Not 'alf a comic the old pot and pan," he thought. "Keeps 'isself to 'isself and why shouldn't 'e? I bet 'e never told 'em nothin'."

George sounded as if the subject of his uncle's nights was the very subject he had come to discuss.

"A most unsatisfactory arrangement, most. Naturally something more suitable must be managed."

With large numbers of people becoming homeless nightly, Henry had already arranged with his post-warden that they would look out for a likely man to sleep in the house at night, but he was not telling George that. He said politely:

"Yes, sir," and looked expectant.

George saw the expectant look and felt he was not making headway with Henry. Henry seemed difficult to impress. He had a dangerously confident air.

"You must understand, my man, that we are a large family and fond of Mr. Hilton, and shall keep a careful eye on both his well-being and his affairs."

When George and Vera had gone Henry went whistling up the stairs to Simon.

"Proper piece of starch, isn't 'e? Didn't 'alf look at me old-fashioned. You ought to 'ave 'eard 'im!"

His imitation of George was very funny. Simon got over his bad temper and laughed until the tears ran down his cheeks.

"You haven't seen the half of it. My brother William had five children. You wait, you'll get to know them all before you're through. God help you."

Simon's prophecy came true. The war years drew Simon and Henry together. The first Christmas news came of the death of William. Simon made a joke of it.

"Gone at last, has he? Been fadin' ever since his wife died. God knows why, shockin' fussy woman Constance was."

Henry was not deceived. William's death had shaken Simon. He was his only brother, and his death brought the digging of his own grave nearer. "Looks proper rough, p'or old B," he thought, and, as a mark of sympathy on his night off, he sat up late with Simon and got drunk with him.

Two years later Peterson's ship was torpedoed. Simon was not able to bring himself to say outright to Henry "Then you're all I've got. You won't leave me, will you?" But when a week or so later in an off-hand way he remarked "Can't you get hold of a bit of paint and do up your bedroom?" Henry interpreted his meaning. The longing of a lonely old man for the feeling of permanence that the newly painted bedroom would give him, so, though Henry considered the bedroom fine as it was, he got hold of some paint and touched up the window and door. As long as the war lasted Henry was a working lodger who received his keep, there was no talk of wages. Henry discovered how Simon liked things done and became something approaching a valet, and Simon accepted a changing world, and not only stood in food queues, but learnt to understand the Food Office, and could, under pressure, wash up or prepare vegetables. Slowly a peace dream evolved. Henry's interests were horses and greyhounds, and so were Simon's. Once in a way they managed to get to a race meeting, and how they enjoyed it. It became understood that peace for them both would mean endless race meetings. At last money was discussed: Henry would earn what Peterson had earned; it was not a lot, in fact it was miserly by the new standards, but Simon added "and pickin's." Henry, who had tumbled to some of Simon's sources of income, agreed happily; he could see there would certainly be pickin's. As the war years passed Henry got to know in person or to hear of Simon's relations. There was Lady Cole. She was Alice. "Married a damned common feller, somethin' to do with the buildin' trade, got knighted for somethin' or other." There was Maurice Hilton. "Silly fool, took Holy Orders, as if a dog collar wasn't bad enough, had to marry a woman called Doris. Maurice! Doris! Idiotic!" There was Sybil. "Married a nasty bit of work called Paul Levington. Nancy type of feller, can't bear him near me. Ought to be a law preventin' that kind of feller breedin'. You'll meet his son, my great-nephew Claud, one day. Disgustin'. I'd have drowned him in a pail of water if he had been mine." The second eldest of the nephews and nieces was the one Henry had first heard of. Clara, the un-married one, who had lived with her father until his death, and been described by Simon as "a proper old maid." Henry saw more of Clara than some of the other members of the family. She was a proper old maid, and the busy sort, always wanting to do good to somebody, but she had her uses. It was she who had found out that Peterson had a mother, and without bothering the old man, had come in one day, packed his things, despatched them, and found out that Mrs. Peterson was for the time being all right for money, and added, evidently considering it a duty, that of course she would keep an eye on the situation and let her uncle know if he ought to do something. What made Clara different from the other relatives was that when she visited the house it was always to do something practical and helpful, and she never wished to see her uncle.

"No, thank you, Henry. I'm sure he doesn't want to see me. And don't tell him I came up with this moth stuff. He would think I was interfering; you and I know that carpets and curtains are unobtainable nowadays, but of course he doesn't, dear old thing."

As well as the nephews and nieces, Henry met the great-nephews and great-nieces. George and Vera's Ronnie and Rita were ordered to call on their uncle when they had leave, the one from his regiment, the other from the W.R.N.S., and their Freda was brought to see him just before she left school. Alice Cole, as instructed by her husband, tried to persuade her uncle to attend her Ann's marriage to Cyril Hind, and when he refused brought Ann and Cyril, again on her husband's instructions, to visit him. Simon had behaved reasonably well during the visit, but as the party left he had called Ann back and whispered "Don't marry him. Feller's a cad, smelt it the moment he came in." Alice's second girl, Myrtle, was already married by that time to a pilot in the Air Force. Henry did not meet her until 1944, after her Frank had been killed. Nobody could fail to pity Myrtle, who had not only sincerely loved her husband, but was very obviously carrying his child. Henry never forgot that first time he met Mrs. Brain, for it caused one of the worst outbreaks of temper from Simon that he had yet seen, and at the same time showed him a new side to his old gentleman. The burden of the angry words which poured from Simon was that it was stupid for boys and girl who married without a penny between them to have babies; but if they had them it was their own responsibility; it was no good making sheep's eyes at their relatives, expecting help. They didn't understand that money was damned tight, and though you might seem to be all right you might have got it tied up in things you couldn't sell at the present time if you wanted to.

"Proper upset 'e was," Henry told his friends at the warden's post later, "but 'e'd kick the bucket rather than say so; but I knew why 'e was creatin'; 'e'd 'ave liked to 'ave told 'er not to worry, 'e'd give 'er enough to live on comfortable, but 'e 'asn't got it, not to be sure of it. 'e surprised me straight 'e did, didn't think 'e cared what 'appened to any of 'em, especially Lady Cole's lot. Any'ow I reckon that Sir Frederick's got plenty, anyway enough to see after 'is daughter and the baby."

Henry met what he called "The Reverend Hilton" and Simon called "My damned fool nephew Maurice," his wife, Doris, and their two schoolgirl daughters, Alice and Marjorie, at the time of Ann Cole's wedding. Henry respected clergy. His father, not one given to respecting anybody, had hit him on one occasion for throwing a stone at the local Roman Catholic priest who was passing on his bicycle. "If I catch you doin' that again you won't 'alf cop it. You treat reverends proper, if you don't need 'em before, you'll need 'em for your buryin'." The warning had taken root, when clergy crossed his path Henry remembered it. It shocked him, therefore, when Maurice Hilton, supported by his wife Doris, spent the whole time they were with their uncle telling him how poorly paid the clergy were, how nothing had been done to raise their income to match the cost of living, and how hard it was to give the girls a good education. Henry had heard these things with his own ears, for they had asked for tea and he was in and out of the room all the time they were in the house. "Sniv'lin' type," he thought, "only come 'ere for what 'e can get, ought to know better seein' who 'e is."

The niece Sybil, her husband Paul Levington and his son Claud Henry only met once during the war, and then merely to open the front door for them for he was on his way to bed; but, fleeting glimpse though it was, he could tell that Simon had not exaggerated when he had described Paul as "nancy type," and as for Claud! Claud had some heart trouble, which kept him out of the Services, and so was working at one of the ministries. Henry, watching him mince up the stairs in his rather too well-tailored suit, remembered what Simon had said about putting the baby in a pail of water and laughed. "'e 'asn't 'alf got a comic lot of relatives, p'or old B."

* * * * *

Henry, climbing the stairs with the paper, heard the angry, prolonged ringing of Simon's bell. When the warden's service was disbanded he had exchanged his blue tunic for the white linen coats that had been made for Peterson. He had disliked wearing them as he considered them degrading, but clothes being rationed he had been glad of anything to wear, and after a time had become accustomed to them, and had even on Simon's behalf ordered himself some new ones. Now, as the bell rang, he took Simon's letters out of one of his pockets. "If I had any sense I'd post this lot down the pan," he thought. "No sense 'is relatives 'aven't got, upsetting the p'or old B." Then he opened Simon's door.

"'Mornin', sir. Thought I'd 'ave you creatin' but that's nothin' to what you'll do when you've 'ad a dekko at this lot." Henry put the letters in Simon's hands. "Looks like they've all wrote. Smells like a put-up job to me."

Simon scowled at the letters.

"I don't see why my post should make you ten minutes late. Not taken to readin' my letters now, have you?"

Henry neatly placed two extra pillows behind the old man's back.

"Our postman's 'ome from 'is 'oliday."

Simon's eyes gleamed.

"How's he been doin'?"

"'orrible. That chap 'e gets 'is information from has been no good lately, because the man 'e gets 'is information from, the one 'o works for a private trainer, has been away. I told the postman to pick us another smasher like that dog 'e gave us at Wimbledon."

Simon was turning over his letters, a look of disgust on his face. It was as if they exuded an unpleasant smell.

"What do they want? They're up to somethin'."

"Don't ask me, sir. You 'ave a nice read of 'em while I get your breakfast."

When Henry came back with the breakfast tray Simon was in a temper. He had never had much colour, and with age the little he had had disappeared. In repose his face had the beauty of a skeleton leaf, the bone structure gleamingly white. His few remaining hairs were the same tint as his face, but his eyes had retained their colour, and in contrast appeared, if anything, more blue than they had in his youth, as they flashed with rage or twinkled with sly amusement. Now, as he looked up at Henry, they had a frosty glint, and there was a patch of colour on each cheekbone.

"What d'you think my damn family have thought up now, Henry?"

Henry placed the bed-table over Simon's knees. It was rising five years ago that Simon had taken to his bedroom more or less permanently. A sharp attack of influenza had affected an already diseased heart. The doctor had said he doubted if the old man would be able to get about much in future. He had added sensibly that he didn't want to bully the old fellow. He had had a pretty good innings, but there was no need to make a prisoner of him, he had a right to depart in his own way. Henry must use tact to get him to stay at home as much as possible, but it was unlikely he would have the energy to do much. The doctor had been right; there was no statement from Simon, but as day followed day, ordinary convalescence from influenza slipped into semi-invalidism, and Simon left such of his affairs, which would take him out of the house, in Henry's hands. In many ways Simon seemed to enjoy life from outside, brought to him second-hand by Henry, more than he had enjoyed the dreary post-war life he had seen for himself. Henry was clever with him. It was bad for the old man to be upset, and with ingenuity almost anything could be told in such a way that he would not be upset. When something he had money in went wrong Henry often held up the news until he could couple it with something that had gone right. Even when that was not possible there was usually a funny side to make him laugh. Trouble always came from the same direction, one or other of his relations. Henry respected relations, however tiresome. Relatives were relatives, and as such had their rights. When alive, if necessary, a share of what you had, even to a bit of your home; in death regular visits to their graves and flowers. Association with Simon had taught him that he was without conscience when it came to relations. Never once, when he had the health and strength to do it, had he visited his only brother's grave. He had never sent flowers, not even a bit of holly at Christmas. It was true his relations only troubled about him because they hoped for a bit when he was gone, but that was natural; if relations had a bit he supposed you would hope for a share of it one day. What he really held against Simon's relatives was the stupid way they behaved. They ought to know the old man hated being visited without notice, yet they all did it. They all knew he hated presents, but at Christmas and on his birthday presents turned up. They all knew letters bored him, but they all wrote, and even made the great-great nephews and nieces write as soon as they could hold a pencil. To-day was the worst ever. Except for special days he never remembered them all writing by the same post. He looked anxiously at the colour on Simon's cheekbones.

"No need to excite yourself whatever they've wrote. We've got better thin's to do than worry about letters. You 'ave a look at the papers and pick us some winners, and 'ave a look what I've got for your breakfast."

Simon looked at his plate, and was pleased but was not going to admit it.

"What is it?"

"A kidney, and you eat it while it's 'ot, I 'ad to crawl to the butcher like a bloomin' snake to get it."

Simon ate a piece of kidney.

"It's about me birthday."

Henry poured out Simon's coffee.

"August. Well, we could do with a bit of cheerin' up in August. No good races and that. I reckon now we don't get away, as a month it's a bit off."

The colour flared more brightly on Simon's cheekbones. He laid down his knife and fork and searched amongst his letters and threw one to Henry.

"Read that. It's from me nephew George's wife."

Henry read the letter.

"DEAREST UNCLE SIMON,

"Your family would like to make an occasion of your eightieth birthday. August is such a difficult month that we have decided that the last Saturday in

July would be a better time and would suit everybody. George could call for you in a hire car with an experienced driver, who can help Henry carry you down. We thought a quiet family luncheon in a private room would be what you would like.

"I believe most of the family are also writing, but if you would let us know your answer we will pass it on.

"Your affectionate niece,

"VERA"

Henry put the letter back in its envelope.

"You can say no. You don't 'ave to go just because you've 'ad an invite. You'll 'ave to be a bit of a 'oly friar, can't say right out you don't want to go, but we'll think up some-thin'."

Simon was not attending to Henry, he was following a private train of thought, and the longer he followed it the angrier he grew.

"July! July! Me family want to celebrate me eightieth birthday in July! August is a difficult month! But I happened to be born in August. I'm goin' to be eighty in August, and nobody is goin' to fob me off with a party in July, because it suits 'em better than the proper day."

Henry pushed the cup and saucer nearer to Simon's hand.

"'ow you do run on. Eat your breakfast and stop creatin'. After breakfast you can write an' say you won't 'ave no party. Matter of fact you far better not, you've only been out once this year, and then you carried on alarmin' when we was gettin' you down the stairs."

Simon pointed at the rest of the letters with his fork.

"Never heard such impertinence. If I keep me birthday at all I'll keep it on the right day, and not on some fancy time picked to suit themselves by me nephews and nieces." He swallowed his last piece of kidney. "Take this plate and pass those letters here, I'll read you some of the charmin' thin's they say."

Spectacles on nose, his eyebrows rising and falling, Simon spat out:

"Here's one from me great nephew Ronnie. He says he hopes July will suit because if he can find somewhere cheap he plans to take Mrs. Ethel, Pansy and Peter to the sea. Pansy! Pansy! Damn fancy name! This is from Mrs. Brain. She says, 'I hope July will suit, because in August I am taking little Frank to Holland to see his daddy's grave.' Disgustin'! Draggin' a small boy half across Europe to look at a grave. Miss Alison and Miss Marjorie, me parson-nephew's girls, are goin' to help with the harvest in August. They say it's the only holiday they can afford. That's a nasty one meant for me." Simon tossed the letter down and picked up another. "Me great-niece Rita writes that in August she's drivin' her husband and the boy to some place I can't read in Scotland to fish. She writes: 'Fishin' is one of the few things Tim enjoys and I can't disappoint Derek.'" Simon looked at Henry. "I daresay, with a couple of false legs, fishin' is one of the few thin's Mr. Tim can manage, but you can fish at other times than August. As for young Derek bein' disappointed, that's a lot of poppycock. How long ago was it Miss Rita got married?"

Henry thought for a moment.

"It was after your influenza, but you was still in bed for

you couldn't come down and the young gentleman 'ad a shockin' time gettin' those spare legs of 'is up the apples and pears to see you. Near enough four an' a 'alf years I should say."

"That's what I thought, so unless they cheated the starter young Derek isn't four yet. Can't disappoint a child of three of his fishin'! Poppycock!"

Henry saw Simon was working himself up again. Each letter he re-read fanned his temper to a brighter flame. He laid a hand on them.

"Pack it up. No need to read 'em all again. They don't want no party in August. You won't 'ave one in July. So what? There ain't goin' to be no party and a good job too."

Simon's eyes blazed.

"Take your hand off my letters. Pass them here. You're gettin' altogether above yourself, Henry."

Simon sorted his letters, his lips pouting, while he muttered under his breath. Presently a line from a letter caught his eye.

"This is from Mrs. Hind. Whinin', miserable letter it is too. But I warned her. 'Don't marry the feller,' I said, 'he's a cad.' Smelt it the moment he came into the room. Listen to this. 'I haven't been well lately, and the doctor said I simply must get away. I could not manage much of course because of the expense, but it is by the sea for the children. I would put off my holiday because of your birthday, but I think it would be wrong for Ursula and Gordon don't have much fun since their Daddy deserted them.' If she'd written because their mother couldn't recognise a wrong-un there'd be more to it." He picked out a sheet of grey paper with the address engraved in scarlet. "This is from me great-nephew Claud. He's goin' to Spain. Never cared for Spaniards, just the sort of long-haired types he would go mincin' about with. This last letter is from me great-niece Freda. Married that fellow Basil Pickering. Breeds like a rabbit, that girl. Says she's spendin' August in Bognor, which will be nice for Poppet and Noel. She isn't feelin' well, but she doesn't think she ought to let the new little brother or sister, who is expected in the autumn, spoil their summer holiday." Simon tossed the letters to Henry. "Whatever's turnin' up in the autumn let's hope she doesn't give it a disgustin' nickname like Poppet. Poppet! That child was christened Constance after me brother William's wife. I never cared for Constance, but it's a good, plain name, and damned disrespectful to the dead turnin' it into Poppet."

Henry gathered up the letters and put them on a table out of Simon's reach and laid the sporting papers near his hand.

"Now you're through with that lot, 'ow about our bettin'?"

Simon did not hear what Henry said. An idea had come to him. A joke, a glorious turning of the tables. As he thought of it he began to shake; a rumbling laugh started in the pit of him, and rolled round until it left him in gusts and gales.

"Give me paper and pen. July indeed! I'll show 'em. Henry, we'll give a party. It'll be on me birthday and no other damn day. I'm going to invite the whole bang shootin', babies and all."

"But they can't come in August. That's why they wrote."

"I'll lay you five pounds they'll all turn up. They think

26

there's pickin's when I've gone." Another gust of laughter shook Simon. "I'm not havin' me eightieth birthday pushed around. They want a luncheon. Very well, they shall have a luncheon, but it will be in August, and it will be here."

Henry gaped at Simon.

"'ere! 'ave you gone crackers?"

"I said here and I meant here. Why not? Get one of those caterin' fellers along. Tell him to fix up the drawin'-room for a luncheon, but, mind you, I choose the menu. None of that breast of chicken, steamed fish nonsense. It's me eight-ieth birthday, and I'll do the thin' in slap-up style."

Henry saw Simon meant to give this luncheon, and when Simon decided to do something he did it. He gave him note-paper and a pen and carried the breakfast tray down to the kitchen. Over the washing up he thought of what Simon had said. Fix up the drawin'-room for a luncheon! Get in a ca-terer! This was a nice how-d'you-do, this was, and the old B was set on it. No turning his mind to other things when it was set on something. Presently he dried his hands and fumbled in the corner of the kitchen cabinet and found a key.

He had never considered the front room as part of his and Simon's home. Since that night in 1940, when he first came to the house, he had never had a real look at it. He had unlocked the door in case of incendiaries, peered in, noted the windows were shuttered and everything covered in dust-sheets, and shut the door again. When he tidied Simon's room there were things Simon was not likely to use, and for which he could not find a place, so he put them in the unused front room. As time went by rubbish collected not suited to the pig-bucket or dustbin, and that went in the front room. When Peterson was killed there were belongings Clara Hilton had not considered worth sending to his mother, which she had told Henry to throw away. Henry had thrown them in the front room. When the war finished other people found it difficult to get rid of gas masks, tin hats, stirrup pumps, sandbags and other such paraphernalia, but not Henry, to him it was merely a matter of opening the front-room door and pushing it in. As the years passed the rubbish dump in the front room became of considerable size, and the people who lived on the top floors and the caretakers who lived in the basement became inquiring and inquisitive, and asked with much meaning in their voices: "It's terrible the trouble we have with moths. Is Mr. Hilton much bothered with them too?" "I never see anybody cleaning that big drawing-room, I suppose there aren't moths in there, are there?" "I can't think why we have so many mice; are you doing anything to keep them down?" Henry had seen moths of incredible size lurching around in the air, gorged with meals eaten in the front room. He knew all about the mice, and wasted no time on them; what was the good of killing the odd one when vast colonies lived unmolested in your front room? But your moths and your mice and anything else you might have in your home were your concern, and he was allowing no busybodies to nose round interfering. He kept the door locked, and hid the key, but he had an uneasy feeling that sooner or later one or other of the tenants would say something to one of the old man's relatives. To prevent this he planned ahead. It was before Simon had become tied to his room, but already Henry was his confidant and handled certain of his affairs. Simon had made a considerable sum of money gambling, and was discussing what he would do with it, and this gave Henry his idea.

"You know what? I wouldn't buy anythin' with it. I'd pay the rent. You've enough there to pay the rent for seven years." Simon had argued. What was the point of paying rent in advance, before you were asked for it? He would thank Henry to mind his own business. Henry waited until Simon had said his say. "You never know what's comin', there's a lot of nasty types about what are tryin' to get 'old of 'ouse property. I've kep' me meat pies on 'o comes in and out, but you can't be too careful."

Henry's words had the effect on Simon that he had calculated that they would. The hint of insecurity was enough. He had given Henry the money and told him to negotiate a seven years' lease.

The landlords, who were always short of money, had received Henry's offer of seven years' rent paid in cash with rapture, and Henry came home with a present of ten pounds in his pocket, and the comfortable feeling that the nosey parkers could be as nosey as they liked, for no matter what they thought, they could do nothing, nobody could turn them out.

Since the tenants shared the staircase Henry had never risked the door of the front room being wide open, so what he had to put away he had tossed quickly through the half-open door. Now that he had to get into the room he found himself pushing his way through a jungle of rubbish. He was not helped by the fact that there was no light. Choked by dust and blinded by cobwebs he at last arrived at one of the windows, and after a lengthy fight succeeded in opening the shutters.

Not much light came through the dirt-coated window, but enough for Henry to see the state of the room in which, in two months' time, Simon intended giving his party. The walls had once been cream, the elaborate mouldings on the ceiling picked out in gold. The cream was now grey and the mouldings almost hidden under festoons of cobwebs. The curtains had been tapestry, but moths had eaten so much of the material away that what was left crumbled as Henry touched it. Under dust-sheets were a sofa and chairs that had also had tapestry covers. The moths had thrived on the material, and what they had left mice had used for nests. Signs that mice lived in the room were everywhere. It also seemed a mouse burial parlour, for there were mice skeletons about, and a decomposing mouse under the dust-sheet that covered the sofa. The electric lighting had fused, but the room had been lit by a vast chandelier. Henry had never seen a chandelier at close quarters, and was puzzled by what seemed to him a collection of dirty glass held together by cobwebs. He kicked at the carpet and found it too had fed moths, and whatever it might once have been, it was now a mass of rotting threads. There were a few good things left, tables, pictures and ornaments, that had not appealed to moths and mice, and time had not ruined, but they were tiny oases in a desert of decayed rubbish. Henry spoke out loud.

"Fix up the drawin'-room for a luncheon! Don't make me laugh!"

It was at that moment that someone rang Simon's front door bell.

* * * * *

Clara Hilton was sixty-two. She had never owned a good figure, and as she had aged she had spread. Spreading was to her something that happened, like your hair growing grey or wrinkles; it never crossed her mind that she might need stronger and better quality corsets; she had always bought the same sort of corsets and saw no reason to change her habits; the result was that sideways she was reminiscent of a cottage loaf. Clara had never been well-dressed. All her life clothes had been to her coverings, not adornments. She liked loose, comfortable things. While her mother lived she had seldom had them, for Constance Hilton had believed in an upholstered look. After her mother's death the change from the upholstered to the comfortable had been slow, for the clothes chosen by Constance had been of good quality and had taken a long time to wear out, and Clara had not been able to get rid of them, for that was waste, and waste was wrong. But at last they had worn out and comfortable clothes took their place. It puzzled strangers where Clara got her plum, maroon or grey dresses with roomy bodices, voluminous skirts and old-fashioned trimmings. They did not know that there were shops which catered for Claras, and that the old-fashioned trimmings were leavings from Constance's day, patiently sewn on by Clara because it was such waste not to use them up. Her nephews and nieces did not think Clara's clothes odd; they were part of her, just as pince-nez spectacles were part of her. Nobody else they knew wore pince-nez, and nobody else they knew wore clothes like that. That was in fact the way she ought to look, and they would have been resentful, in the way they would have resented furniture moved without permission, if she had made any alteration in her appearance.

It had been convenient for George, Alice, Maurice and Sybil that Clara had not been what they called "the marrying sort." That Clara had small opportunity to marry had she wished was not discussed. She was the eldest daughter, and as their mother was not strong somebody had to stay at home. It was very nice for her, they told Clara; it was no joke being married and bringing up babies; in her sheltered life, with nothing to do all day and servants to wait on her, she did not realise how fortunate she was. Clara, rushing about the house for things her mother had mislaid, bicycling into the village for something her father wanted, pacifying the latest cook, whom Constance had, as usual, offended by petty criticism, or busy on one of the hundred and one tiny jobs which completely filled her day, had no time to think about herself. She was doing her duty in the way she supposed God intended, and that was as far as her inner probings went.

Not that Clara's life was spent wholly in Somerset. It was an understood thing in the family that in an emergency she must be lent, and emergencies arose frequently. Maurice, struggling along with his Doris, first as curate and later parish priest, in ungetatable spots in Essex, was constantly crying out for assistance. There was no telephone in Clara's home and the telegraph boy was a common sight. The messages from Maurice had a familiar ring. "Come at once children measles." "Come at once Alison mumps." "Come at once Doris influenza." Alice did not really need Clara, for her Frederick was well off and could pay nurses when there was illness, but Frederick was not to be deprived of a right on that account. Because someone might mention nurses, Alice's telegrams gave nothing away. "Great trouble come immediately." George always wrote when help was needed, firm solicitor's letters, which permitted no hedging or excuses. "The children have whooping cough. Vera is over-tired and must rest. I shall meet your train on Wednesday. It arrives at Brighton at 6.25 precisely." Sybil cried for help down the chemist's telephone, and the chemist's boy brought the messages to Clara. Sybil's Paul was head of the advertising department of a metal firm. His taste, which was reflected in his advertisements, was for ultra-modern pictures. The rest of the family disliked Paul, and said his house with its startling colour schemes and weird pictures gave them the horrors. Clara never wondered if she liked Paul or not. Sybil had married him, he was her brother-in-law. That was that. She did not think much about the house either. It was Sybil's home, and though not what she cared for herself, presumably Sybil liked it, and that was all that mattered. Besides, she saw very little of it. Claud was a fretful child, difficult to please when he was ill, and Clara was only in the house when he was ill, so she spent most of her time in his bedroom.

When their mother died, Clara's brothers and sisters had grudgingly to admit that Clara's place was looking after her father. For years she never left Somerset. She was contented.

Her father was less demanding than her mother had been, and she was able to give time to other things. She taught in Sunday School. She was a pillar of the Women's Institute. She was the backbone of the women's branch of the British Legion. She looked after the books in the village lending library. She cleaned the church brass. She arranged and provided the flowers in the altar vases, unless the coming Sunday was an occasion, when someone who considered themselves important took over. She did all the little tiresome jobs in the parish the Vicar had no time for; leaving parish magazines, seeing the parish nurse, seeing the school mistress. Her reward, though she wanted none for she considered she was doing no more than her duty, was that nobody called her Miss Hilton, she was just Miss Clara. But that this was so, and that it was a sign of affection, escaped her, for she never thought about it.

When in 1940 George brought Simon to Somerset, he had explained to Clara that of course the old man could not be left in London without Peterson, and with air-raids every night. He had explained too that he had pretended the arrangement was only temporary as a means of getting him away, but that actually Vera had packed everything in Simon's flat, and put it under dust-sheets for the duration. Clara had asked: "But will he be happy here?" The question had infuriated George. It was past bearing when you had done more than your duty to an elderly uncle to be asked about happiness. Sharply he told Clara that he failed to see that happiness had anything to do with the matter under discussion, it was safety not happiness they were considering. Clara, who had been dealing with evacuees since the beginning of the war, had answered: "It won't work, you know. People of his sort like bombs and being uncomfortable better than being bored. You'll find he'll drift back."

When Clara had proved right about the drifting back, George blamed her. Blaming inwardly is annoying when the one blamed is ignorant that blaming is taking place. George would not have admitted it even to himself, but he was pleased when, after his father's death, it was found there was no special provision for Clara in the will. There was a pittance through a marriage settlement, but the pittance without house or furniture would not be enough. George felt Clara had received her deserts. Naturally, as he said to Vera, something must be done for her, a room in the village perhaps; he would think it over and discuss the matter with the rest of the family. In the middle of the passing of letters round the family Clara wrote to George. The postmark, he was surprised to see, was London. The heading on the paper, he was startled to read, was "The Mission House." Clara wrote as casually as though she were writing a Christmas or birthday letter. She said through the Vicar she had joined the mission. She was not being paid, but she was kept and fed, which was splendid, because it meant that with what dear father had left she was quite comfortably off. That was when George used the expression "I wash my hands of Clara." He did more than wash his own hands, he wrote suggesting a family hand washing. Clara, he pointed out, was middle-aged, it was not for ever that missions would wish to keep her. Had she waited until her family had planned for her it would have been different. In return for rent paid she could have found many little ways of saying thank you, for times were difficult and extra hands needed. But if she imagined she could give her best years to a mission and then expect charity from her family she was mistaken. They must be careful and watch the situation; it would be more than trying if, in ten or fifteen years' time, they found themselves landed with an impoverished dependant.

In spite of the family hand washing, the family continued to use Clara, for it was a habit not easily broken. She was no longer sent for in times of illness, for that meant her sleeping in the house, and sleeping in a house could sneak into a permanent arrangement. Instead she was ordered to meet trains, take children to dentists, and to shop. It was on the way back from taking Ann Hind's Ursula to the station after a visit to the dentist that Clara called on Simon. A little exhausted, for the day was hot, and Ursula had screamed at the dentist, she rang Simon's bell.

* * * * *

Henry was immensely relieved when he saw Clara. As he locked the drawing-room and scurried down the stairs, he thought with bitterness that it could only be one of the relatives who would choose a day like to-day, and he would be lucky if it wasn't that Mr. and Mrs. George. He grinned thankfully at Clara.

"Oh! It's only you, miss."

Clara looked Henry up and down.

"What has happened?"

Henry had forgotten how he must be looking. He wondered what Clara meant. His dislike of nosiness, especially nosiness from those not given to nosing, was in his voice.

"Nothin' special. What should 'ave?"

"Your clothes! Look at you. Are you spring cleaning?"

Henry examined those parts of himself that he could see, and understood Clara's surprise. He shook his coat and brushed his trousers while he considered what explanation he should give. Not easy to fox Miss Clara, she knew he wasn't the spring-cleaning sort.

"Just givin' me kitchen cupboard a turn out."

Clara, with years of mission work in south London to guide her, knew that something was going on which Henry did not intend her to know about. She respected Henry; he was in charge, there was no reason why he should tell her what made him look as if he had been travelling in a dust cart. She changed the subject.

"I have been taking my little great-niece Ursula to the dentist. Mrs. Hind's little girl, you know, and she told me that there was going to be a family party for Mr. Hilton's eightieth birthday, I understand not on his birthday but in July. I wondered what you thought about it. Is he fit for it?"

Henry jerked his head in the direction of Simon's room.

"He won't 'ave it. Created alarmin' when the letters come."

Clara was relieved. She would have tackled her family if Henry thought the party might be too much for Simon, as she tackled anything she knew to be a duty, but it would have been a difficult task if not a fruitless one.

"Oh, splendid. There's nothing to worry about then."

Henry looked at Clara's kind blue eyes gazing at him through her pince-nez. Miss Clara was no trouble-maker, she was the busy sort, but not one to run to the old gentle-man. It might be she would see a way of putting it to him that the front room was not suitable, without upsetting him. His voice took an inflection which had been much used in his home when there was trouble. It was accompanied by another upward jerk of his head, this time indicating the kitchen.

"Could you come in for a minute?"

Clara recognised the inflection. She heard it almost daily in her mission work. It meant that over the kitchen table she was to hear of disgrace, a wayward child, illness or money trouble. She always obeyed that inflection, and always hoped to help, or if that were impossible, to comfort. Without further words she followed Henry upstairs.

Henry had to put in some strenuous work before it was possible to get the door wide enough open for Clara to get into the drawing-room. While he worked he looked round. This was a nice to-do, this was. He oughtn't to have showed it to Miss Clara, not till he'd done a bit of tidying. Enough to turn anyone over seeing it like this.

Clara walked round the drawing-room. She examined the walls, she studied the woodwork, she instructed Henry to force open the shutters of the other windows to give more light, then she looked at the ceiling. Her inspection over, she said:

"No bugs. Isn't that splendid!"

Henry had grown up in a world where bugs were taken for granted, and though it was years since he had lived with them, he still thought no worse of a house for harbouring them.

"Come to think of it I 'aven't seen one since I come to the 'ouse."

Clara's years of mission work had taught her what neglect could do to a house. She had come into the drawing-room, not to criticise, but to find out for herself how bad things were, so that she knew what steps to take.

"Really this is a job for the local authority's public cleansing department." Henry gave a low, dismayed whistle, which Clara interpreted correctly. "But we won't send for them. Their coming to the house would be bound to be noticed, and there might be unpleasantness which might reach Mr. Hilton, and of course that must be avoided. I can find a team of women to clean and scrub, but what is worrying me is how to get rid of all this." She swept a gloved hand over the decayed rubbish. "Do you know any men you could trust?"

Henry's mind went back to his warden's post. There was Nobby, he was in the log business, he had a cart and he would know how to get someone to help and where to dump the stuff.

"There was a chappie was a warden with me, 'e might do it. 'e's workin' in the daytime but . . ."

Clara recognised the caution in Henry's voice. It did not mean he was doubtful if he could get the help of his warden friend, but merely that it was against his upbringing to commit himself.

"Good." Clara lowered her voice. "The best time would be when everybody's in bed, if it could be done quietly, and it would be so much easier to dispose of everything at night. It should be burned, but that is so difficult in London;

perhaps in the middle of a large bomb site it couldn't do any harm, I doubt if moths fly far."

Back in the kitchen, over a cup of tea to lay the dust, Henry and Clara discussed ways and means. Clara explained that though her little income was ample for her needs it could not be stretched to pay for Henry's warden friend or for the army of cleaners that would be needed before a caterer could be brought to see the room.

"I don't like doing things behind Mr. Hilton's back, dear old man, but if he insists, as you say he does, on this luncheon in the drawing-room in August, we must deceive him, I'm afraid. Is it possible to get him to spend a quite considerable sum of money without knowing what it is for?"

"No. 'e leaves most of 'is business to me if it means goin' to see anyone, but 'e goes through 'is books like a dose of salts. Wonderful spry 'e is for 'is age. No flies on 'im. If I was to 'old back a bit to pay for this 'ow d'you do 'e'd spot it in a minute."

Clara spoke gently but reprovingly.

"I did not mean that, Henry, and you should have known it. Taking money, even for his good, would be dishonest. I am glad to hear he still has a grasp on his affairs. I find that old people are apt to rust away and become senile, unless they use their brains."

Henry jerked his head in the direction of Simon.

"No fear of that for 'im. 'e's as bright to-day as when I first set me pies on 'im, September 1940 that was."

Clara's mind was searching for an answer to their problem.

"It will have to be part of the caterer's bill. You must find out what your warden friend will charge, and I will find out what women I can get to clean. There are some old friends who come to the mission who would do it for nothing, but I couldn't allow that, and then, of course, there will be their expenses in getting here. I think it might be as well to prepare Mr. Hilton for considerable expense."

Henry thought of Simon lying comfortably in his bed laughing his inside out at the thought of his party, while he and Miss Clara got themselves all over dirt fixing things for him. He answered with a glint in his eyes.

"You leave that to me, miss. I'll see 'e coughs up the needful."

Clara got up and dusted herself. She took a card from her bag and wrote on it.

"That's the mission telephone number. You can get me there between nine and ten any morning. Let me know when your friend will have finished removing the rubbish and I'll bring my cleaners up." Clara was turning to go when a thought struck her. "And Henry, don't tell my uncle I've been here. I don't think he would like it if he knew I was interfering in his domestic arrangements. It must be a secret between you and me."

Henry looked at Clara. Funny how different brothers and sisters could be. If any of the others had popped in and seen the front room they couldn't have waited to run to their uncle and, supposing they were doing as much to put it right as Miss Clara was doing, which they wouldn't, they couldn't have waited to tell him that either. Any chance of putting themselves forward and they weren't backward; never took an eye off the old man's little bit hoping to be in on the share-out. It was a shame Miss Clara was so simple; she'd more right than most to anything there might be when the old fellow kicked it.

"I won't say nothin' now, but when the room's spruced-up it'd be only right 'e should know. I'll tell 'im you 'elped me over the caterer and that."

Clara put on her gloves which she had taken off for the tea drinking.

"You'll do nothing of the sort. Old folk are apt to get strange ideas, and I'm afraid my uncle might think I was hoping to be remembered in his will. Dear old man, as if I cared what happens to his money; all that matters is that he should enjoy it while he's alive."

Henry thought for a moment Clara was pulling his leg. She couldn't really be as simple as that. She must know what the others were up to. Then a look at Clara and the idea melted as if it were snow. Miss Clara had said what she meant, she was good all through. Poor thing, she didn't ought to be let loose, bound to be done in the eye her sort was.

"He did ought to know. Others would tell 'im, if they took the trouble you're takin'; after all, what 'e's got 'as to go to someone."

"Nonsense, Henry. In any case I want nothing. I've more than sufficient for my needs."

Henry felt an urge to guard and protect.

"Still, if anythin's to come you did ought to 'ave your cut."

Clara could feel that Henry was trying to be helpful, so, though talking of dividing Simon's money while he was still alive was distasteful to her, she answered kindly.

"You remind me of a dear old hymn we sing nearly every week at the mission. 'Lord I hear a shower of blessing— Thou art scattering full and free—Showers the thirsty land refreshing; Let some droppings fall on me—Even me!'" Henry only knew one meaning of the word droppings and was surprised it should be mentioned in a hymn. While he was thinking this Clara added: "You understand, Henry, any help I may give is not to be mentioned. If I find it has been I shall cease to help."

* * * * *

"DEAR NIECE,

"Thank you for your letter. It was kind of you all to plan a party for the occasion of my eightieth birthday in July. I was, however, born on August the fifteenth and shall not therefore be eighty until that day. I had not thought of a celebration but since you suggest it, I have decided to give a luncheon party here, at which I hope my family will be present, including my five great-great-nephews and my three great-great-nieces. The luncheon on August 15th will be at one o'clock. You will perhaps be good enough to pass this information round the family.

Your affectionate uncle,
SIMON HILTON"

This letter, telephoned round the family, caused first anger and then dismay. As Vera read Simon's words telephones snorted as if fire-breathing dragons lived in them. "August!"

screamed Ethel. "But Ronnie's taking us to the sea. Pansy and Peter are so 'cited about it. I couldn't disappoint them. Ronnie must write to Uncle Simon and say we can't be there." "But, Aunt Vera," Ann Hind whined, "I can't change my plans now, I've not been a bit well, my nerves are all to pieces, and anyway I've promised Ursula and Gordon they're going and I couldn't disappoint them now. I do feel, as their Daddy has deserted them, their Mummie must be extra careful not to let them down." "Oh, Vera, how tiresome!" said Sybil. "We shan't be there, you know. We're going to Spain with Claudie; well, not with him exactly, because he has a friend going with him, but near him. It's all arranged." "It will be impossible for Marjorie and Alison," Maurice explained. "They've promised to help with the harvest, and I think they will consider that promise a sacred trust." Myrtle sounded grieved. "August! But, Aunt Vera, he can't have read my letter. I told him I was taking little Frank to visit his daddy's grave." "Let him hold his old party," Freda said. "I simply can't come to London in August; if he'd ever had a baby he wouldn't suggest it. Anyway, I wouldn't dream of disappointing Poppet and Noel. They're already playing sandcastles in the nursery." Rita lost her temper. "Inconsiderate old beast! I've fixed fishing and everything for Tim, and I'm not upsetting my plans for him and Derek for a selfish old man."

By the next morning second thoughts prevailed. The general home talk put the subject on a high plane. Simon was very old, and relations should be good to the very old. The telephone calls were from parents to children. George rang his three. He had not seen his uncle's will, but it was likely that, as the eldest nephew, the money would pass to him. That being so, he thought it would be a suitable gesture if they were all present at this luncheon, and there was no need to tell the rest of the family they intended to attend. Maurice came down to breakfast wearing the face his daughters recognised as the one worn after wrestling in prayer. It was not Maurice's way to make a clear statement about anything, but as the porridge was cleared off the table and fishcakes took its place, it did emerge that God had hinted that if two duties conflicted then the duty of eating lunch with an aged uncle superseded the country's need for help with the crops. God also seemed to have hinted that His advice was to Maurice and family only, and not to be passed on. Sybil had trouble with Claud. "But, Mumsie, you know how cross Freddie gets at the weest change in his plans. He'll be mad with rage if I put him off. He's been so Spanish lately, he uses castanets instead of ringing his bell. Still, I suppose I could fly back for one day, but don't yatter about it. Let's be the only ones to make the supreme sacrifice." Alice left the telephoning of her brood to her husband. Sir Frederick Cole never minced his words. "Don't be daft," he told Ann and Myrtle, "put off anything, and bring the children. I reckon you two are well in the running. A widow, and a deserted wife ought to be remembered. It's only right. And keep the fact that you and the children will be there to yourselves, no harm in out-smarting the family for once."

It was not until July that Vera remembered Clara. She was cleaning her face before getting into bed, when George whistled a bar of a hymn which brought her to mind.

"Oh, dear, I've forgotten to tell Clara about Uncle Simon's lunch. I'll write to-morrow."

George got into his bed. If Clara knew of the luncheon she was sure to come to it. She could not be going away, for she had no money. Since the frantic telephone messages after the reception of Simon's letter the luncheon had not been mentioned in an inter-family way. It was to be hoped none of the others were upsetting their plans for it. It was likely, and much to be desired, that he, Vera, their children and grandchildren would be the only guests. It would be a mistake to have Clara there.

"As she's been forgotten until now, I should leave Clara out. It might hurt her feelings if she knew it was planned in June and she did not hear of it until July."

Vera finished cleaning her face, while she considered the implications of what George had said.

"I daresay you're right, it would be an expense for her to come up and I'm sure she's nothing fit to put on, poor dear. It will be kinder not to mention it."

* * * * *

In the weeks before Simon's party Clara and Henry saw a lot of each other. The money needed for cleansing and doing up the room had, as Henry expected, been easy to acquire.

Simon, gloating at the thought of the effect of his letter, would have paid far more than Henry asked to feel his plans were going ahead.

"Here's a cheque. Take it to the bank and cash it. If there's any over after the party you can keep it. But, mind you, I want a slap-up affair; flowers, champagne, the whole boilin'."

While Clara's flock of women cleaners scrubbed and cleaned Henry and Clara conferred in the kitchen. Clara learned of the skilful way in which Nobby and his friend Sid had disposed of the rubbish.

"Proper scream it was. They comes of a night-time, after eleven, it was, and seein' we don't want anyone gettin' nosey, they leaves their boots in the 'all. I told Nobby to bring somethin' to park the stuff in, and what 'e brings is a coupl' a long wooden cases for all the world like coffins. When they was packed and 'e an' Sid was carrying the first one out, he laid a bit of pampas, what I'd put in the front room, on the top of the box, and 'e says to me, 'Where's yer manners 'enery, get yer tit-for and 'old it with your 'ead bowed; weren't you taught no proper respec' for the dead?' Laugh! Do you know, miss, Sid laughed so much that as near as possible 'e tripped at the bottom of the old apples, and if 'e 'ad it would 'ave brought Mrs. What-not up from the basement; she's a woman 'o screams at sight of a mouse, so what she'd a done at seein' a coffin creepin' by at midnight, Gawd knows."

Together Clara and Henry decided what redecorating the room required. The floor under the carpet was found to be parquet. To Henry parquet was bare boards, fancy boards but nevertheless bare. Bare boards were something to be ashamed of in any home and certainly you hid them when you had company. Clara appreciated Henry's view. Naturally he did not know parquet when he saw it, why should he? She understood exactly what drew from him "Even a bit of cheap lino would be better'n nothin'." She was sure Henry would not believe that parquet should not be covered up if she told him so. He knew she had little money, and her home was one small bedroom at the mission. He had never seen the house in Somerset in which she had been brought up, and though, with the flawless seventh sense of his class, he would know exactly to which stratum of society she belonged, that would not mean he trusted her judgment about floorings, and indeed why should he? Instead she said that now the place was clean a caterer should be asked to call, it might be he would have a suggestion to make about the floor.

Neither Henry nor Clara had the faintest idea where you found the sort of caterer required for a grand luncheon. Clara had never employed a caterer at all; parties at the mission were managed by the workers because it was cheaper, and the food supplied was of the sandwiches and buns order. Henry had attended a victory dinner of wardens and he knew a caterer had been used, but he doubted if it was the sort of catering his old gentleman had in mind.

"Soup we 'ad, miss, tasty but tinned, sausage and that with a salad, and for afters there was jellies and the like. Very nice, but I think 'e's lookin' for somethin' a bit more posh."

Clara could picture the meal, and knew that Simon was expecting something more posh.

"I'm such a silly ignorant woman, Henry, when it comes to anything grand. I ought to know who to go to; my sisters and sister-in-law would know in a minute, but . . ."

No word was spoken; both Clara and Henry accepted

that the other knew no sister nor sister-in-law could be asked to help. Clara was aware of the fuss there had been when the July party was suggested, and how it had led to this luncheon; but when Henry tried to tell her how the old man was gloating over the replies to his invitation, how he laughed every time he thought of the plans he had upset, she refused to understand. "Dear old man, of course he was upset, after all, a birthday is a birthday. I've always thought it very good of the King to allow his birthday to be kept on the wrong day." And over the family: "It was natural they should suggest July, Henry. August is the children's holiday month, isn't it? But when they knew dear old Mr. Hilton was determined to have his party on the right day I'm sure they changed their plans gladly." In spite of this talk Henry knew that Clara knew how furious the old man would be if one word were said to his family about his party; hadn't she spotted that straight away when she had told him he must not mention that she was helping?

The "but" hung in the air answered only by their eyes. Clara's eyes looked so distressed that Henry felt upset. It was a shame she should look like that after all she had done, bringing those scrubbing women along, and never a word of thanks from anybody. He would have liked to give the old gent a piece of his mind, upsetting everybody just to hand himself a good laugh. Thinking of Simon gave him an idea. He jerked his head towards his bedroom.

"'e'd know the way to go about it."

Clara considered this.

"He would, but doesn't he think we already have a caterer? I thought you had allowed him to believe it was the caterer who had sent the women to clean the place. I'm afraid, Henry, our sins have found us out. We've been deceitful, and that never pays."

Henry was by now accustomed to Clara's queer views. It was obvious the cleaning of the front room had to be done on the Q.T. and a very nice job they had made of it between them; it was downright silly to talk of deceit never paying, it had paid this time all right.

"'e does, but I reckon I could put it to him so it would sound on the level. I could let 'im think it was two jobs, 'iring tables, china and that for one, and the grub was another."

Clara sighed. It was a pity that so much had to be done behind Uncle Simon's back. It felt unpleasantly as though she and Henry were conspiring together. Of course God understood she was doing the best she could in a difficult situation, but was God restraining Henry from telling actual lies?

Henry had no difficulty with Simon. Simon had enjoyed hearing the noise made by Clara's women. It was natural the room needed turning out, it hadn't been used for years. Provided Henry reported nothing but progress he could do what he liked. He was quite happy that the contractors who were turning the drawing-room into a dining-room should not be the firm to handle the catering. He wrote a note to the secretary of his club, explaining what was in the wind and asking who were the best people to get hold of. The secretary, who had supposed Simon, if not actually dead, long past entertaining, sent the name of the most august caterers he knew.

From that moment the party took shape. The caterer looked at the drawing-room and approved it.

"Lovely bit of parquet," he said of the floor. "Nothing to touch it for entertaining. I never like a carpet, things get stamped in no matter what care is taken." He dismissed the gas stove as beneath contempt. "We shall make our own arrangements. You cannot cater for twenty-nine with this equipment." He even seemed pleased there were no curtains. "Quite unnecessary in August. I shall place flowers on the balcony." He refused to discuss food or wine with Henry. "Explain to Mr. Hilton I must see him personally."

Henry reported all this to Clara.

"Funny, 'e says the floor should be left; I didn't say anythin', no need, 'e should know we was ignorant, 'e's not usin' me gas stove, bringin' 'is own fixin's. 'e's seein' Mr. Hilton about the grub. I've warned 'im to try and keep the old gentleman's mind off shellfish, death to 'im, that is. I've told 'im there's eight children, the youngest bein' a baby. 'e says 'e'll put a special table for them, and bring girls to look after'm."

Clara was most relieved to hear how well everything was progressing. It was heart-warming to think that in spite of all difficulties the dear old man was having his party just as he wanted it.

"Splendid! I shall be here early on the 15th. I don't suppose there will be anything for me to do, but I shall be about if I'm wanted, for you'll be busy dressing Mr. Hilton, won't you?"

Henry grinned in the direction of Simon's room.

"Too right I will. If we 'ave anythin' like the trouble we 'ad the last time 'e come down, it'll be quite a mornin'."

* * * * *

Awake in the early hours of his birthday, Simon made the decision that the occasion should be honoured by his wearing morning dress. A dream decided him, for it remained with him after waking, and he was confused between it and reality. In his dream he had attended some long past festivity which called for smart dressing, and had been shocked at the slovenly appearance of some fellow guest. He awoke murmuring "Disgustin'! Fellow shouldn't have come at all if he couldn't come properly turned out." Then he preened himself, admiring his young, slim figure in its sartorial perfection. Gradually he came back to the present; he was no longer young and beautiful to look at, he was not wearing a frock coat and striped trousers, he was wearing flannel pyjamas. From there it came to him what day it was, and Simon groaned. It would be tiring, it would be boring, he never had liked his family, he couldn't imagine what had made him do such a damn stupid thing as invite them all to the house. Then the morning dress of his dream floated back to him, and he chuckled. He could see his nephew George's face when he realised he had made a gaffe, and come in the wrong togs. Some hours later, when Henry called him, he remembered his early morning decision.

"Get out me striped trousers, me frock coat, and me grey waistcoat."

Henry knew that Simon was sometimes confused, when

he woke, between the past of which he had dreamed, and the present.

"You lean forward and let me give a shake to your weepin' willows. 'appy birthday and all the best. 'ere's your papers and the post. No cards nor nothin', reckon they'll bring the presents with them."

Simon poked Henry with his first finger.

"Did you hear what I said? Get out me striped trousers, me grey waistcoat and me tail coat."

Simon's morning dress had been in poor condition in Peterson's day. It was only worn at Ascot, and a good thing too, Peterson had said, for the Lord knew how old it was. It would not have surprised him if it had been made for Mr. Hilton when he was first up at Cambridge. It had been good in its day all right, but clothes could not be expected to stay good for fifty years, especially when they had been let out to fit middle-aged expansion, and taken in to fit shrivelled old age. Peterson, because it was worn so seldom, and was therefore a nuisance to look after, had disliked the outfit and when war was declared had packed it away thinking to himself "He's never likely to wear that again, praise be." When Henry had taken over, Simon's morning suit had been an early discard into the front room. The old man never wore it, was never likely to wear it, and it cluttered up the bedroom. Now, hearing it mentioned, Henry, while placing an extra pillow at Simon's back, racked his brains to think if he had seen any part of the outfit when the rubbish was carried out. All he could remember was Nobby and Sid having a bit of fun with what once had been a grey topper. Now he came to think of it he seemed to remember he had thrown away that grey topper at the same time as the frock coat, and the rest of the fancy clobber. He supposed the moths had eaten everything except the grey topper for he couldn't remember seeing anything else. He made a face at Simon's back. "You old B," he thought, "you would create about that lot this morning seein' I've 'ad your blue suit steamed and pressed special."

To Simon he said:

"There's no striped trousers, frock coat nor grey waist-coat in this room, nor never 'as been since I been 'ere."

The battle raged. Cupboards were opened. Henry was called every name Simon could lay his tongue to. When it was proved beyond doubt no morning dress existed, Simon, his eyes sultry and his lips pursed like the lips of a small, spoilt boy, refused to accept defeat.

"I said I'd wear mornin' dress, and I'll wear mornin' dress. I don't know who is to blame, you or Peterson, but I have a feelin' it's you. Now you'll take a taxi-cab and get along to Moss Brothers and hire the thin's. You know me measurements. If you're back without the doin's I'll stop your wages."

When Henry had left on his mission Simon, thoroughly pleased with himself, lay back against his pillows. He was fond of Henry, knew in fact that he couldn't get on without the fellow, but that did not mean he could do what he liked. Laying down the law about what he should wear for his luncheon party! Who did he think he was? Why, the fellow had never had more than one suit to his name, didn't know what morning dress looked like; probably cut it up to clean the silver or some damn thing. Simon slipped for a few minutes into a doze, from which he was awoken by sounds from the catering staff, at work in the drawing-room. He listened a moment, slowly taking in what the sounds meant, who was making them and what the occasion was. He looked round his room. He ought to be dressed. Been talking about clothes to Henry only a few minutes before. Where was Henry? Gossiping with those fellows downstairs most likely, wasting time! Angrily he put his finger on his bell and kept it there.

Henry, running downstairs to get a taxi, had run into Clara. He had been thankful to see her and, watching for a taxi, had explained to her what had happened.

"What put it into 'is 'ead to think of that lot this mornin' beats me. 'e was quite 'appy with 'is blue suit yesterday."

Clara had not lived for many years with an ageing father without gaining understanding.

"It may have been a dream. Old people get mixed up, you know, and Mr. Hilton was what was known as a dandy in his younger days; I often heard my father say so."

Henry sighted a taxi.

"I shouldn't think he'll want anythin', 'e never does of a mornin', but bein' to-day with the noise and that, 'e might. If 'e does would you go up, miss, and tell 'im I'll be back with 'is clothes in a coupl'a shakes of a lamb's tail."

Clara caught Henry's arm as he was climbing into the taxi.

"What did happen to the clothes, just in case he asks me? Was it moths?"

Henry lifted his shoulders.

"I don't know, reckon it must 'a been. All I know is I put

'em in the front room, and when we comes to turn the place out there wasn't a sign of 'em."

The caterer was a competent man. He hurried to and fro supervising and directing. This luncheon was the type of business he liked, an almost free hand and no expense spared. All that was missing was that member of the household that most homes who engaged caterers possessed: the one who stood about ready at the lift of a hand to hurry forward, prepared to admire. Clara had no sooner reached the first floor than the caterer accepted her as this missing fixture. She was, for she told him so, a niece of Mr. Hilton's. She was there, for she told him so, just in case she was needed. Immediately she was needed. The balcony under the caterer's instructions had been massed with hydrangeas. He knew they looked beautiful, but he needed to hear some member of the family exclaim at their beauty, and his taste in choosing just that shade of hydrangea. Clara loved flowers, and needed no pressing to admire. They were lovely; she had planned to sit at the children's table because, she had thought, it might give their mothers a rest, and now she was so glad she had, for the children's table was laid in front of one of the windows; why, it would be almost like eating lunch in a garden! From the hydrangeas Clara was led to see the flowers being arranged for the table, and from there to the table appointments. The caterer recognised, in spite of her appearance, she knew what was what, and could appreciate that everything was being done in the best taste. He had planned a little surprise for the children's table, an arrangement of dolls sitting round a cake which had "eighty" on the top in pink sugar. Clara was charmed, but asked what the cake was made of; the eldest children were nine and six, but the others were babies, and ought not to eat anything too rich.

The caterer was leading Clara to where boxes were being unpacked in order that she should sample a small cake made of the same ingredients, when Simon's bell not only rang but pealed. Clara made a distressed sound.

"Oh, dear! That must be my uncle ringing, I didn't want him to know I was here. He might resent it. You know what old people are, they dislike being interfered with, but I must go to him for Henry is out."

Simon peered at Clara.

"Who the devil are you, ma'am?"

Clara came to the bedside.

"Your niece Clara. It's quite a while since we met. It was in 1940 when you came to stay with Father."

Nineteen forty still rankled. Simon scowled.

"Damn disgrace! George got me there on a trick."

Clara understood how he felt.

"I told him you wouldn't stay. I was afraid you'd hate the country."

Simon pushed his spectacles up his nose, the better to look at Clara.

"What are you doin' here?"

Clara spoke in the slow, comforting voice she had found soothed the old.

"Henry's fetching your clothes. He said he would be back in the shake of a lamb's tail."

Simon had already recalled where Henry was. He did not like it suggested his memory was faulty.

"I know where Henry is. I sent him. Can't think what the fellow's done with me clothes. Damned rogue, that's what he is."

"Never mind, there's plenty of time, it isn't eleven yet. What time are you expecting everybody?"

Simon frowned. What time? His letter to Vera was as clear to him as the day he wrote it. He had often thought it over, chuckling at his choice of words. He had given his orders. There could be no mistake. "The luncheon on August 15th will be at one o'clock. You will perhaps be good enough to pass this information round the family." A horrid suspicion came to him.

"Didn't Vera pass on me invitation to everybody?"

Clara saw the idea of Vera not having passed on the invitation was upsetting Simon.

"I'm sure she did. She's most particular about such things."

Simon pointed to the table he used as a desk.

"There's some letters in the drawer, bring 'em here." Clara found the letters and brought them to him. Simon, his lips pursed, muttering under his breath, went through them. "Here's Alice's, all her gang's comin'. Here's Sybil's, they're all turnin' up. Maurice is bringing his lot. Here's Vera's, they're all comin'. Funny I never noticed that." He looked up at Clara. "I never had a letter from you. Why not?"

Clara had been so busy scheming with Henry for the success of the party that she had overlooked the fact that she had only known of it through Henry. What a foolish woman she was! She should, of course, have written. It would fidget the old man if he thought some of the family did not know about his party.

"It was very rude of me I'm afraid."

Simon was following a thought.

"What did you think of the first idea?"

"The July party, you mean . . . I think a birthday should be kept on a birthday . . . don't you?"

Simon saw Clara was flustered. She looked a silly woman, and God knew she was plain, poor creature, but she seemed a damned sight pleasanter than that tiresome wife of George's. He wouldn't put it past George's wife to have got up to some jiggery-pokery.

"Did Vera give you me invitation?"

Clara was torn. Nobody should tell lies, but equally nobody should upset an old person on their eightieth birthday.

"I'm so forgetful . . . I feel sure . . . actually I knew through Henry . . ."

Simon wagged a finger at Clara.

"She didn't. Why not?" A thought came to him, a gorgeous, glowing thought, which, if true, would turn the day into a sublime joke, a joke to outdo all jokes. He tossed his letters to Clara. "Read those."

Clara read the letters. Each was an acceptance from the nieces and nephews on behalf of their children, and where there were any, of the grandchildren. Each described the sacrifice of plans that was entailed in the acceptance, and each stated how gladly the sacrifice had been made for such an occasion. Each stated how much they looked forward to lunching with their uncle and how their children were looking forward to lunching with their great-uncle, and Vera and

Alice wrote of their grandchildren's excitement at the thought of lunching with their great-great-uncle. No one mentioned the pleasure of meeting the other members of their family. Clara folded the letters.

"It's going to be a real family occasion, isn't it?"

Simon's eyes were twinkling.

"You weren't told and I know why. They haven't told each other they're comin'. They all think they're the only ones puttin' off their holidays. I shall dress as soon as Henry's back. I wouldn't miss the look on their faces when they see each other for a winnin' ticket in the Irish Sweep."

Clara put the letters back in the drawer.

"But why should there be any secrecy? It's such fun all being together."

Simon looked at Clara's rounded behind, and shook his head reprovingly at it. She was simple, this niece of his. Funny one of the family turning out so different from the rest of the batch.

"Where d'you live since your father died?"

Clara was delighted he had got away from the family. She did not like having thoughts lacking in charity, but after reading the letters she had a feeling that Uncle Simon was right, that her not being told of the party had been deliberate, and that perhaps the others were hoping that only their immediate families would be present. It was very unpleasant if it was true, for it meant they were thinking, as Henry had hinted, of the poor old man's money. She drew up a chair by the bed, and eagerly and happily described the mission and those who worked in it.

Simon listened in amazement. His life had been a full one;

he had met most types of person in his time, but never before had he bothered with a Clara. It was news to him that anybody could enjoy living the life she described. It was news to him that you could be happy when you were as poor as a rat. It was news that anybody could enjoy visiting a lot of dirty homes in back streets. It was news that anyone except a parson like Maurice actually liked going to church, psalm-singing, and all that. Yet he had to accept that Clara did like these things, for as she talked her eyes beamed at him contentedly through her pince-nez, and he could feel a glow of happiness emanating from her.

"Bless me soul!" Simon said when Clara paused for breath. "And you enjoy it! It beats me."

"Oh, but it shouldn't, Uncle Simon. I think the only really happy people are people with so much work to do they haven't a dull moment. There's a hymn we often sing at the mission which says exactly what I mean, but so much more beautifully than I can say it. 'Work, for the night is coming, Work through the morning hours, Work while the dew is sparkling, Work 'mid springing flowers; Work when the day grows brighter, Work in the glowing sun; Work, for the night is coming, When man's work is done.'"

It was during Clara's recitation of this hymn that Henry arrived home with the hired clothes.

* * * * *

It was always a slow job dressing Simon. In hired clothes, especially clothes that to Henry were fancy dress, it was, as he told Clara later, "a proper picnic." It would have been

61

more of a picnic if the old man had not been in an exceptionally mellow mood.

"You wait, Henry me boy, you'll see more sour looks than ever you saw on a race course when an outsider came home. That niece of mine, Miss Clara, hadn't been told about me party, and take that surprised look off your face, for it was you who told her about it, she told me so."

Henry passed Simon a soaped flannel.

"Give your neck a nice wash. What if I did tell 'er, it's no secret, is it?"

"Didn't know you knew Miss Clara. Extraordinary woman! "

Henry was annoyed on Clara's behalf.

"If you ask me, she's a bitta all right, she is. She comes 'ere now and again, same as they all do, but when she comes it's to do us a bitta good, not to sit up 'ere moanin' and groanin' about 'ow bad times is. As you're so nosy I don't mind tellin' you she 'eard about the party because one of the kids told 'er it was goin' to 'appen in July, and she wanted to know from me if you ought to 'ave a party."

"What's she doin' here at this time? The luncheon's not till one."

Henry did not intend to break faith with Clara, but there was no harm in the old B knowing a little of what she had done.

"Miss Clara's the busy sort. From what I can 'ear she's been runnin' after 'er relatives whenever there's illness or that for years. For all she's livin' at that mission, she's still at it, takin' the kids about, meetin' trains and that. When

62

she knows you're 'avin' this do for your birthday it come natural for 'er to pop along and lend an 'and."

Simon seemed to accept that. At intervals as he dressed he murmured "Extraordinary creature," but he asked no more questions. Now and again he shook with laughter. When Henry asked what the joke was he refused to say.

"You wait. You'll find out when the time comes."

Shaved, washed and dressed in his hired clothes, Simon looked impressive. Henry felt a creator's pride in his work. The relatives, whatever else they might say, couldn't say the old gent was not nicely kept. As a final touch he had a present for him, a pink carnation for his buttonhole. He fixed it in place and stood back to study the effect as a whole.

"You look a bitta all right, and 'ere's 'opin' you be'ave nice to go with it. Your relatives may be what we won't put a name to, but they are your relatives and as such should be respected. You don't want they should feel awkward-like because you keep laughin' about nothin' at all."

Simon examined himself in the glass and approved what he saw.

"You stop talkin' and get me chair and someone to help you take me down."

Henry looked at the clock.

"No 'urry for 'alf an hour. You don't want to be longer on your plates than you must be."

Simon rapped on the dressing-table.

"I said I'd go down now and I'm goin' down now."

Henry shrugged his shoulders.

"All right, all right, don't create; if you want to kill yourself it's not my business. And talkin' of dyin' you eat reasonable; I don't want to spend me night rushin' round with a basin."

A low, rumbling laugh shook Simon. When it was over, his eyes were still twinkling at his private joke.

"It's me birthday and I'll go downstairs when I like, and I'll eat what I like, and I'll drink what I like, and if I want to laugh and share the joke with no one, that's me business too. Now get me chair."

* * * * *

On a hot day in August when, at great inconvenience, a sacrifice has been made for an old man's birthday, it is hard when the sacrifice loses its splendour by its universality. As the family converged on Simon's front door, and the contents of cars and taxis drifted and poured out on his doorstep, voices cried, disguising their surprise with difficulty, "Fancy seeing *you*, dear" to be answered by "Fancy seeing *you*." Vera had arranged that her family should meet herself and George on the doorstep at five minutes to one. The arrangements had worked. Ronnie's old Morris, with Ethel in the back with Peter on her knee and Pansy beside her, had drawn up at the front door, Freda and Basil, with Poppet and Noel, were already on the doorstep, and Tim's Ministry of Pensions' car, driven by Rita with little Derek hanging out of the window, was turning into the street as she and George arrived. How aggravating, in fact how infuriating then, to see on the doorstep with Freda and her family, Alice, and, as far as a quick glance could gauge, all of her family. How maddening to have the door opened, not by Henry, but by Claud, who had apparently arrived a few seconds earlier together with Sybil and Paul. How it caused the soul to suffer to see walking briskly up the square Maurice and his family. Alice was not incensed but nervous. Frederick was not a man who liked his plans upset. There was not time to say much before he was involved in greetings, but he had managed, out of the corner of his mouth, to whisper "You're a damned fool, Alice, you ought to have known this would happen." Maurice was hurt. He felt God had let him down. He would pray for understanding later, but his immediate reaction to the sight of his entire family on his uncle's doorstep was a mutter in the direction of Heaven, "You promised it should be only us." Sybil's dismay at the sight of her family came from fear that Claud would be cross with her. Only too well she knew what her family and friends said about her Claudie; but the very fact that so much that was unkind was said bound her to him the more closely. He was Mumsie's boy, Mumsie understood him, Mumsie was proud of her original, amusing son. He filled all her heart, which was comforting for Paul's demands on her, though many, were not for her heart. As she was swept up Simon's stairs on a tide of family, Claud, though he said nothing in words, said clearly with his expressive brown eyes "I'm utterly furious. When I gave up going to Spain with Freddie you promised there was to be none of this family nonsense."

George, already hot, cross and out of humour, had his day further ruined by his first sight of Simon. He had come by train from Brighton and had spent the journey deviating between outbursts on the idiocy of going to London in

August, and pompous statements about giving pleasure to a dear old uncle. The least that Simon should have done in return for sacrifices, was to have looked frail, and like somebody worth upsetting your summer holidays to please; it was inconsiderate, to put it mildly, that he should not only appear in admirable physical condition, but dressed like a prize poodle in a dog show, and should greet his eldest nephew, not with the pathetic air of one getting old and glad to lean, but with a tiresome air of levity, as though the occasion was in some way funny, and no one could have looked less like one wishing to lean. It was when George saw the arrangements made for the luncheon that his day was ruined finally. A quick glance round at silver, napery, flowers and, a pride of waiters, and he had made a rough estimate of what was being spent, and it was clear it worked out at a pretty penny. What right had an uncle with a bad heart to be spending pretty pennies on his eightieth birthday? Frugality would have been fitting, so that pennies were hoarded for those who inherited.

Vera and George, though surprised to see Clara, felt, since all the family had turned up, it was as well someone had invited her for she could be of use. The rest of the family took her presence for granted and were relieved to see her. In no time she was bustling about, running children upstairs to tidy for lunch, carrying little Peter's food to the imported chef to be heated, changing the seating at the table so that Freda, whose baby was expected in two months could get out easily: "You've never had a baby, Aunt Clara, the pressure's awful"; pausing as she ran to hear complaints about journeys, heat and postponed holidays, and, though she had no time for many words, managing with understanding smiles and pats to show sympathy.

The luncheon, in spite of its excellent, if indigestible food, flowing champagne and admirable service, was enjoyed only by Simon, Maurice's girls, the children and Clara. The seating at a long narrow table had been arranged by the caterer and was correct as regards precedence. Simon was seated in the centre; on his right was Vera, on his left Alice, and the husbands were reversed so that Alice had George and Vera Frederick. Maurice, with Sybil on his right and Ann on his left, faced Simon; the rest of the family were carefully arranged so that the sprigs from the various branches were as far as possible mixed. "So much more fun for them," Clara had said to the caterer, "to sit next to relations they don't often see." The caterer had accepted this; his only quibble with Clara's plan had been her own place at the table. He had wished her to sit facing her uncle, in the seat she had given to Ann. Clara had brushed this suggestion away. "It will be nice for my niece, Mrs. Hind, to sit there, she's had rather an unhappy life . . ." Her voice had trailed away on these words, for she was not, of course, telling the caterer that Ann's husband had left her, nor, as she spoke the words, could she see why sitting opposite a great-uncle was to be nice for Ann. She came back to herself. "I want to sit at the children's table, near your beautiful hydrangeas."

What prevented gaiety at the table, or indeed much conversation, was not the seating, but that plans had been laid for certain things to be said and certain conditions drawn attention to. When it was accepted by all that the day had changed form, for all the other branches of the family unfortunately were present, wordless understandings were arrived at. Husbands, by lifted eyebrows, said to wives, "There may not be a chance in this crowd," and wives, putting their answer into their eyes, replied, "You watch out that the others don't push themselves forward." The result was the conversation sounded rather like a conversation on an ill-working telephone: a spate of words, silence, and then a sudden effort to pick up words that had been missed. As the party sat down there was a babble of talk which died as it was seen that Alice, prompted by a look from Frederick, was speaking quietly to Simon. The silence was followed by a relieved burbling, as it was seen that Alice had been drawn from Simon's ear by George, who, to attract her attention, had given her a sharp tap on the arm. Immediately Vera, in a voice which by its clipped, clear precision, reproved whisperers, said to Simon:

"We ought to have a photograph taken of you, George, Ronnie and wee Peter. It would be a unique photograph of four generations all males."

George snapped off the laboured conversation he had started with Alice to account for snatching her from Simon, and added:

"And all Hiltons."

Frederick never stood for what he called "being shoved around." He was, moreover, given to making after-dinner speeches.

"I think we must in fairness add the situation is only unique because so many fine lads have shed their blood for their country. You take my Myrtle, if her Frank . . ."

Sybil felt somebody should draw attention to Claud.

"I think it would be fun to have a photograph of all the men and boys, don't you, Uncle Simon? You've got two great nephews, Ronnie and Claud . . ."

Vera was not having her plan for a Hilton male descendants' group forgotten because Frederick had dragged Myrtle's widowhood across the trail. She spoke to Frederick, but her words were intended for the whole table.

"Even had Frank lived that would not have made little Frank a Hilton."

Simon had not spoken. He had turned his blue, twinkling eyes from speaker to speaker, with the eagerness of one watching players at a tournament. Now he silenced the table by first a low rumble, and finally a roar of laughter. Henry, who had been watching the old man from the doorway, hurried over to him. He was ashamed of him, he felt he was letting the household down roaring with laughter at nothing at all. His voice had the crossness heard in the voice of an adult whose charge has committed a solecism at a children's party.

"Is somethin' the matter, sir?" The "sir" was jerked out a little late; it would not have been there at all if the family and the waiters had not been listening.

Simon wheezed through his laughter.

"Nothin's the matter. What should be the matter? I suppose I can laugh on me birthday without askin' your permission."

Henry looked at Simon's glass.

"You didn't oughter drink that champagne."

Simon had difficulty in controlling his laughter. This was a day of days. No sooner was one glorious joke conceived than another more stupendous eclipsed it. He made a gesture to Vera.

"Mrs. Hilton here wants a photograph taken." Another rumble of laughter shook him.

Henry was disgusted and showed it.

"And very nice too, a picture should be took. I'll ask 'o should be telephoned to, and see to it right away."

As Henry hurried off on his errand a spate of chatter arose, relative asking relative what was funny in the idea of a photograph. Maurice, who had decided to be guided from above as to what, if anything, he should say to Simon about his personal affairs, felt at that moment not merely guided but almost a celestial shove. He leant over the table.

"So fortunate the birthday fell to-day, for we could get cheap day returns. They make a great difference to us clergy, for you know our stipends have not been increased, so the high cost of living . . ."

Frederick boomed across Vera.

"I think we shall all agree that though the high cost of living hits everybody, the worst hit are the housewives, especially those housewives who are left alone to struggle along without a man to support them . . ."

This produced another spate of conversation, this time on the subject of Cyril Hind, and how understandable it was that he had left Ann. Vera made another effort to hold Simon's attention. This time she kept her voice lowered, for she was drawing attention to Freda. How splendid girls were nowadays, didn't Uncle Simon think so? Such courage to have big families in spite of the difficult times.

It was not until they were all served with cold lobster, and were engrossed removing meat from shells and claws, that it was generally realised that Simon had no intention of bothering himself to talk. It was as if he were a rock against which waves of words washed, merely to sink back, leaving no impression behind. It was clear he was enjoying himself, he ate and drank with gusto, and acknowledged that he was being spoken to by turning his twinkling eyes on the speaker, but his only contribution, if it could be called a contribution, was chuckles and deep laughter. As the room grew hotter, indigestible food mixed with champagne caused gloom to descend on the elder members of the party. Eyes of wives caught eyes of husbands. "He's so aggravating," Vera's eyes said to George, "and there was so much I could have said." "Don't be angry with me," Alice's eyes pleaded with Frederick, "he won't listen to Vera either." Sybil's eyes tried to be amused as they held Claud's. "Don't blame Mumsie, Claudie." Doris did not try to catch Maurice's eyes, for though bodily he was still at the table, mentally he was on his knees wrestling, she knew the look. Slowly efforts at conversation died. It was hard work making conversation intended for, but not actually addressed to, somebody. It was especially hard since it had to be general, and general conversation had not been intended when the luncheon invitation was accepted. As the elders gave up the struggle they caught the eyes of their offspring, and made it clear that all further efforts were to come from the younger generation.

It was with thankfulness, coffee finished, that the party dispersed, waiting for the photographer. Common suffering drew the women together. Sybil murmured:

"Oh, dear, I don't know when I've been so bored."

Vera replied:

"You didn't sit next to him, dear. He did nothing but laugh, and there was nothing to laugh at."

"Poor Maurice was hurt I'm afraid," sighed Doris, "he's very sensitive."

Alice kept her thoughts about her brother Maurice's sensitivity to herself. She had received a look from Frederick which had deepened her gloom.

"Frederick feels it has been a wasted day I'm afraid. If only it hadn't been August."

Clara, hurrying by with children to be washed and brushed up before the photograph, paused to say:

"Wasn't it fun? I think it's the nicest party I was ever at."

The eyes of Vera, Alice, Doris and Sybil followed Clara's loaf-shaped figure to the door. Alice spoke for them all.

"Poor Clara. But I suppose she's happy in her own way."

An hour later when Simon, back in his room, was being divested of his hired finery, Henry said much the same thing.

"Reckon Miss Clara was the only one what 'ad a really good time, but she's easily pleased she is."

Simon chuckled.

"I made 'em come. July indeed! It's me birthday, and I had it kept on the right day. Did you see my nephew George's face? That's the damn fellow who got me to me brother's on a trick."

"I saw all their faces, proper disgusted they was and no wonder. 'old up your arms so I can get off your dicky dirt. They was proper browned off with you, sittin' at the cain and abel laughin' fit to bust yourself about nothin'."

72

Simon waited until the shirt was off, then he poked Henry with his forefinger.

"How d'you know it was about nothin'? You wait and see, me boy."

* * * * *

Simon died two weeks after his party. Excitement, lobster and champagne proved too much for his digestion. The night after the party he was very ill. Henry looked after him efficiently and kindly; to him, if you chose to be ill after a blow-out, it was your own affair; the silly old B knew he couldn't digest shellfish. The morning light showed a blue tint in Simon's cheeks and that his nostrils seemed pinched, as well he was short of breath. Henry believed it did a patient good to hear they were causing anxiety.

"You do look rough and no mistake. Now don't you move until I come back. I'm sendin' for the doctor."

The doctor with treatment and care got Simon almost to the condition he was in before his party. He told Henry that the old fellow had put paid to trips outside his bedroom, and that really, with a heart in the condition his was in, he ought not to leave his bed, which would mean, of course, nurses. He laughed when he saw Henry's reaction to this. It was all right, for the present he was not suggesting nurses. He thought the effort of getting out of bed and going to his bathroom was at the moment less likely to kill the old man than the temper into which he would fly if nurses were suggested. He must not, of course, be left alone, and he must be humoured. He was not to see people likely to irritate him.

73

The doctor held the highest opinion of Henry and this was in his voice.

"Nobody knows better than you do how to look after him. I'll drop in every day, and of course telephone at once if you see anything to worry you."

Simon was exceptionally easy to look after in the last weeks of his life. Although it had nearly killed him he was still proud of his party and could ruminate happily on it for hours, chuckling at especially pleasing memories. Now and then he shared a joke with Henry, but mostly he kept them to himself. He was as happy as a child with a first watch with the photographs when they came. He pointed out the figures to Henry.

"Look at me nephew George. Got a face on him like a judge passin' the death sentence. Look at me parson-nephew; must have had a glass of champagne and is afraid it's goin' to keep him out of Heaven. That's a very stupid-lookin' child, wonder which that is."

Henry at the luncheon had familiarised himself with the children's names and to whom they belonged.

"Reckon that's young Poppet Pickerin'. I remember Miss Clara speakin' of 'er curls."

"Poppet! No wonder she looks stupid with a name like that. She was christened Constance after me sister-in-law. I never cared for me sister-in-law, but it's damn disrespectful turnin' it into Poppet. Look at me nieces, Henry. What a collection! Mrs. Levin'ton looks the best of a bad bunch, and she had to pick that shockin' fellow for a husband." Simon tapped Vera's photograph. "It was her idea to have this picture taken." He looked up at Henry with a wicked twinkle in his eye. "I'd give a lot to be there when she sees the thin'."

Henry thought the photograph a very nice souvenir. Everybody had not come out well, but you couldn't expect that in a big group, and where the likeness was bad, as in the case of Mrs. George, who seemed to have moved, it would hand everybody a good laugh; there was one portrait nobody could speak against. His old gent looked a bit of all right.

"You've no call to come the acid, you've come out a treat."

Simon studied his portrait, and as he looked at it he began to chuckle. The chuckle grew to a roar. He spoke between gusts of laughter.

"So I have . . . I do look a treat, don't I, Henry? . . . If you looked at that you'd think it was me lookin' at you, wouldn't you . . . ?"

Later that day Henry had orders to send for the photographer, as Simon wished to see him.

"And you can keep to your kitchen while he's here, I don't want you hangin' around. You tell him it will be worth his while to come at once, I'm goin' to give him a damn fine order. I wouldn't like any of me family to miss the pleasure of lookin' at this picture."

In the last days of Simon's life Henry scarcely left the house. The doctor was most considerate; whenever he called he told him to pop out and get a breather, for he would stay with the old man for ten minutes, and one afternoon when he and Simon's solicitor were there together, he told him he could go out for an hour, he would distract the old man's attention if he asked for him. In the evenings, if he went out for a few minutes for a drink, he bribed the caretakers from downstairs to listen for Simon's bell. Often, as he looked at the telephone, he thought longingly of Clara; she would be the one to help, and glad to do it; what stopped him from ringing her up was the way Simon looked at him. The old man would never admit to being dependent on anyone, but since the night after his luncheon, when Henry had nursed him, he seemed to like to be sure he was at hand. It showed in little things: a worried glance as he left the room, a query as to where he was going, usually followed by:

"And you can leave the door open, I like to hear you workin', you lazy devil."

On the last day of his life he was in especially good form. He was in reminiscent mood and kept Henry constantly in the room.

"'member Sheila's Cottage? That was a good pick, that was. Cold weather though, that's the worst of the National. Remember that time you heard about that screwy-lookin' beast? Where were we? Kempton, was it? You couldn't get hold of me, so you put a fiver on for me with me book-maker."

Henry grinned at the memory.

"I won't forget your face in a 'urry when you opened the envelope Monday, expecting to 'ave somethin' to pay and out drops a cheque for close on fifty nicker."

In the evening once again Simon re-lived the incidents attached to his birthday luncheon. He made Henry read the letters from his family telling of the original plan for a lunch party in July, and also the letters accepting his invitation to his party in August.

"I diddled 'em, Henry. July! Damned impertinence! I noticed they all managed to turn up all right, I wonder why?" He lay chuckling as he recalled each point. George's face when he saw his morning dress. Vera's suggestion of a photograph. He was in the middle of a chuckle when he murmured, "Get out, you bastard," and fell asleep. Henry turned out the light, and tiptoed from the room.

It was a tremendous shock to Henry next morning when he came in with the papers and letters to find the old man dead. For a moment or two he could not believe what his eyes and touch told him. He whispered:

"'opped it, the old B."

Downstairs he found it difficult to telephone the doctor; he could not see the letters on the dial, for his eyes were blinded by tears. When at last he got through his voice was unsteady.

"'e's gone, doctor. I reckon it was while 'e was sleepin'. It was a beautiful end. 'Get out, you bastard,' he says to me. I reckon 'e never moved after that."

* * * * *

Simon, when fighting in South Africa against the Boers, had known a brother officer called Tom Willis, who in civilian life was a solicitor. Simon had made something of a friend of Willis, so when shortly after his return to England his father died, leaving a will, which would have meant his taking an interest in various family business concerns, he put his affairs in the hands of Willis, instructing him to find out how to liberate him from boring ties, and what could be sold to whom, in order to leave him free to lead a life of his own choosing. This Willis had done to admiration, leaving Simon with a feeling of extreme confidence in him; so, though their tastes differed widely as they grew older, and they saw little of each other as friends, any business Simon had which required legal advice went as a matter of course to Willis and Willis. Both Tom Willis's sons were killed in the 1914 war, and soon afterwards he himself died. Simon read of Tom Willis's death in *The Times*, wrote to sympathise with his widow, and attended his funeral, but since there were still Willises in the firm he retained his feeling of confidence in his solicitors.

With the passing of the years Simon had become something of a legend in the firm of Willis and Willis; nobody ever saw him and any business they transacted for him was as a rule of an unusual nature, and when he wanted advice it was frequently on matters on which advice was not asked in the ordinary way of Willis and Willis. So when in the week following Simon's birthday luncheon his secretary told young Charles Willis, a great-nephew of the original Tom, that there was a doctor on the telephone, who said he had a message from Mr. Simon Hilton, Charles picked up the receiver with interest. Charles was holding the fort in August while his father and uncles were away, for it was not a time of year when much cropped up, but after the doctor's telephone call he rang his father in St. Jean de Luz and asked, since he had never set eyes on Simon and knew little of his affairs, to be put in the picture, for Simon wished to make a will. Charles's father was not very helpful; they had advised and occasionally negotiated, but he had no knowledge of Simon's money affairs. Charles had better look carefully through the documents and letters concerning him, which went back to the beginning of the century, and he should try and get access to Simon's pass-book, for the old boy must be quite eighty and might not know exactly what he had to leave. As far as Charles's father knew there was no previous will, certainly they had never drawn one up. It was tiresome the business cropping up while he was away, Charles must do the best he could; it was to be hoped the doctor was right and the old man might last for some time yet, which would give an opportunity for either himself or one of Charles's uncles to go into the matter in September, for if, as was likely, they were appointed executors, they did not want a muddled will on their hands.

Had an elder member of the Willis firm been available when Simon made his will, there would have been remonstrances and efforts made to change certain arrangements, but they were not available and Charles was. Charles had spent the larger portion of his adult years as a commando. He liked legal work, it was in his blood, but there were times when he found it tedious. He was captivated by Simon, and Simon was captivated by Charles. Simon wanted his will enjoyed, and Charles enjoyed it. Simon did not want curbing, and Charles saw no reason to curb. The old boy might be eighty, but he was certainly of sound mind, and if his will was unusual, it was perfectly clear and would give no trouble to his executors. He listened enthralled to Simon's word pictures of his relations, while studying their likenesses in the family group, and promised to embody all Simon's instructions in the will, and to send the will to him with the least possible delay. As well he agreed to act as one of the executors. As he left he gave Simon his word that when news reached him of his death he would be responsible for seeing that letters were sent to the nephews and nieces worded as Simon wished.

Amongst Simon's wishes which Charles had been ordered to see carried out, was that the will should be formally read by Charles to the relatives after the funeral, and that everybody concerned should be given a glass of port before the reading. Never had Charles been asked to read a will to assembled relations. Port and reading a will made him feel as if he belonged to the reign of Queen Victoria; he would have liked to have hired clothes for the occasion and to have worn side-whiskers. He had only to close his eyes to hear the chuckle before the old man had said: "It's one way of usin' up the port. Put quite a bit down at one time, very nice, too, but this feller," he had pointed to the doctor, "stopped me drinkin' it years ago." Simon had evidently seen an inward vision of his family drinking port, for later he had added, "See they all drink it, even me damn parson-nephew Maurice; one glass won't keep him out of Heaven, and he'll need consolin' for not havin' been allowed to do his psalm-singin' at me funeral."

Charles looked in on Henry before the funeral, to see the port-drinking arrangements were in order. Henry was in the kitchen dusting some glasses. He had a black band round his arm and wore a black tie. To him funerals called for respect, even if you were not interested in the person who had died. Mourning should be worn, faces look solemn, and voices lowered. For Simon's funeral these things came naturally, outward display to show a sad heart. Charles saw this was how Henry felt, and exchanged a few friendly remarks about Simon and funerals before getting down to business.

"You got the port Mr. Hilton wanted served?"

Henry looked worried.

"Four bottles come yesterday. They was kep' at a wine merchant's. I didn't know where to put 'em. 'Lay 'em on their sides' was the message what come with 'em." Henry jerked his head in the direction of Simon's room and lowered his voice. "I put 'em on 'is bed. Seems disrespectful like, but the old gent wouldn't mind; fond of port 'e was, though it served him cruel."

Charles did not say what he thought about a bed as the place to lay good port, but suggested it had better be decanted before the funeral, and he and Henry went up to Simon's room. It looked noticeably empty. When Charles had seen it with Simon in the bed it had seemed a crowded room, now it was probably just as crowded, though tidier, but bleak was the word it brought to mind. Charles looked round and made a face.

"Looks a bit dim without the old boy."

Henry picked up a bottle of port.

"You've said it. I don't mind tellin' you I can't get out quick enough to please meself. It's been somethin' chronic 'ere since they took 'im to the mortuary."

Charles nodded understandingly.

"Not a bad innings though, and life goes on and all that,

you know. You wait until after they've downed this port before making any plans, and don't shake that bottle, the old boy would turn in his grave if he saw you at it."

Henry cautiously picked up another bottle.

"It's not so much missin' 'im. I know we've all got to go and 'e made a lovely end; it's all of them," Henry jerked his head towards the window. "'Course I know they're relatives, and relatives 'ave their rights, but if I 'adn't promised the doctor I'd stay till to-morrow I'd 'ave gone the day the corpse was took out, straight I would. You see I've been 'ere a long time, and though perhaps everythin' 'asn't been done as nice as some could wish, I suited 'im and no one can say different. Ever since 'e was took it's been jaw, jaw, jaw. Mr. George Hilton is a grief and pain and 'is missus is worse. You tell me nothin's to be touched nor taken from the 'ouse, but to 'ear the way they carried on you'd 'ave thought it was me 'o fixed it. They created alarmin'. 'My good fellow,' 'e calls me, and goes pokin' 'is big nose where it wasn't wanted, and she runs her finger over everythin', and when she sees it's dusty, which is only natural in London, she says nothin' but shows 'er finger to 'im with ever such a sarky look."

Charles gently picked up the other two bottles and carrying them reverently followed Henry back to the kitchen.

"I've only talked to him on the telephone. Sounds a bit of a blimp."

Henry got out four decanters.

"I've 'ad the Reverend round tryin' to make me say the old gentleman 'ad said 'e wanted 'im to take 'is funeral, which 'e never. You can't speak plain to a Reverend, but when 'e says don't I remember the old gent sayin' so, when I was bringin' the tea one day, I near as possible said you 'oly friar you, you know 'e never."

Charles looked with a pleased eye at the decanters. He saw in his mind Henry gravely pouring out port, and himself accepting a glass as he opened his papers, and increasingly felt as if he were playing the lead in a Victorian drama.

"Sandwiches! There ought to be sandwiches. I believe ham's the right thing."

Henry gave Charles a reproachful look. He had followed every instruction to the best of his ability; to be asked for ham sandwiches just before the funeral was hard.

"Nothin' wasn't said to me about sandwiches."

Charles recognised injured feelings.

"It was only a thought, forget it. Better let me decant the stuff. Two bottles will do as a start. Did all the relations turn up?"

"Lady Cole come, thinkin' the corpse was 'ere. Mrs. Levin'ton is away, so Miss Clara said."

"She been?"

"Not 'er, got plenty to do on 'er own. She telephones; very nice she was too, wanted to know 'ow I was placed, if I'd anywhere to go and that, and if there was anythin' she could do to 'elp over the funeral. She did ask if there was to be 'ymns, proper set on 'ymns she is, but I told 'er I didn't know, but that you would, sir."

"That's right. They've all been on to me. Mrs. Levington got back yesterday. I told Miss Clara that Mr. Hilton wanted a quiet funeral, and she said she quite understood. She sounds the best of the bunch."

"You've said it, sir. She's a real lady, Miss Clara is, you wouldn't know she was one of the family, straight you wouldn't."

Charles looked at his watch.

"We needn't go for five minutes. How about bracing ourselves with a glass of this before we start?"

Henry looked doubtfully at the port. To him it was a woman's drink. He liked the look of Charles, he didn't seem the nosy type.

"There's a little whisky up there. I 'aven't touched it, but no one doesn't know about it but me; what the eye can't see the 'eart can't grieve after."

Charles decanted the second bottle. He put the stopper in the decanter.

"Too true." He waited until the whisky was poured out, then he raised his glass. "Here's to the will reading. I hope the old boy gets a chance to look on, he'll enjoy himself."

Henry swallowed some of his whisky and felt slightly less depressed and therefore able to speak more easily.

"You seen the photo what was took?" Charles nodded. Henry lowered his voice. "There 'e's sittin' dolled up to the nines, lookin' out so natural it seems as if 'e was back. It's comic, but, d'you know, sir, I couldn't seem to fancy seein' it no more when 'e was gone, so I put it face down in a drawer. You see 'e needed such a lot of lookin' after, 'e needed me like."

Charles was used to cockneys; several had served under him in the commandos, through them he had learned to pick sorrow and tragedy out of totally inexpressive words. He understood that Henry was truly grieving for his old man, that his death was going to leave a gap in his life he would find hard to fill; probably he had needed the sort of attention a mother gives a child, and towards the end had been as dependent on Henry as a child on its mother. It was no wonder he felt cut up. He opened his cigarette case for offering a cigarette was an expression of sympathy Henry would recognise.

"Liked the old boy myself only time I saw him. Which reminds me, after you've given the relatives their port you are to stay in the drawing-room while I'm reading the will and you're to drink a glass of port yourself."

"Me, sir! They won't like that, sir, especially Mr. George 'ilton won't."

"I couldn't care less what any of them like." Charles raised his glass towards Simon's room. "His instructions; though, mind you, if you can get away with having a drop of this instead of port I shouldn't think he'd mind." He looked at his watch. "Drink up. We shan't half get our ears pinned back if we're late for the funeral."

George, Alice, Maurice, and Sybil, with wife or husband, and Clara on her own, obeyed Simon's summons to attend his funeral and will reading. Clara excepted, they were out of humour. George, Vera, the Coles, and the Levingtons considered it inconsiderate of their uncle to have died when he did. Plans had been upset once to attend that ghastly birthday luncheon, and little less than two weeks later they were upset again. Maurice was put out—and a put-out Maurice meant a put-out Doris—not by upset plans due to tactless timing of dying, but by upset feelings caused by the tactlessness of the one who had died in not making the right requests. When a family owned a parson it was customary to ask him to take part in services which concerned the family; it was, thinking charitably, thoughtless to put it mildly, not to have done so. It was especially hurtful when the only parson in the family was poor, and because he was poor apt to be slighted by brothers and sisters and brothers-in-law and sisters-in-law.

Before the funeral there had been partial solace for inconvenience caused by an early September funeral, in the knowledge of the letter each had received from Willis and Willis. A straightforward letter stating that it had been the special request of the late Simon Hilton that *they* should be present when the will was read. It was tiresome and very like old Uncle Simon to wish his will to be read; why could not the contents be passed on by his solicitors by letter in the ordinary way? Still, it was satisfactory to know that Uncle Simon had especially asked for *their* presence. It was only after the funeral when, walking towards motor cars, a little conversation of a quiet kind not being out of place, that the bad news filtered through the family that everybody had received the letter; it was far from unique, in fact it might be described as stock.

George did not mention the subject to Vera until they were in the privacy of their Austin car. Vera drove, so he was able to give his full attention to gloomy thoughts, which he passed on to Vera. He did not like the look of things at all. Everybody had received the same letter, even poor old Clara. Had Vera had a look at that young man who was representing Willis and Willis? He knew the type, come back from the war thinking he could teach his grandmother to suck eggs. Extraordinary that a firm of the class of Willis and Willis should send a young jackanapes like that to represent them. It looked to him as if the old man had left a stupid will, a bit all round perhaps, nonsense in these times, with the death duties as they were it meant there would be nothing for anybody. Vera, at this point, saw the Coles' chauffeur-driven Bentley in her mirror. The road was crowded and she had to give her attention to driving, but she could not look at that rich glossiness behind her in silence. She said bitterly it would be a real miscarriage of justice if any of Uncle Simon's money went to Alice, Frederick was rich as Croesus. George ought to have heard the way Alice, at the luncheon, had tried to draw Uncle Simon's attention to Ann and Myrtle, as if Frederick wasn't more than able to do anything for them that needed doing. It was to be hoped, if the money was split up, Uncle Simon had remembered how many descendants he had. It would be too unfair if he had overlooked the fact that Alice and Frederick had only three grandchildren while they, with far less money in the family, had five.

Alice, out of the corner of her eye, saw Frederick's face and wilted. At some time he had got it into his head that she had told him she expected to come into Uncle Simon's money, or at any rate the greater part of it. She was sure she had never made so definite a statement, and if she had it had been made in a moment of fright, and was meant to placate temporarily, not to be remembered and quoted. When she had received her letter from Willis and Willis, forwarded to the hotel in Torquay where they were finishing their holiday, she had shown it to Frederick with pride and thankfulness. Torquay was not suiting Frederick, and he blamed her for having chosen it; the letter, with the news it clearly hinted at, was just the tonic he needed. It had proved a tonic, Frederick's mood had in a moment changed from morose to hearty. He had interviewed the hotel manager and browbeaten him into allowing him to cancel their rooms, which were booked for another two weeks, without payment, and uplifted by this feat, he had, on returning to the bedroom where Alice was stooping over a suitcase she was packing, pinched her behind, a sign of jollity and affection she had not been given for years. His mood of gaiety had continued until, the body of Uncle Simon finally disposed of, he had spoken to Sybil as they walked to the cemetery gates. Alice had simultaneously spoken to Paul. Desperately she turned over words which might soften, but nothing came to her mind. It was Frederick who spoke the only words spoken on the drive to the will reading.

"If there's been any monkey business I'll have something to say. You told me it was as good as promised. Nobody is going to double-cross me, I know what's right, and don't make things worse by opening your big mouth."

Maurice, Doris and Clara travelled to and from the funeral in a very old Rolls Royce belonging to the undertakers. Henry drove to the funeral with them, sitting in front beside the driver, on the return journey he was given a lift by Charles. Driving to the funeral Maurice's eyes were shut and his lips moved. Clara, seeing this, had addressed herself to Doris: how lucky it was it was such a lovely day for dear old Uncle Simon's funeral; shocked signals at Maurice from Doris silenced her. Clara would not, in the ordinary way, have stopped talking because her brother appeared to be praying, she was always praying herself and knew there was no need for people to keep quiet while you talked to God, but she was glad not to make conversation. It had worried her that there were to be no hymns during the funeral service. She had to accept that Simon had said he would like a simple service, and she felt that might be because no one had suggested hymns to him. There was something very comforting about the hymns they sang at the mission; there was nothing sad about the dear old man dying, he was eighty and his time had come, but she would have liked to hear at least one of the old favourites sung, it was like waving good-bye to a friend. To make up for what would not happen at the service Clara sang, in her head, hymns all the way to the cemetery. To concentrate she too closed her eyes, and though she did not know it, her lips also moved. This was observed by Doris; admittedly poor old Clara lived in a mission, but that was not an excuse for imitating Maurice; if you were in the presence of a parson, even if he were your brother, you should leave any praying that required doing to him; amateurs did not perform when professionals were present. They were nearing the cemetery when Clara, carried away by a hymn, sung out loud "When we see a precious blossom, That we tended with such care, Rudely taken from our bosom . . ."

The sound drew Maurice from wrestling in prayer. He had started the drive by praying for Uncle Simon, but soon he was stating his own case. "If only I had been asked to take the service. I don't mind for myself, but . . ." He was not making himself clear, so was glad of an excuse to stop praying. He opened his eyes and gazed at Clara, while Doris, incensed that a mere sister had power to distract a parson from his orisons when so often a wife had not, said "Clara!" in an unmistakable tone, and backed up the tone by a nudge from her elbow. Clara laughed.

"Did I sing out loud? What a silly old thing I am! But, you know, it's a lovely hymn. I wish we could have sung it at the funeral."

The words Clara had sung, though new to him, were repeating in Maurice's head. He cleared his throat.

"Many of the old hymns are beautiful, but I scarcely think that one applicable to Uncle Simon. Do you?"

Clara sang the lines again.

"Oh yes, Maurice. I do. After all, though he was old to us, I expect he's a tender blossom to God."

Maurice, first giving Clara a look sadly lacking in the Christian spirit, returned hurriedly to his prayers. Doris quivered visibly, hoping thereby to show Clara she had offended, for if things like that were to be said at all Maurice was the one to say them. Clara, quite unconscious she was responsible for an unchristian look or quiver, returned to her mental hymn-singing, and the rest of the journey passed in silence. Because of the silent outward journey there was no mention of the will reading, and it came as a complete shock to Maurice and Doris when, as they drove away from the cemetery after the funeral, Clara said:

"I suppose we must all hear Uncle Simon's will read, as he specially asked us to, but I've such a lot to do at the mission . . ."

"Us!" exclaimed Doris.

Maurice could not believe he had heard aright. During the funeral he had come, he thought, to an agreement with God that he would not grumble any more about the apparent slight, for after all joy was coming in the morning, or rather after the funeral. The days of being the poorest member of the family were over. God was looking after his own, or rather Uncle Simon, prompted by God, had done so.

"Us? Why do you say 'us,' Clara?"

"It is us. We've all had the same letter, you know."

Maurice tried not to let his face show his thoughts. Us. That meant everything was to be divided. A share of Uncle Simon's money was, of course, better than nothing, but why divide it? It was obvious who needed it most. He closed his eyes, his face was full of suffering.

Paul knew just what Sybil's family thought of him, and, knowing it, took pleasure in being present at family occasions. They bored him, but he was able afterwards to be immensely amusing about them to his friends, and it pleased him to feel how it aggravated Sybil's relatives . . . with the exception of poor old Clara, who was never aggravated about anything . . . when he put in an appearance. He had attended the funeral with some expectation of entertainment. He knew Sybil believed that she was to hear that Simon's money had been left to her, and through her to Claud. He had let her think this would happen. It was pleasing to picture her disappointment. He could not imagine why she had heard from Willis and Willis; some little memento perhaps. He had not missed the expression on Alice's face when she heard that Sybil had received the same letter as she had, nor had he missed the expression on George's face, nor the look Frederick had given Alice. The moment he and Sybil were in his car he began to laugh.

Henry found it hard to throw off the gloom that had fallen on him at the funeral. Charles sensed this and gave his attention by one dodge or another, to getting his Jaguar through the traffic ahead of any other vehicle. It was this feat of driving which caught Henry's attention, and pulled his mind from Simon's decaying remains.

"You don't let nothin' come it over you, do you, sir?"

Charles oozed the car round a delivery van to arrive at the head of the queue waiting for the lights to change.

"Too right I don't, in this world it's push or be pushed. Anyway, I've got to step on it if we're to beat the family to it. You want to be there to open the door and pass that port."

"I won't be a jiffy. Just want time to put on me white coat. I got a new one what 'asn't never been worn, reckoned the old gentleman would like me togged up."

Charles shot forward as the lights changed.

"You bet he would." He let his mind dwell on the will reading. It was a pity he did not look his part. He spoke this thought out loud. "A frock coat would have been the ticket."

Henry was horrified.

"Oh no, sir! You mean what 'e wore in 'is photo. I never worn one of those; anyway, we 'aven't one, the moths 'ad ours. That was 'ired that was."

Charles grinned.

"Not you, me. I wish I'd hired something. An old-fashioned frock coat, and a heavy watch chain; you know I've an idea if I'd had a chance to speak to him about it Mr.

Hilton would have liked a bit of dressing up."

It was as if a voice spoke from a long way off. "Get out me striped trousers, me frock coat, and me grey waistcoat."

"Shouldn't wonder neither. Pity you only met at the end like, you and 'im would 'ave got on a treat of roses."

They reached the house. Charles stopped the car and looked round.

"Beaten the lot to it. Good. You mark my words, Henry, if there's such a thing as a ghost you'll hear your old man splitting his shroud laughing in half an hour."

Henry gave a quick glance towards Simon's windows.

"Don't say that, sir. You give me the creeps. As true as I'm standing 'ere I says to 'im after 'is party 'e ought to be ashamed of 'imself laughin' at 'em all about nothin', and d'you know what 'e says, "ow d'you know it was about nothin'? You wait and see, me boy.'"

Charles stood aside to let Henry unlock the door.

"How right he was. You wait and see."

* * * * *

Charles looked round at the family, and cleared his throat in a manner he felt suitable to a will-reading with port.

"I Simon Augustus Hilton of the maisonette known as flat 17A, Gorpas Road, Kensington, S.W.7., in the County of London, Esquire, hereby revoke all former Wills and testamentary dispositions and declare this to be my last Will. I appoint my solicitor Charles Frobisher Thomas Willis of the firm of Willis and Willis of Longacre London, and my

93

doctor William Edward Bing of Drayton Gardens London, to be the executors of this Will and I give to each of them who shall prove my Will the sum of fifty pounds."

Charles paused and collected the eyes of the family. He hoped he was wearing a suitably grave expression, but feared he merely looked comic.

"Then comes the directions for the funeral, which have of course already been carried out." He returned to the will. He lifted his voice slightly as he read out the words. "The following pecuniary and specific legacies." He was rewarded by rapt attention from everybody except Clara, who chose that moment to let her prayer-book slide from her knees to the parquet floor.

Clara picked up the book and smiled apologetically at Charles.

"I'm so sorry, you see I was thinking of something else."

Nobody answered, but family looks were exchanged. Who but poor Clara would think of other things when the solicitor was about to read out the legacies.

Charles did not want the prayer-book to drop again, so he got up and came to Clara.

"You don't want to hold it, do you? Shall I put it on the table?"

Clara beamed at him.

"Please do. I was thinking about the last time we all met; it was in this room; I'm so glad Uncle Simon had his party, I mean that it was in time."

The family exchanged more looks. Really Clara was getting ga-ga. Why mention that miserable luncheon? George said in his most pompous voice:

"I think, Clara, that Mr. Willis should be permitted to read the will without interruption."

Charles glanced round to see Henry was attending.

"To my valet Henry the sum of one hundred pounds, if . . ."

The rest of the phrase was missed, for the family was turning to smile kindly at Henry. One hundred pounds. Very nice, very suitable. Some also felt relief; you never knew with old people, they did foolish things, it might have been a thousand.

Henry, standing in the doorway in his clean white coat, his hand discreetly hiding that the liquid in his glass was not port, nodded in the direction of Simon's bedroom. A hundred nicker. Not so dusty. Very nice of the old B, he hadn't expected anything.

The little flutter towards Henry died abruptly as Charles read.

"To Gladys Smith of 1, Liptons Grove, Paddington, W.2., the sum of one hundred pounds and to the following ladies if they still live and can be traced the sum of fifty pounds each, in gratitude for the pleasant times we spent together."

As the names of the ladies were read out, the Lilys, Roses, Victorias, Daisys and Nellies, it was as if others, and raffish others belonging to the last century, had joined the family group. Charles laid down the will.

"I should explain that, although of course careful search will be made, it is not likely many of these beneficiaries can be traced. Mrs. Gladys Smith was the only one Mr. Hilton had seen of recent years."

"The old B," thought Henry admiringly. "All those bits of brass wrote down in 'is will, 'e 'adn't 'alf gotta sauce."

Charles picked up the will again. He read slowly, as if savouring each word.

"To each of my nephews, nieces, great-nephews, great-nieces, great-great-nephews, and great-great-nieces who were present at the lunch party which I gave on my eightieth birthday, a copy of the photograph of the family group taken on that occasion . . ." There were small sounds as breaths were caught, disgusted inflections checked. Charles, enjoying himself enormously, added: "I have all the copies here," he pointed to a large cardboard box. "Mr. Hilton himself purchased them."

George felt Charles was amused at their expense.

"I think, Mr. Willis, you can leave the copies of the photographs for the time being and let us hear the rest of my uncle's will." There was the faintest pressure on the words "my" and "uncle," suggesting that this was a family matter and, outside his duty as executor, no concern of Charles's.

Charles nearly smiled, but covered it by a slight bow, saying, "Of course, Mr. Hilton." He looked round. Yes, they were all attending.

"I give the residue of my property wheresoever and whatsoever including all property over which I may have a general testamentary power of appointment to my niece Clara Alice Hilton absolutely . . ."

Clara had been dreaming. She found legal phraseology boring. She had heard that Henry was to have a hundred pounds and nearly had run across the room to shake his hand. Dear Uncle Simon, how thoughtful of him! A hundred pounds would be such a help to Henry while he was settling down in a new situation. She had heard with pleasure they were all to have a copy of the family group. Clara was a hoarder of photographs, never in her life had she thrown one away, her bedroom at the mission was full of them. She had wanted a copy of the group and had meant to ask Henry to find out the price, and now dear old Uncle Simon had left her one. From hearing it was hers it was natural for her mind to turn to her room; it would be quite a big photograph, it might fit in that gold frame she had bought at that last jumble sale, in which case it could hang . . . It was not the words Charles had read which brought her back to Simon's drawing-room, but a strange silence, a silence which almost had shape, and not a nice shape but cold with evil in it. Moving her cosy figure to dispel her feeling of unease, Clara glanced up to find everybody looking at her. At once horrid ideas passed through her mind. Had she dropped off for a moment and snored? Surely she had not spoken out loud, she had got into a habit of doing that. It couldn't be that, without her being aware of it, she had made a rude noise.

Charles saw that Clara had not heard what he had read. He was amused. What a comic old girl she was! He could see why old Simon could not stop chuckling when he had worded his will.

"I had just read out to you, Miss Hilton, that you are your uncle's heir."

"Me! Oh, surely not. Why me?"

Vera could not control herself. She said, and there was no hiding the bitterness in her voice.

"Why indeed?"

Frederick was convinced now of the monkey business he had feared. Clara must have been snivelling round the old man when no one was about. He looked at Charles.

"On what date was that will made?" Charles told him. Frederick turned to the family with the triumphant smile he wore when he silenced a heckler at a public meeting. "I don't think we need trouble ourselves why Clara comes into everything. That will isn't worth the paper it's written on. Not a week after that luncheon party, and you all saw him then, laughing at nothing, the poor old chap was senile."

Charles was about to answer, but Henry spoke first.

"That 'e never was, the old pot and pan 'ad more sense in 'is 'ead than some I could put a name to what's sittin' in this very room."

Charles's voice rose above the outraged family's. He spoke to Clara.

"I don't, of course, know the value of the estate for death duty, so I will, if you don't mind, leave that for the moment and go on to the assets." He picked up a sheet of paper. "The lease of this flat together with all the contents. Fourteen racing greyhounds. Four race horses. The freehold licensed premises at 10, Orland Lane, Ashford, Kent, known as 'The Goat in Gaiters.' Preference and Ordinary shares in 'Gamblers' Luck Limited.' A leasehold property at 1, Liptons Grove, Paddington, W.2., together with all the contents. And in addition there is cash at the bank and sundry small items."

There was an inclination on the part of all the family except Clara to speak, so Charles held up his hand for silence. "I've read you the contents of the Will, and my notes about the assets, but as well the testator left a memorandum of Wishes. Here it is. It's addressed to you, Miss Hilton, and, in accordance with the instructions your uncle gave me when he made his Will, I am to read it in full. I, Simon Augustus Hilton, having to-day made my Will and having after certain bequests given my residuary estate to my niece Clara Alice Hilton desire to state my Wishes in respect of it. These Wishes are: That my niece will take an interest in Julia and Andrew Marquis, circus artists of Borthwick's Circus of whom I am alleged to be the putative father, it being my wish that they shall be kept from want. That Gladys Smith caretaker at my leasehold house at 1, Liptons Grove, Paddington, W.2., shall be adequately provided for. That my valet Henry shall be retained in my niece's employment at his present salary and for his present duties so long as he shall be able to fulfil them and that thereafter suitable provision shall be made for him. That my niece will arrange so far as she can both in her lifetime and after her death that the present even tenor of life and sociability at 'The Goat in Gaiters' and at No. 1, Liptons Grove shall remain unimpaired, and finally that the racing dogs and horses shall have consideration and kindness for the remainder of their lives and shall be well looked after. I do not wish to fetter the discretion of my niece about selling any of my assets since I feel confident that she will respect the spirit of my Wishes and as a Declaration of Faith I add that while I know that these Wishes are not legally binding on my niece I know all the more that being morally binding they have the greater force. As witness my hand, etc."

There was silence for a moment when Charles finished reading, then Frederick burst into a spluttering laugh. As he mastered it he turned to Clara.

"Sorry, old girl, but I can't help laughing. You, with greyhounds, race horses, and a couple of by-blows in a circus . . ."

Vera had been considering how best use could be made of Clara's odd possessions.

"You'll have to sell everything, of course, but you might keep this place; it would be fun for you because it means you can see us all, and perhaps sometimes put up one of the children."

George had decided that, from the sound of things, he was well rid of Simon's property. All the same, it would be as well to keep in with Clara, so he spoke kindly.

"Mr. Willis will look after everything for you, but you know where I am if you want me."

Sybil got up to go. It had been a tiresome, wasted day, and very disappointing, but she would have the fun of telephoning Claudie and telling him all about it. He had such a sense of humour, he would adore repeating the story of Aunt Clara's greyhounds.

"Go back to your mission, Clara, and let Mr. Willis look after everything."

Maurice was utterly appalled by the will and still more by the wishes: "alleged to be the putative father!" What a mercy the girls had not been able to leave their harvest work to attend the funeral. All the same he had to see Clara in a new light. He had not had time to inquire how God looked upon money earned by racing dogs and horses, and from shares in something called "Gamblers' Luck Limited," but God knew all about the small stipends of the clergy and deplored them, and perhaps on that account He might consider that it was not necessary to ask where money came from provided it came. He gave Clara a kiss.

"Dear Clara. You mustn't do anything in a hurry, must she, Doris? Why not come and visit us in Essex while you're thinking things over?"

Doris picked up her cue.

"What a good idea!"

Paul had listened to all that was said, but his eyes had been on Clara, now he minced over to her.

"But I don't think Clara is in need of advice. You know what you are going to do, don't you, Clara?"

Clara had not listened to the others, her mind was on Simon and his wishes, but she did hear what Paul said. She clasped her hands, her eyes shone happily at her family from behind her pince-nez.

"But of course I know what I'm going to do. Uncle Simon's wishes are a sacred trust. I shall try my best to look after everybody and everything exactly in the way he would wish. I shall move in here immediately." She looked towards Henry. "And you will stay and look after me, won't you, Henry?"

* * * * *

Charles arranged things so that three days later Clara moved into Simon's flat.

"He has been so helpful," Clara told Henry. "I'm such a muddle-headed person about business, but he makes everything so easy. Although my uncle left me some money Mr. Willis says I can't have it yet, but he has talked to the bank manager who has very kindly arranged that I can have a little to go on with; so wonderful of him, Mr. Willis, I mean, because I find bank managers rather unapproachable myself."

Henry, though he liked Clara, was extremely doubtful how they were going to get on living under one roof; it was Charles who had persuaded him to give the arrangement a trial.

"It won't kill you to try it out for a week or two, and you'll be doing her a good turn, you know all about everything and can see to everything; just imagine her hopping off to look at horses and greyhounds on her own, let alone everything else."

"I don't see what good she'll do lookin' at any of 'is property; much better stop on at that mission, and let you see to everythin'."

Charles had laughed.

"You're no psychologist, Henry. You heard what she said, her uncle's wishes were a sacred trust, and if that lady says something's a sacred trust you mark my words they'll be a sacred trust. She'll go into everything like a dose of salts."

Henry's face was gloomy.

"That's what I'm afraid of, 'tisn't right a nice lady like that. I'll do what I can, sir, but I won't say for 'ow long, not bein' used to lookin' after a lady, more especial not a religious-minded lady."

It was therefore a cautious Henry who greeted Clara on her arrival, carried her cases up to Simon's bedroom, and heard her views on bank managers. Clara felt a change in Henry's manner and appreciated its reason. He had his ways of doing things, and of recent years without interference; it must be hard for him to see her, a comparative stranger, in his old master's room, and he would naturally dread changes. The first of Uncle Simon's wishes that she must carry out was seeing Henry happy. She opened a suitcase and from under a dress took out her copy of the family group, now framed in the gold jumble sale frame. She placed it in the middle of the mantelpiece.

"Dear old man, it's a speaking likeness, isn't it, Henry? I'm so glad to have it, because when I'm in doubt as to what he would have wished I shall look at it and I'm sure I shall know."

Henry's face expressed nothing, but he thought a lot. It was a speaking likeness all right. He could see the old B dolled up in his flash togs, laughing fit to bust himself because he had thought of leaving all he had to his niece Clara. If the old man were alive Henry would have given him something to laugh about. Ought to be ashamed of himself, playing a joke on a nice Christian lady like Miss Clara.

Clara, still peering at Simon's portrait through her pince-nez, disregarded Henry's silence; it was her duty to make him trust her, that was what Uncle Simon wished.

"Except that I shall clean my own room, for I've always done so at The Mission, I don't want you to change your ways, Henry; my uncle especially mentioned in his wishes that you were to have your present salary for your present duties, so of course you're to go on exactly as if he were still alive, for his wishes are sacred to me."

Henry swallowed. The old pot and pan ought to be here to see what he'd done. It was a shame, playing Miss Clara up like that. His wishes sacred! They wouldn't be if he could help it.

"That's all right, Miss Clara." Henry hesitated. "Miss 'ilton I should say."

"Oh, no, call me Miss Clara. I am called all sorts of things at the mission, Miss Clara is one of them; sometimes I am elevated to Lady Clara, and a lot of people call me 'our lady'; it is not meant blasphemously, you know, but quite literally; I am their lady, the one they know. Now, about plans. The first thing I must do is to find those children. Do you know anything about them, Henry?"

Henry had already been asked this by Charles, so he had his answer ready.

"Not really. I did 'ear 'im leadin' off one day after a letter come; it was from someone 'e called Ruby. I reckon she was the kids' mother; in 'orspital she was when Mr. 'ilton let fly; I think she was askin' 'im to see after 'er kids and sayin' 'e was their father, which, accordin' to 'im, 'e never was." Henry struggled for suitable words. "You see, miss, Mr. 'ilton didn't think nothin' 'appened what could account for it; what 'e said in a manner of speakin' was he was gettin' on a bit at that time and . . ."

Clara, experienced from her mission training, understood Henry's embarrassment.

"Of course. All the same, I have my duty to do to the

children, that was his wish. Do you know what age they are?"

"Mr. Willis asked me that. It was in '44 when the letter from that Ruby come. I remember it was just about the time the rockets started comin' over."

"They were babies at that time I suppose. What happened to the mother, do you know?"

"She died, that I do know, because 'e told me so. I don't think they'd 'ave been babies, you see 'e 'adn't seen that Ruby since before the war."

Clara calculated on her fingers.

"They're in their teens perhaps. Do you know anything about circuses, Henry, how you find out where they are?"

Circuses had not been a part of Henry's life. They could be seen on the south London roads, passing from place to place, but he could not imagine they had an address. He replied, and as the words left his mouth, he felt they were to be used very often.

"I couldn't say, Miss Clara, I should telephone Mr. Willis."

Charles was delighted to search for Borthwick's Circus; he was, and he made it clear on the telephone that he was, delighted to advise Clara on anything at any moment. The truth being that Clara and her strange possessions filled his mind; she was, in spite of her appearance, a figure of romance in a drab world, and he had a frustrated feeling, as if he had missed an instalment of an absorbing serial, when he thought of that flat with Clara and Henry in it, and he not there to know what was going on.

"Of course I'll get the address right away. I'll ring you back."

Clara found Henry in the kitchen.

"How good people are, Henry. That young Mr. Willis is kindness itself, nothing seems too much trouble. Now, I want to know about Mrs. Gladys Smith; I must call on her, of course."

Henry kept his face on the potatoes he was peeling.

"I've met 'er like."

"What sort of person is she? You see, my uncle wished she should be provided for, and should go on living her life as it was lived in his lifetime and, though I must call, it will only be to tell her this, not interfere in any way."

Henry dug his knife into a potato.

"I don't think I'd visit. She's a woman what does thin's 'er own way and always 'as."

"Is it a nice house?"

"Well, for them as likes Paddington it is." A helpful memory came to Henry. "Church property it is, so I 'eard Mr. 'ilton say."

"Church property! How splendid! I shall look forward to meeting Mrs. Smith, but I'll leave her for the moment. Now, tell me about 'The Goat in Gaiters'; I'm teetotal myself, it's the one wish of my uncle's I'm rather worried about. Having taken the pledge it's difficult to own a public house. I wonder if he would understand that? What do you think?"

Henry cast an eye towards Simon's bedroom. He could picture the old man sitting up in bed doubled up with laughter. It was not right to think badly of the dead, but at that moment he would have given a lot to tell him what he thought of him. He was spared answering for the telephone bell rang. Clara answered it, she sounded happy.

"Eastbourne. How clever of you, Mr. Willis. You'll write?

Oh no, I think I must write to them myself. I'm sure that's what Uncle Simon would wish, and carrying out his wishes exactly in the way he would like is what we all want, isn't it? Oh no, Mr. Willis . . ."

"Strewth," said Henry feelingly to the potato he was peeling.

* * * * *

Borthwick's Circus was preparing for the first house when Samuel Borthwick received Clara's letter. Sam was not one who enjoyed reading letters, he left letter reading and letter writing to his wife Bess; but he did glance at the signature and it bothered him. As ringmaster he did not get much time to think of anything but his artists and animals during the show, but at those moments when he could take his mind off his work he turned over the name Hilton, trying to remember where he had heard it before. As soon as the show was over he went in search of Bess. He found her sitting on a chair outside their caravan; he tossed Clara's letter into what had once been her lap, but as she grew older had become a well-padded incline from waist to knees.

"That come. I haven't read it."

Bess read the letter, folded it, put it back in its envelope, then tucked it down the front of her dress between her gigantic breasts, and waddled laboriously up the caravan steps to prepare the tea. Increasing fat had in no way dimmed Bess's wits; by the time the tea was ready and she and Sam seated at the table, she had digested Clara's letter and decided what to do about it. There was fried fish for tea; she ate half hers before she was ready to speak.

"When you saw Ruby that last time in hospital before she passed over, what else did she say except about the children?"

At all times Sam dreaded Bess getting on to the subject of Ruby, but as a rule it was something he had done which started her off; to-day he had done nothing, so his tone showed resentment.

"Why bring her up now? You know all she said. I told you a hundred times, she asked if I'd train . . ."

Bess stopped him with an imperiously-raised fork.

"Did she say anything about a person called Hilton?"

Sam put down his knife and fork. Of course, that was it. Fool that he was not to have remembered. He could have kicked himself for giving Bess the letter to read. Not knowing what Clara had written he answered with caution.

"Come to think of it I believe she did. Why?"

"What was it she said?"

"Nothing really. Something about there being the name and address of a Mr. Hilton amongst her bits of things which she had given Julie when she was brought to see her. She said it was someone the kids could get help from if needed."

"Didn't you ask who he was?"

"No. Ruby was wandering a bit. Mentioned several names, but you know how she was about men."

Bess eyed him sternly.

"I ought to."

Sam hurried to cover his slip.

"Never thought of the name again till it caught my eye on that letter; it's been nagging at me where I'd heard it."

"It's from a Clara Hilton, a niece she says, of the Mr. Hilton Ruby knew. Mr. Hilton's just passed over and she's come into what he had, and left her a list of things he wanted done, and one was to look up Julie and Andrew."

"What for?"

Bess's voice was carefully disinterested.

"How should I know? This Mr. Hilton knew Ruby at some time I suppose."

"Maybe admired her act, there's many remember that."

Bess's voice was heavy with sarcasm.

"Most men knew her closer than on a flying trapeze, as I've reason to know."

Sam slammed down his teacup and got up.

"It's a nice thing to spoil my tea raking up that past history which should be forgotten."

"Can't very well forget it with Julie and Andrew around."

"That settles it. I'll let them go; we're lucky Andrew's stayed with us so long, he's had offers enough."

Bess had not intended to goad Sam that far.

"How you do carry on. Of course they're not going. We adopted them, didn't we, and whatever I may think of their mother they're like my own children, and you know it. Sit down and finish your tea." She waited until Sam had resettled himself. "I'll write to this Clara Hilton and tell her our next date is Hastings. If she could come on the Wednesday she could see the show, and the kids after."

Sam pondered this while he finished his tea.

"Be all right I suppose; seems funny though, you'd think he'd have come himself if he was interested, not leave it to his niece to do when he was gone."

Bess's mind was on Clara's visit.

"I'll have a word with her during the show. I'll ask her to say it was her was a friend of their mother's. If they knew it was her uncle who was, it might get them thinking things, and we don't want that, having brought them up to suppose Ruby had her marriage lines."

"Julie's still got the things Ruby left; it was Mr. Hilton she said was wrote down."

Bess got up to clear the table.

"On your way to the big top send Julie to me. I'll make it all right. Brought up nicely the way they've been they won't get thinking things unless someone puts them into their heads."

When Julie reached the Borthwicks' caravan Bess had finished her letter to Clara and was stamping the envelope. Julie was a slim, well-made girl, with brown eyes and what should have been brown hair, but was peroxided and dyed a brassy gold, for neither Sam nor Bess thought brown hair good for show business. She was dressed ready for the parade in a pink tarlatan tutu; she had her wrap round her shoulders and clogs over her pink shoes. Bess looked at her, a loving smile on her lips.

"Hallo, dearie. There's a friend of your Mum's written to say she's coming to see you and Andrew at Hastings. Name of Hilton, Clara Hilton."

Julie sat on the table. She looked at Bess with amused affection.

"When did she know Mother?"

"I don't know, dear, perhaps a school friend. She'll tell you."

From where Julie sat she could see down the front of Bess's dress, and had spotted the envelope folded between her breasts. She asked, though she knew the answer before she spoke, if she could see the letter, and her eyes twinkled as Bess looked round in a puzzled way, and told her of course she could, but she did not know where she had put it, then, lest she was bothered with further questions, dismissed her by asking her to post her letter to Clara.

Julie clattered up the steps of her caravan. Andrew was lying on his bed in the outer room, reading a paper. Their mother had been red-headed and Andrew took after her. He had an athlete's body, and the shut-up face of one who, dedicated to physical achievement, finds thought a burden. Julie rushed into her room and pulled open a drawer.

"Have you seen Mother's envelope lately?" Then, triumphantly, "I've got it." She brought an envelope into the outer room and sat down at the table. "Aunt Bess says there's a friend of Mother's coming to see us at Hastings, a woman called Hilton. I'm sure the name Hilton's on Mother's list."

"There isn't a woman on Mother's list."

"Of course not. That was only what Aunt Bess said, you know how she is. I thought so, here it is, Mr. Simon Hilton. He comes high on the list, so it looks as if he was one of the ones who was told he was our father."

"Why's a woman coming then?"

Julie put her mother's letter back in its envelope.

"I don't know. I couldn't get hold of the letter, it was parked down Aunt Bess's front. I should think he's sending her, perhaps he's ill or something. You know Aunt Bess only parks things down her front that are secret, so it would be my guess there was something in it about Mr. Simon Hilton being our father, for she'd never let Uncle Sam know anyone else thought they were if she could help it; after all, look at the things she makes him do because she pretends she thinks he is."

Andrew sat up and went to the door and looked out.

"Nice queue for the cheaps. Perhaps she's coming to see if we look like Mr. Simon Hilton, who's her husband I suppose."

"Won't do her much good looking at me, it isn't even as if I took after Mother, but you know what people are, they always see likenesses that they want to see. Look at the way Aunt Bess makes herself pretend to Uncle Sam we look like him, though she knows, except for your hair, you're the image of that American Mother was doing her act with when you were thought of, and that everybody knows it."

Andrew put his clogs over his ring shoes.

"I'd be glad if Mrs. Hilton did think we looked like Mr. Simon Hilton. I'm sorry for Uncle Sam, he'd be glad to have that cleared up."

Julie looked at Andrew as if he were a child of eight instead of a youth of sixteen.

"Idiot! He'd hate it. Of course he doesn't like Aunt Bess getting at him, but when she isn't there he doesn't mind people pretending we're his, it makes him feel sort of manly; after all, Mother was the sort of person all kinds of men liked, and though Aunt Bess is an angel, nobody could say she was a glamour-puss."

Andrew turned and looked at Julie.

"I shouldn't think Mr. Simon Hilton's wife could think

you like him; he's probably a very ordinary man, and Mother told you your father was a marquis, at least you think she did."

Julie went into her room and put the letter back in the drawer.

"I wish I could remember exactly, but it was all such a muddle, and I was frightened in the hospital. I was thinking about it when we worked Maidstone. On the way we passed a big pub in South London called 'The Marquis of Granby.' You see, Mum couldn't speak properly any more, and she might have been telling me she was staying there when I was started . . ."

Andrew, now that the evening show was about to start, had lost interest in anything outside his work. Julie accepted this, it was always so. Resignedly she dropped the, to her, intriguing subject of her parentage, and followed Andrew towards the dressing tents.

Clara was having her breakfast when Bess's letter arrived. Henry ran up the stairs with it, for he knew how pleased she would be. Clara had all her meals at a small table in the drawing-room. Henry stood in the door waving an envelope.

"They've wrote. Look, Miss Clara, it's got Borthwick Circus printed."

Clara read Bess's letter. Then she looked anxiously at Henry.

"It's from Mrs. Borthwick. She says they will be at Hastings next week, and if I go down on Wednesday I could see the show; she says Mr. Borthwick would be pleased to pass me in, do you know what that means?"

"Get in on the nod, free like."

"How very kind, and I can meet the children afterwards. What's worrying me is Mr. Willis. I don't like not to tell him that we're going, it would seem deceitful as he was so kind finding out where the circus was and everything, but I'm afraid he's going to be cross with me."

"You didn't write to the kids, did you, not after promising 'im you wouldn't?"

"Not to the children, to Mr. Borthwick, in the way Mr. Willis advised me not to. Not because I don't trust Mr. Willis, but because before I wrote I looked at the family group. You know, Henry, it may sound foolish, but it's a very speaking likeness of the dear old man, and I felt, looking at it, that he would not have liked any deception. He wrote openly and bravely in his will about the Marquis children, and looking at his portrait I knew that he would wish me to write quite openly to Mr. Borthwick. So I did."

Henry thought of Simon, and his thoughts were not respectful to the dead. He could see him sitting up in bed, spectacles on nose, his eyebrows rising and falling as, choking with laughter, he described Clara looking at his portrait. "Lookin' at me as if I were somethin' in a church." The worst of it was Henry could not say any of the things he knew about Simon to Clara, not out of loyalty to the old man's memory, but because Clara would not so much disbelieve him as brush away what he said. "Oh, Henry, you don't mean that, you were very fond of him, and try just as hard as I do to do everything as he would have liked it done." Since Simon's death Henry had time to see his friends. Amongst those he had looked up was his friend Nobby. To Nobby, after he had described Simon's end and the contents of the will, he had struggled to explain the situation.

"Lovely lady she is, very religious-minded with it. It's a shame leavin' all those wishes, just'avin' 'er on 'e was, and so she'll know later when she sees everythin'."

Nobby, though known as a rare one for a good laugh, did not laugh at the story of Clara's inheritance; taking a religious-minded lady into places where she did not belong and had no right to be was no laughing matter.

"You did ought to tip 'er off 'enery. Straight you did."

Henry fumbled for words to explain.

"You can't. You see, she never knew 'im like, not to know 'im, and she thinks leavin' 'er everythin' was a sacred trust, those are 'er words. Well, what can I say? 'urtin' 'er would be like kickin' a cat, you know, what can't do nothin' to protect itself."

"What about the mouthpiece, what's 'e say?"

Henry shook his head.

"Mr. Willis. Very pleasant gentleman, but I couldn't fancy talking to 'im, not seein' what I know. I keep me mouth shut when 'e's around, what 'e finds out 'e finds out for himself. You take the dogs. Well, it's all right really what's done, and Perce treats them wonderful and Mrs. Perce is like a mother to 'em, but you know 'ow mouthpieces are, and Perce wouldn't thank me bringin' one along askirt' questions and that."

Now, as Clara admitted that she had done what Charles had advised her not to do, Henry thought of this conversation with Nobby. Mr. Willis might be a mouthpiece, and as such not far removed from a copper, but he had his uses. Nobby had been right there. He looked at Clara's kind blue eyes gazing at him trustfully from behind her pince-nez, and spoke as he would have spoken to a well-intentioned but wrong-doing child.

"You didn't ought to 'ave done that, Miss Clara, not after Mr. Willis tellin' you not to, straight you didn't; you don't want to go tellin' people thin's what maybe they needn't never know, it isn't 'ealthy; next thin' you know they'll be askin' for money."

"They won't unless they are in need, and if they're in need, then they must have it; it was Mr. Hilton's wish they should be kept from want."

"You oughtn't to be allowed out, that's a fact. I tell you one thin', if you don't ring up Mr. Willis I will, 'e says to me, I was to look after you; 'ow was I to know you was writin' on the sly, tellin' them thin's what there was no need they should know."

Clara got up.

"I'll tell him myself. I don't really mind his knowing now. I wrote what my conscience told me to write, and even if he's cross he can't take that letter back."

Charles groaned when he heard Clara's confession. He had tried to persuade her if she must write, to let him rough out the letter she should write. Clara had refused, but he thought he had got a promise out of her that her letter would not mention the possibility of Simon being their father.

"Miss Hilton! You are difficult to help. Don't you see what you may have done? You won't have a farthing for yourself if you go round telling people your uncle might be their father, and they are to be kept from want."

"But it's what Uncle Simon wished."

"Well, you can't go to Hastings alone."

"Oh, I'm not. I'm not used to circus people. Henry's coming with me, and imagine, Mr. Borthwick is passing us in, which Henry says means free seats, isn't that kind? Do you know, nobody ever gave me a free seat for anything before."

Charles, apart from not caring to miss anything, could not feel Henry would be sufficient guard. He could picture Clara, pleased with the circus, making reckless promises right and left.

"If you like I'll drive you down."

Clara gave a pleased squeak.

"Oh, how very kind! I'll tell Henry at once. What a treat! A drive to Hastings and a circus: I'm afraid you'll think me very silly, but I'm like a child at the thought of the circus, I haven't seen one for years."

On the next Wednesday the first house was about to begin when Charles's green Jaguar turned into the circus parking ground. Bess, from the door of her caravan, watched Charles open the door for Clara. She was not close enough to see more than Clara's outline. "Looks a bit homely for a friend of Ruby's," she thought. "Still, she needn't have been in show business, and I daresay Ruby would have gone off a bit herself if she was still alive."

Andrew did not see the car arrive, but Julie had been watching out for it.

"She's in front, I saw her passed in," she told Andrew as she climbed on the rosin back for the parade. "She came in a posh car, with two men. I shouldn't think it's her car, she looks poor. I hope Mr. Simon Hilton isn't ill or something and expects us to cough up."

"Us! Why should he?"

"I'm your poor old father stuff."

Andrew walked on stilts for the parade. He climbed a stepladder and sat on the top of it to fasten the stilts. When they were on and someone had pulled his trouser legs over them, he had digested what Julie had said. He leant down to her.

"If he's really poor, we'd have to do something I suppose; we've got a bit in the Post Office, and if he knew our mother I expect she had quite a bit off him."

Julie fluffed up the skirt of her tutu.

"Don't you dare mention our savings. I suppose we might help a little if he knew Mother, but she's got no real right to ask us to help him, and don't you let her think she has."

Clara was given a pass for a plush-lined ringside box seating four. Charles, not usually given to thinking of the effect he might have on others, glancing round, wondered with amusement what anyone looking their way would make of their party. To meet the Marquis children Clara was wearing what she considered her best outfit, a grey dress in her usual voluminous style, trimmed with beaded braiding, over it she wore a loose black coat, and a rather end-of-summer black straw hat, trimmed with what had once been expensive flowers. Utterly unself-conscious, she beamed happily at the ring and the audience through her pince-nez, uttering at intervals pleased, childlike chirrups. "Isn't this a treat?" "Oh look, Henry, that's where they are coming from, do you see those horses?" "What lovely seats, how kind of Mr, Borthwick!" On her left sat Henry in a shiny blue suit, holding a black bowler, which had belonged to Simon. His body was rigid, but his sparrow-like eyes under his thinning hair darted from side to side missing nothing. No one around them looked as though they were psychologists, but had they been how would they place Henry in juxtaposition to Clara? Or himself in relation to either? To visit the circus he was wearing ordinary country clothes; he might, of course, be taken for Clara's son, only Clara looked so virginal.

The start of the parade took Charles's thoughts off themselves and to the Marquis children: which amongst these riders, stilt walkers, clowns and floor acts were they? The programme said the thirteenth turn would be "The Marquis Duo" in their remarkable aerial novelty, but obviously they were part of the parade in some other capacity. Were they two of the Red Indians on horses? Were they part of the group in fleshings and spangles who marched? Then he saw that the girl in pink riding the rosin-back had turned to have a look at Clara. He pointed this out.

"Look, Miss Hilton. I bet that girl in pink is Julia Marquis, she's looking at you."

Clara turned, but Julie and her horse had disappeared through the exit.

"That pretty fair girl on a horse! I don't think it can be, nobody ever has been a rider in our family."

Charles looked round to see if anyone were listening, for Clara's elderly but still youthfully eager voice had a carrying quality; but only Henry had heard. Henry's face and tone had the disapproving quality of a shocked headmistress.

"There you go again. If I told you once I told you a 'undred times you didn't ought to talk that way." Henry saw Clara was not listening, her eyes were glued to the clowns who were fooling before the first turn. He spoke to Charles across her. "You see 'ow it is, Mr. Willis, she won't be told nothin'."

Bess had waddled across to the entrance to the big top from which she could see Clara. Bess had been born in a circus. Her father had owned sea lions and her mother had been a trampoline artist. She herself had not been particularly gifted, but had been well trained, and by the time she was twelve had performed regularly with both the sea lions and on the trampoline. Her parents had joined Borthwick's when she was sixteen, and there she had met Sam, who was eighteen, and had married him a year later. She knew no world but that of the circus. The spot where the circus performed in summer, and where it stood in the winter, was her village. However close to a town the circus ground might be it was as a foreigner, string bag in hand, she visited it to shop, and it was only when she was passing through the gate, and was back on circus ground, that she relaxed, no longer an alien. Sam had rather more dealings with the outside world; he visited public houses and had to talk to local dealers and tradesmen. He had been too, separated from the circus world during the First World War and was, as a result, less uneasy in a non-circus atmosphere; but he too looked upon the spot where his circus stood as his village. In talking together Sam and Bess spoke of "we" and "they," and to them both the "theys" were a strange, inexplicable lot. Bess, peering at Clara, Henry and Charles, knew nobody with whom to compare them. It took all kinds to make an audience; she was used to the outing and the village bus load, so there was nothing to her odd in the look of Clara's party. But Clara herself puzzled Bess. Was she the sort to agree to admitting to having known Ruby? Would she take the hint to keep the possibility of her uncle being the children's father to herself?

Although the matter was important to her, Bess did not hurry, for acting with caution was part of her, so it was not until the sixth turn was in the ring that she opened the door of Clara's box.

"Good afternoon. I'm Mrs. Borthwick."

Clara turned unwillingly from watching a comedy horse.

"How do you do? Won't you sit down and watch the horse, he's so funny."

Bess looked at the horse. The two augustes who on that tour were working the horse act were poor. Bess marvelled, as often before, at how easily pleased "they" were, and how indiscriminating.

Charles stood up and offered Bess his chair.

"I'm afraid you won't get Miss Hilton's attention until the interval, she's a circus fan." Bess sat. Clara, having neither eyes nor ears for anything outside the ring, it was Charles's chance to protect her. "It was kind of you and your husband to give her this box, and to arrange she can meet the Marquis children."

Sometimes when he had guests Sam would come and speak to them in the interval, it added lustre to their afternoon to be seen talking to the ring-master in his scarlet coat and top hat; Bess was at no time fond of small talk, and on this occasion, with the interval near, time certainly could not be wasted on it. She paid no attention to Charles, but drew her chair closer to Clara's and tapped her arm.

"I've told the children it was you who knew their mother."

The tap drew Clara's attention from the horse, Bess's words held it.

"Me! Oh, you shouldn't have done that, it isn't true."

"There are times, Miss Hilton, when a lie is best."

Clara gave Bess her full attention.

"Never. It couldn't be. I mean, how could what's wrong ever be best?"

Bess valued respectability, and in Clara she saw respectability in bulk. It was to this quality she addressed herself.

"When Mr. Borthwick and I adopted Ruby's children we never told them she hadn't her marriage lines."

Charles, from Bess's first words, had jumped to it that for some reason he had an ally in Bess. He tried to prompt her as to the best way to approach Clara.

"You mean they had no idea that their father was not perhaps somebody called Marquis?"

The comedy horse turn was coming to an end, the liberty horses would follow and then there would be the interval. Bess had no time to waste on Charles.

"They've been brought up respectable, Miss Hilton, and Mr. Borthwick and I would take it kindly if you wouldn't upset them by putting ideas in their heads."

Clara had never been talked to in that way before. It had been she who had pleaded for the not putting of ideas in the heads of children. She found Bess wholly admirable, but that did not mean she agreed with her.

"But my uncle wished they should be kept from want, and I think he wanted them to know he wished it. I mean . . ."

Charles spoke firmly.

"That wish is covered if you keep an eye on them." He turned to Bess. "From the look of everything here nobody is likely to be in want, are they, Mrs. Borthwick?"

Bess was nobody's fool. It was unlikely Julie and Andrew would need help, and they were the last to ask for it, but it was always nice to know there was something behind you. In their work there could be an accident any day. She addressed Charles for the first time.

"We none of us know what's coming to us."

Clara came to a decision.

"I needn't lie. I shall say they must look upon me as somebody they can come to whenever they need anything and I won't say why." She turned to beam at Charles. "That will do splendidly, won't it?"

Charles had not liked the tone in which Bess had spoken of a possibly gloomy future.

"I think you should explain to Mrs. Borthwick there's very little you could do. You see, Mrs. Borthwick, although Mr. Hilton left his property to Miss Hilton there's not much . . ."

"Don't listen to him," Clara interrupted, "all I had was one little room at a mission, and now I've got a beautiful flat full of furniture, and racing dogs and horses, and a public house, though that distresses me rather because I'm teetotal, and there's some shares in something, and some

Church property in Paddington; Mr. Willis is a lawyer, and lawyers are used to people with money, so I don't seem rich to him, but to me what Uncle Simon left is a fortune."

Bess gazed at Clara in wonderment. She had met many simple and generous people in the circus world, where the hint of a hard luck story opened every purse; but even the simplest had either known how to guard their own interests, or had someone to guard them for them; this Miss Hilton needed looking after. She got up.

"I'll be going now to prepare tea. We're having it outside our caravan." She looked at Charles. "There's no need for Miss Hilton to worry about Julie and Andrew, they're not the sort to go asking favours." Clara was about to say she wanted favours asked but Bess, with an imperiously-lifted hand, stopped her. "If Mr. Borthwick should come to speak to you in the interval I would be glad if nothing was said about Mr. Simon Hilton. You never know who's listening and we don't want talk."

Charles had moved to open the box door for Bess. With amusement he watched her enormous back fade, with immense dignity, out of sight. As he sat down again he said to Clara:

"That was an order, Miss Hilton, and don't you forget it."

Bess had filled Henry with awe.

"S'trewth, I wouldn't like to get the wrong side of 'er."

Clara had decided what it would be right to say to the Marquis children. As was her way, once she had decided what was right, she let the subject slip from her mind until the need arose to act on that decision. She had liked Bess, but was no longer thinking of her for the liberty horses had all her attention.

"Oh, look, Mr. Willis, aren't they clever? Every one of them is putting up the same hoof at the same moment."

Sam did not have time to go to Clara's box in the interval, but instructed by Bess, he collected her and the two men after the show, and conducted them to his caravan. Although she often described herself as an old muddler Clara was not muddled when it came to remembering what had been said. Much of her time at the mission had been spent standing on doorsteps, or sitting at kitchen tables listening, sorting out what she was being told, picking fact from fiction, and, where action was needed, reporting later what had been said. Her brain recorded that Mrs. Borthwick did not wish her to mention to Mr. Borthwick that her Uncle Simon had stated he was alleged to be the Marquis children's father. It had noted that the reason Mrs. Borthwick had given for this was that what was said might be overheard by somebody, and she did not want talk; it had also noted that this did not appear to be the true reason, but that since it was the wish of Mrs. Borthwick, who seemed a very nice woman, and did not affect what she was intending to say to the children, it would be right to do as Mrs. Borthwick asked. So, as they walked across the show ground, to the amazement of Charles and Henry, Clara said nothing about the reason for her visit, but talked enthusiastically of the circus, and in particular of the aerial act performed by the Marquis children.

"Quite extraordinary! Right up there. I can't think how

they learned to do it. You know, when Julie swung that thing for Andrew to catch hold of and he left go of the one he was holding, well in that moment he stopped looking like a boy and was like a bird."

Mr. Borthwick was used to the fact that "they" were ignorant, and used strange, awkward words to describe circus apparatus. As Clara spoke he mentally translated what she was saying, and knew the exact moment of which she was speaking. He liked her simile.

"That's right, he does look like a bird. Wonderful good artist that boy's turning out. It's in the blood, of course. His mother, as maybe you remember, worked a wonderful flying trapeze act."

Charles felt they were touching unsafe ground.

"The girl does less, but she's good too, isn't she?"

It was not Sam's way to discuss Julie's work, not even with Bess. Julie and Andrew had never been separated but he could see it happening. He took his time before answering; it was doubtful, even if he explained things, Miss Hilton and her friends would know what he was talking about, how ignorant they were stood out a mile from what Mr. Willis had just said, but he felt bound to try and make them understand, for Miss Hilton seemed really interested in the kids; why else would she come all the way from London to have a look at them?

"Julie's a fine girl, and very useful tenting, can turn her hand to most things, but she's not up to Andrew. Rightly speaking he ought to be teamed up with an act in his own class. He's had offers but he won't leave Julie; you see, they've always been together, right from a child Julie was a mother to him, it's hard for her to know what's best for him."

Clara answered with shining belief.

"Oh, but it shouldn't be. If she prays she will be given the answer. You know, like in the hymn. 'O Brother, life's journey beginning, With courage and firmness arise . . . Look well to the course thou art chosing; Be earnest, be watchful, and wise! Remember . . . two paths are before thee, And both thy attention invite; But one leadeth on to destruction, The other to joy and delight.'"

Charles was enchanted. Who else but Clara Hilton would choose to recite a hymn to a circus owner she had only just met, and who else, in that confident way, would talk about the power of prayer? He glanced at Sam; what was he going to reply to that?

Sam, like many of his kind, was not a church-goer, but a great respecter of churches. Once or twice while tenting, their arrival in a town had synchronised with a civic occasion, and he had been asked if a service could be held in his big top. He had been delighted and had taken an infinity of trouble over the arrangements. It did him good to hear hymns rising to his canvas roof, it was proper that prayer should be said. If a service could have been held every week he would have liked it, a nice sensible service with good hymns, and prayers for the King and the Royal Family, and a bit of a sermon about doing what was right. It was going out to a church that did not appeal to him; he felt any praying and hymn singing that he took part in should take place amongst the things he knew, with the scent of sawdust in his nose, and the roar of old Popeye, his lion, as accompaniment. From the manner in which Clara spoke of the power of prayer, and in the way she quoted a hymn, he recognised a faith simple as his own, and so answered without embarrassment.

"That's right, that is. But I don't think Julie gets wind of what's being offered to Andrew before he's turned it down. He keeps it from her."

Henry felt responsible for Clara. His views on the laity praying or hymn quoting in public were those of Maurice and Doris. They were nearly at Mr. Borthwick's caravan, for he could see Bess putting the finishing touches to her tea table. He did not want Miss Clara making a show of herself when those young Marquis kids were around, maybe sniggering.

"If you must pick on a 'ymn, Miss Clara, you didn't oughter 'ave picked that one; those words about leadin' on to destruction aren't lucky seeing what they do."

Charles, listening to Sam and Clara, had forgotten Henry. He had been knocked off his usual perch by what they had said. He never thought much about himself. He supposed in a dim way that a mixture of public school ethics, commando standards, legal codes of behaviour, and the words dropped about life by an exceedingly successful father and uncles had fixed him up all right as to what was what. Listening to Sam and Clara he began to wonder. Funny the way they both used the word "right." He was damned if he was sure anything was "right" in the way they meant it. Henry's remark snapped him out of what to him was surprising thinking. There was no time to answer, for they were within hailing distance of Bess, but he grinned at Henry. Old comic, he was, proper watch-dog, but he would have his work cut out if he hoped to make Clara obey his bark.

Julie and Andrew, nervous as colts, sidled up to the tea table. They had changed; Julie was wearing a plain flowered cotton frock and white sandals on her bare brown legs. Andrew had put on a clean shirt and grey flannel trousers. The usual summer clothes of the young of any walk of life gave anonymity to the children. The glamour of the circus was gone, and they became any shy sixteen-and-eighteen-year-olds. Sam introduced them.

"These are our boy and girl, Julie and Andrew Marquis."

The seats on either side of Clara had been left vacant. She pointed to them.

"Mrs. Borthwick has put you next to me. I have been so looking forward to meeting you."

Passing round the table Julie was able to give Andrew a nudge, a reminder to be cautious and keep off savings; there could be no reason why this Mrs. Hilton was looking forward to meeting them, unless she wanted something.

Julie and Andrew sat, but it was clear from their expressions that they were only doing what they were ordered to do, if they had their way they would not be there at all. Bess and Sam exchanged the gloomy glance of parents burdened with inexplicably sullen children. Sam cleared his throat while he thought of something to say. Bess was quicker. She told Clara she hoped she liked a meat tea; she had planned it because they would need something in them before their long drive back to London.

Clara's mission life had taught her how to behave when faced with large meals at the wrong hours. She had been, she thought, "guided" when she had refused Charles's offer of lunch on the road, and had said she would rather have an early lunch at home. She was aware that Bess had only mentioned the tea to cover the hostile attitude of the children. She was sorry for Bess and Sam, but sympathetic with Julie and Andrew. They probably thought she was an old busybody come to ask questions and meddle with their affairs. She beamed at Julie as well as at Bess before she answered.

"It looks lovely, and we're all very hungry." She nodded to Henry who was seated opposite her. "This will save you cooking our supper when we get home."

During the performance Julie and Andrew had examined Clara and her party. While they were standing on the swing waiting to start their act they had discussed them. Andrew had thought Charles might be Clara's son, but Julie said no, Charles, she thought, was too smart and different to be the son of the dowdy old lady. Both agreed that Henry, in spite of wearing no uniform, must be the chauffeur. Clara's remark to Henry surprised Julie so much that she stopped feeling on the defensive. It was unusual in her experience for husbands to cook, but obviously this one did.

"You're Mr. Simon Hilton. We never guessed you were him."

Bess's eyes were thoughtful. So Julie and Andrew did know there had been a Mr. Simon Hilton. Sam could have shaken Julie, speaking out of turn like that. Not but what it was Miss Hilton's fault, she had distinctly said "our supper"; she didn't seem the kind of lady for that kind of thing, and he would have thought she was past it, but you never knew. Henry struggled not to laugh; he might be getting on but he hardly looked like Miss Clara's uncle. He must tell Nobby that one, he wouldn't half scream. Charles's mind jumped to what Julie thought, and he was enraptured. What a picture I Clara was unworried by Julie's mistake.

"No, dear, that's not my Uncle Simon, he's dead. That's Henry who lives with me to look after me."

Henry did wish Miss Clara would be more careful how she put things.

"What Miss Clara means is it was me looked after the old gentleman till 'e was took, and in 'is will 'e left me money and wished I'd stop on to keep an eye on 'er. You see, I did everythin' for 'im, collectin' rents and that."

Clara appeared to give her attention to helping herself to salad, while she decided what it would be best to say next. It was clear from Julie's words that she had heard of a Simon Hilton. If that was so it was doubtful if the children believed it was she who had known their mother. She turned to Julie.

"Tell me what you know about my uncle."

Charles saw from Bess's face how she disliked that question; as well, from every angle, he felt it had better not be asked. Julie seemed the sort of girl who blurted out what came into her head. If she said she had heard Simon Hilton might be their father, there would be no holding Miss Hilton, she would be sure to make the most unwise promises. The thought of how foolish a statement Clara could make in front of all those witnesses made him look for a means to change the conversation. He was sitting next to Julie, her hand was about to pick up her fork, he put his over it and felt her fingers, and asked in a voice calculated to draw attention to his words and away from what had been said, whether especially strong muscles were needed for her job.

Andrew was sitting between Bess and Clara. Bess followed Charles's effort to change the conversation. She knew Andrew, being such a dreamer, was unlikely to have heard what was said. She gave his arm a poke.

"Wake up, Andrew. Tell Miss Hilton about your training and how strong you have to be, and of that offer you had Christmas time."

Henry felt glad that Charles was with them; that was the sort of silly question Miss Clara would ask. He pointed his knife at Andrew.

"That's right, you tell 'er 'ow it's done. Proper turned me over seein' you nippin' about up there."

Sam was proud of Andrew. He had natural gifts, but they no had been fostered by careful training. Season after season Sam had engaged aerial acts, often more expensive than he liked, so that the artists could give Andrew lessons. On the ground he knew Andrew did not seem much, boys of sixteen were often shy, and there were times when, if you didn't know Andrew, you might think he was lacking in wits, but in the air he was wonderful. Sam had not the words to say what Andrew in the air meant to him. He would never get his tongue round "poetry of motion," or "inspired," but watching Andrew working he knew complete artistic satisfaction. He did not use a microphone in the ring, he had a fine voice to roar out "My Lords, Ladies and Gentlemen . . ." He used it now to get Andrew started to talk of his work; once over the tongue-tied stage he would do all right, for enthusiasm for his work would make him forget himself.

"Andrew came to us when he was only a nipper, Miss Hilton; they had been tenting with their mother, so they'd picked up a bit, but not regular, you understand. The first proper lessons Andrew had was from a Swede. Andrew, tell Miss Hilton about Sven."

Andrew thought back. He saw himself and Julie very small beside the blond Sven. He could hear again Sven's voice as he said, "First we must see every muscle does as he is told; when all muscles obey, then we can begin to work." His shyness dropped from him, eagerness to speak of the great Sven took its place.

Henry and Clara listened to Andrew, Bess and Sam waited to prompt him if he should become self-conscious; no one was watching Julie and Charles. Julie was a gauche eighteen; she had grown up with Borthwick's, had her behind slapped, her pigtails pulled, and been hunted off to school by all Sam's permanent staff. As she grew up many eyes turned to look after her as she passed to and fro, and many thoughts lingered on her, for she had a beautiful body; but Bess was strict about behaviour, and nobody liked to think what she would do if anyone touched Julie. Moreover Julie had an elusive wild-flower quality which quelled ideas of snatched pleasures in dark corners. When her hand was held by Charles it trembled and fluttered as if he held a scared bird. After a second she snatched it away, and looked up at him.

"Why did you do that?"

Charles was unused to young women thinking anything of a held hand.

"I was only interested. I say, what luck having those

brown eyes! Brown eyes and fair hair are a bit of all right."

Julie felt he was teasing her, but she was more at ease.

"You can see it's dyed. Uncle Sam and Aunt Bess like fair hair for show business. You held my hand so that I shouldn't answer Mrs. Hilton, didn't you? Why?"

"It's Miss Hilton. She's quite a woman, but she needs looking after."

Julie relaxed, for she liked plain speaking.

"I told Andrew she would. Of course we know she wasn't a friend of our mother's; the Mr. Simon Hilton who is dead was on the list mother left of people who could help us." She looked round to see Sam and Bess were not listening; although both were attending to what Andrew was saying she dropped her voice. "He was high up on the list, so we guessed he was one of the men who had been told he was our father. We can't do much for Miss Hilton, because we haven't much, but as her uncle knew our father we'll help . . ."

Charles warmed to Julie.

"Was it because you thought Miss Hilton had come for help you looked so cross when you sat down?"

Julie felt increasingly at ease with Charles.

"Yes. Andrew doesn't care about anything but his work, he'd give away all our savings, but I can't because I haven't got the gift."

Charles, remembering what Sam had said, did not answer that.

"He seems brilliant."

"He is. Of course our mother was good . . ." once more Julie looked cautiously round before she whispered, "but we think his father was an American who worked with mother. We never saw him because he broke up the act when Andrew was coming, and when he was working in Zurich he was killed, but people say he was one of the best trapeze artists there ever was."

Charles followed Julie's example and dropped his voice.

"Was his name Marquis?"

"No, that was my father."

"Was your father a trapeze artist?"

Julie smiled. It was the first smile Charles had seen on her face except the synthetic one she put on when she bowed to her audience. It was a charming smile; it lit up her face as if the sun had appeared on a grey day. As well there was a slight flush on her cheeks. Her whisper was embarrassed.

"You'll laugh when I tell you, and it is funny. Mother always told me my father was a marquis. She said she met him in Paris when she was working there, but I think she made it up; she was always making things up like telling her uncle . . ." Julie made a tiny motion with one finger to indicate Clara, "that he was our father."

"I don't see why your father couldn't have been a marquis. France is stuffed with aristocratic types."

Julie sighed.

"I'd like to think that, but the more I look at myself the less blue blood I see. When we were on the road to Maidstone in August I saw a pub called 'The Marquis of Granby.' I dare say I happened there, it's more likely."

Charles laughed.

"You are a scream. If you want to know, I think you might well be partly French, and oozing with blue blood. In fact I'm sure you must be; only a girl oozing with *noblesse oblige* and all that would think she had to help the niece of an old man she never met, who it is most unlikely was her father, as he only died the other day and he was eighty."

"I don't know what *noblesse* means, was it French you spoke? But if she . . ." there was another tiny gesture, "has nothing, and the uncle was a friend of our mother's, it's right we should help, for Mother is sure to have had a lot of money from him, she always did."

Julie had finished eating. Her hands were in her lap. Charles laid his hand over them, and though again they quivered Julie did not this time draw them away.

"You're pretty nice. I'm going to trust you. Miss Hilton came to offer to help you."

Julie's eyes widened.

"Us! Why? Why should we want help?"

"You don't. But that's why she came. To find out if you did."

Clara was still hanging on Andrew's story, which was to her like a fairy tale. Julie glanced at her, then turned back to Charles.

"That was very good of her. I should think she is very good."

"She is. So good she's going to be disappointed she can't help you." Charles felt Julie was about to move her hands. Casually, as though he had been about to do so anyway, he took his hand away. As he did so he thought it would be nice to see her again. She was a funny girl, not a bit his type, but all the same he would like to have another look at her. An idea came to him, and as he mentioned it he saw how admirable it was. It would suit Clara and as well it would suit him. "If your blue blood is telling you to be nice to Miss Hilton, why don't you ask her if you and Andrew could come and stay with her? You must get a holiday sometime."

Julie looked scared.

"Would she like that? Andrew and I have never stayed with anyone."

"She'd adore it. It won't be grand. There's not much room, it would mean more or less camping I think."

"Would you be there?"

"Not in the house, Henry looks after her, but I'll see you. You'll find me popping up like a cork."

It was evidently a great decision for Julie to make.

"We have a little time when tenting is finished . . . Uncle Sam goes to winter quarters, but he has an engagement for Popeye our lion with a circus in Brighton . . . it could be managed if it'll really please her."

Charles spoke with immense authority.

"It will please her. Before we leave we'll fix it up."

* * * * *

Clara spent her Sundays at the mission. She enjoyed the services and meeting old friends. The first Sunday after she came to live in Simon's flat she had tried to persuade Henry to come with her. Henry had refused.

"No, Miss Clara, I likes to enjoy me Sundays in me own way. I wouldn't fancy that mission, straight I wouldn't."

One Sunday in each month they planned to spend to-gether, visiting Simon's grave. Clara was an anxiety to

Henry, but there were qualities in her which he liked, her respect for graves was one. The Sunday following their visit to the circus they decided to make a Cemetery Sunday. It was the end of October, so the wreath was chrysanthemums. Brilliant weather had given summer warmth to the last weeks, but that Sunday was autumnal. Dying leaves scratched along the pavements blown by a chilly wind, and the decaying autumnal smell, together with the sharp scent from the chrysanthemums, blew up Clara's and Henry's nostrils, and turned their conversation to graves, which made the walk to the bus stop pleasant for both. Clara told Henry exactly what the stones on her father's and mother's graves were like, what flowers she had planted round them and how, though she lived too far away now to visit them herself, she arranged for holly wreaths at Christmas, daffodils at Easter and roses on their birthdays. Henry said "and very nice too," and told Clara about the graves of his family, and of the difficulties of keeping them looking nice.

"Somethin' chronic it is, people are that dishonest you wouldn't believe when it comes to pots. Put a jam-pot down 'alf a cock linnet and before you can say 'Bob's your uncle' someone's lifted it. You wouldn't think, would you, Miss Clara, there could be people sunk so low they'd rob a cemetery?"

Clara made distressed sympathetic noises. Pots, she was afraid, were a great temptation to those who lived near a cemetery; of course they shouldn't be, but when there were cheap oranges about and you had the sugar, and wanted to make marmalade . . . Her voice tailed away. She had learned at the mission of many little things which, before she went to the mission, were clearly wrong, but with more under-standing of other people's problems, though not becoming right exactly, belonged more nearly to the childish word "naughty." She could see both points of view so clearly; Henry's very proper anger at a robbed grave, and the ha-rassed mother held up in her marmalade making for the want of a couple of jam-pots. She changed the subject to one about which she had been giving much thought.

"Of course it's too soon yet, Henry, but I want to have all the arrangements made for a stone for Mr. Hilton's grave. I shall order it, and Mr. Willis is arranging to keep the money on one side to pay for it. What is troubling me is what would the dear old man have liked. I know he was not a churchman in the ordinary sense of the word, but he led a Christian life, and I feel his generosity and consideration, as shown in his will, should be in some way remembered; did he ever men-tion any text or verse he was fond of?"

Henry's face took on a look which Simon had known well. "Take that damn disobligin' look off your face." Dis-obliging was the wrong word, the look was a shutter be-tween Henry and those who wished to nose into matters which were not their concern. Not that he believed Clara's question came from nosiness, he knew it did not, but her constant appeals to him for advice as to whether Simon would have considered this or that right or wrong embar-rassed him. He could never get over the feeling that the old man was somewhere around listening, a wicked gleam in his eyes. He could almost hear him say, "What was that she was askin' about me?" Even in the street he could catch Simon's laughter. His ears carried the sound of that low rumble, and he could recall exactly the tone and voice in which Simon had said, "How d'you know it's about nothin'? Wait and see." The more Henry knew of Clara the less he liked to think of that laugh and what it had meant. For that was the day Simon had planned his will, and though Henry felt it was no laughing matter he knew now why the old man thought it funny and said, "Wait and see." But much as he was growing to like and respect Clara he could not bring himself to tell her the truth. For one thing the truth was not easy to tell; he had been fond of the old man, there had been a lot to like in him but the things he liked about him were not the sort to appeal to Miss Clara, and just telling her that the will had been his best joke, and that he had been laughing up to the last minute, was only half true, and it would upset Miss Clara if she believed it, which more than likely she wouldn't, and it wouldn't be fair to the old man.

"'e wasn't much of a one for texts or that, 'e was never one for troublin' much about graves."

Clara heard the reticence in Henry's voice, and thought she understood it. Dear Henry, he was so loyal he would not like to remember faults, and to him not visiting graves was a fault.

"You are thinking he never visited my father's, his only brother's grave, but that was understandable. It was during the war he died, remember, and we were asked not to travel unnecessarily, and there were plenty of us children to see to everything. I feel sure he took a great interest in the stone that was chosen, and the words we selected; I expect he talked it all over with my brother George, or perhaps my clergyman brother Maurice."

Henry thought how it would surprise Miss Clara if she knew what her uncle had thought of her brothers, but the mention of them turned his mind to something he had overlooked. Gravestones were not put up to please the dead, but to show the neighbours you were doing all right, and knew the way to behave. Miss Clara was not one to notice what others thought about her, but it would be nice if she could manage a really showy stone, so the relatives couldn't say she had been mean.

"I see a lovely stone once. Great big angel it was, with a finger pointin' up showin' the way like."

Clara did not admire angel tombstones, but if Henry did she was prepared to consider it.

"It depends on money. There is not a great deal, you know, and it's only mine in trust, I have such a lot of people to look after."

They had reached the bus stop. Henry glanced at the queue to be sure they were not overheard.

"'ow often am I to tell you you don't want to keep 'arpin' on lookin' after people that are all right as they are, you don't want to give 'em ideas. You look at the Marquis kids. They didn't want anythin'."

Clara did not care who was listening.

"I'm glad you mentioned the Marquis children, Henry. Do you realise they are coming to us in about three weeks?"

Henry had thought the matter over, but he waited until they were seated in the bus before he answered.

"That's right. I thought Julie could 'ave me bedroom, and I'd doss down with young Andrew in the front room, 'ave to get a coupl'a beds, but it'll be easy fixed."

Clara beamed.

"You are kind, Henry. I never thought of your bedroom. I was thinking of Julie sharing with me, and I'm such a staid old thing, she might be shy. But it wasn't the bedrooms I wanted to speak to you about. You mustn't misunderstand what I am going to say. I am very lucky in my family, so many nephews and nieces and so affectionate and kind, but I don't want any of them to know I am having the Marquis children to stay. You see, I don't look on Mr. Hilton's flat as mine. It's your home too, he said so in his wishes, and though Mr. Willis says it's very unlikely he'll trace them, there are my uncle's other friends and he might find one who is in want." Henry thought of the Lilys, Roses, Victorias, Daisys, and Nellies, and a low whistle escaped him. Clara did not notice, but went on: "Then there's Mrs. Gladys Smith . . ."

"She's all right, she is."

"But you never know, she might get ill and need looking after."

"She's all right," Henry repeated stubbornly.

"Perhaps, but I must keep her in mind; then there are the people at 'The Goat in Gaiters,' I thought I would go there this week. In spite of my uncle's wishes I might find my conscience won't let me keep it, and if so there are the people living there to be thought of. Anyway, I have decided it's my duty until I have seen everybody, including the animals, that my uncle left in my care, to keep the flat ready. I am sure my family would understand if I could explain to each of them how I feel, but I can't and I would so hate them to feel hurt, so if you don't mind, Henry, if any of them should telephone or call we won't mention the Marquis children. It sounds rather deceitful, I know, but I'm sure you understand."

Henry could barely hold back a grin. He wished the old B was alive, so he could have heard that. It wouldn't half have made him laugh, to know the rest of the family were being kept out and why.

In the cemetery Henry regretted that wish. Both were standing quietly by Simon's grave, when Clara, who had been saying a prayer, opened her eyes and with pleasure announced that her uncle had himself selected a text for his tombstone. Henry was at that moment re-living an immensely successful afternoon he and Simon had spent at Goodwood. With a jump he returned to the present, for Clara's statement had sent a shudder down his spine.

"That 'e never." Clara raised her face towards the sky where she knew Heaven, and her uncle, to be. Henry anxiously touched her arm. "Better be shiftin', Miss Clara, it's gettin' cold, you can't 'elp gettin' fanciful of a late afternoon in a cemetery."

Clara continued to look Heavenwards. She quoted softly, as if memorising what she was being told.

" 'Let your light so shine before men, that they may see your good works . . .' "

Henry was shocked. It wasn't nice carrying on like that. He knew the old man, he would never have chosen any text, let alone that one. Good works! He gave Clara's arm another pull.

"If that's what you think 'e's picked, Miss Clara, you put it, but come 'ome now, no good standin' 'ere."

Clara's eyes glistened behind her pince-nez.

"I heard something else too. It's pleased me very much. I'm such an old muddler, but it's true, I do my best."

Henry took hold of Clara's elbow, and pushed her towards the path.

"It's the nip in the air what does it, and the smell of the chrysanths and that. Before we go 'ome you'll 'ave a nice cuppa, soon put you right that will."

* * * * *

The shock of discovering Clara to be their uncle's heir having faded, and the news, handed round to families, having passed from being news to being an accepted fact, schemes were considered.

George had felt from the beginning that Charles would be hard to handle. He was, as he told Vera, seldom wrong when it came to sizing up, and he had sensed right away the young Jackanapes was the officious, know-all type, likely to be offensive at small notice. But on thinking over the list of Clara's possessions his mind kept returning to "The Goat in Gaiters," and ten days after Simon's funeral he sent a clerk down to Ashford to look at the place, and make discreet inquiries. The clerk's report was satisfactory. "The Goat in Gaiters" was doing well, and moreover, as a free house, was being angled for by the big breweries. George, after brooding over the matter for two days, revealed his thoughts to Vera. It was not the sort of property he would touch as a rule, but it looked as if there was a good chance to make money. Clara had been teetotal all her life, hadn't even touched her port at the will reading, it was not likely, whatever she might have said at the time about a sacred trust, that her conscience would allow her to own a public house. It was no good underrating young Willis, he was not likely to miss that there might be a good sale for "The Goat in Gaiters," but a letter to Clara suggesting, if it was to be sold, Uncle Simon would have preferred it to remain in the family, might influence her.

Vera could not recall the reading of the will, especially the part about everyone who was present at the eightieth birthday luncheon receiving a copy of the family group, without an uprising of rage which brought a red; blotchy look to her cheeks; but she too had been turning over ideas by which she and her children and grandchildren might gain something in the end. She turned her mind to George's plan; it sounded all right, and they could do with some extra money, especially if it could be arranged that the government didn't get the lot, but she saw a difficulty. There had been that nonsense about things going on as before, life and sociability or something; that was the kind of wish that might make Clara hold on to her pub even if it did sell drink. Could George so word a letter that Clara would think he meant to keep the place going as it was? The question of selling need not be mentioned, need it? George did not reply to that. It was a mistake, even to Vera, to commit himself, but he exchanged a look with her which said clearly that selling need not be mentioned. "Good," said Vera, "and write nicely to the old thing, and suggest that if she would like to discuss business we'll come up. It's nonsense her keeping that enormous front room as it is. She ought to turn half of it into a spare bedroom, it would be so useful. Freda says Poppet may have to have remedial excercises for her spine, and that means London at least once a week. It will be fun for Clara to put them up."

Frederick had soon ceased to find the will funny. Only too often Alice heard mutters of "monkey business" and "double-crossed." But time does heal and moreover Frederick had a retentive memory. Before George's clerk had received instructions to go to Ashford, Frederick had been to Ashford and was home again. He was so pleased with what he learned in Ashford that on his return he startled Alice by giving her a slapping kiss. There was, he told her, a chance she might get something after all. She was to write to Clara and ask to see her. She was to learn what to say to Clara by heart, he didn't want that young lawyer getting inquisitive, so Alice was to watch her step, if she said one word too much she would ruin everything. Trembling at the thought of her responsibilities, and sinking inside at the thought of failure, Alice went to her desk, and, notepaper before her, waited pen in hand to be told what to write.

Maurice had spent much of the week following the will reading and wrestling in prayer. It was no good starting off by feeling hurt, that matter had first to be cleared up. It took time, for Maurice had understood clearly that God, knowing about the smallness of his stipend, had intended righting matters through that unlikely instrument Uncle Simon. At last however, rather worn from the struggle, Maurice told Doris he understood; God had not felt he should be burdened with such unsuitable property as his uncle had to leave, but had thought it better he should receive help indirectly. Doris had been feeling offended with Clara since the day of the funeral. She had not got over the way Clara, because she worked in a mission, had dared to behave as though she were Maurice's spiritual equal. That Clara came into everything, even an undesirable everything, was more than Doris felt she should be asked to bear. At least before the will reading there had been Clara to share the position of being the poor members of the family, and now there she was with a flat in London, and probably quite a lot of money. It was therefore in rather a soured voice that Doris asked how the indirect help was to come. Maurice said it had not been vouchsafed to him the exact means that were to be used, but he understood that God, though disliking gambling on principle, felt that if money were made by gambling it had better be put to good use. Doris looked sorrowfully at Maurice, and wished, as often before, that he would get more decisive answers to his prayers, and repeated her question. They were in Maurice's study. It was a small crowded room unsuited to pacings, but Maurice paced. As he paced he told Doris that it had come to him that what was intended was help for Alison and Marjorie. Alison's work at the cottage hospital was useful and splendid, but if she were properly trained as a secretary she might take a really good position anywhere. Marjorie, dear child, had been so good working as assistant to the doctor, but now she ought to have her chance. She had always wished to be a masseuse, and with free board in London it should be possible, the fees would not be much and surely Clara would see her duty. Doris thought of Simon's flat, and asked, in a tone which showed impatience, free board where?

Pointing out that the flat had no spare room. It was then that the speed of Maurice's pacings increased, and his words grew involved, and he became unable to look Doris in the face. Gradually, however, Doris discovered that Maurice, apparently together with God, though that was left a little vague, felt it was not nice Clara living alone with Henry. It might be that up till now they had been inclined to look upon Clara as past the lusts of the flesh, but nevertheless she was a woman, and Henry was a man. Maurice suggested, rather than stated, that he had been given a celestial hint that he should tell Clara how things looked, and that would ensure Henry's departure. Doris, who had never thought of Clara from an attraction angle, took a moment to adjust her ideas, but adjusted they were, and when Maurice finished pacing and speaking she had seen two beds in Henry's room, with Alison in one and Marjorie in the other. So clearly did she see this that all she asked when the pacing and speaking ceased was, "Will you write to Clara, or go and see her?"

Paul Levington kept his friends in a roar for days describing the reading of Simon's will. He was a good raconteur, and therefore many people, repeating his story, said, "But you must hear Paul tell it." The result was that he found himself in great demand to drop in and drink here, and eat dinner there. It was while dining with one of the clients of his advertising firm that an idea was handed to Paul. He had wound up his story of the will reading, as had become his custom, by a superficially brilliant imitation of Clara, in which he even succeeded in looking her shape, saying, "But of course I know what I'm going to do. Uncle Simon's wishes are a sacred trust." As usual his friends were enraptured, a roar of laughter rose round the table, eyes had to be mopped and voices weakened by laughter murmured "a sacred trust!" As generally happened, Paul had to repeat parts of his story, his host was especially tickled at the set-up for the will reading. "You don't mean to tell me you really sat round drinking port. I bet it was terrible stuff." Paul had not been asked about the port before. He recalled now that it was far from being terrible stuff. It had not been treated properly, that queer fellow Henry had probably shaken the bottle before decanting it, but it had been good port; now he came to think of it no reason why it shouldn't be, old Simon, from all accounts, would know good wine when he tasted it, probably had quite a cellar before the war. It was strange he had not thought of a cellar sooner, for part of his imitation was Clara refusing her glass of port while explaining to Henry that she had been teetotal all her life. Paul could not explore the wine idea at the time, but later he thought deeply about it. It was a lovely night and he was not far from his home so he decided to walk. As he minced along he wore a pleased but cruel smile. It would be amusing to get hold of some of the old man's property, which Sybil had so wanted for Claud. He could see his dinner table, and a carefully planted conversation: "Yes, it is good, isn't it? I bought some wine recently, belonged to an old uncle of my wife's." Sybil would give no indication that others could see that she minded that he had got something out of her family, when Claud had nothing, but he would see that he had hurt her. The little flinch, the sudden eager conversation to hide her feelings. The thought of that moment gave him great pleasure. He must, too, let Sybil's family know. He had always aggravated them, but if they knew he had bought their uncle's wine cheap, and that it was good stuff and that he enjoyed it, they would be more than aggravated, they would be angry. Delicious thought. He must be careful how he approached Clara. Paul never overrated his chances. Having seen Charles he was convinced he would do everything in his power to guard Clara's interests, therefore the deal must be kept from him. A picture of Henry's funereal expression as he handed round the port came to him. Henry would be the one to deal with. He had been with the old man, and would know all his business. Wine had not been mentioned in the will, the chances were Clara, being teetotal, would not know she owned any. He must find an excuse to go along and have a word with Henry. Perhaps for a fiver the fellow would tell Clara he had a good offer for her wine, might even say who had bought it, and make out he had been generous about the price; the old girl wouldn't know if she was being done or not. Paul paused at the bottom of the steps to his front door to get out his latchkey. He had a methodical mind; before he went to bed he always considered outstanding things to be seen to. In that pause he wrote on the tablets of his memory, "See Henry."

* * * * *

Nobby, his left ear directed to Henry's mouth, leant on the bar, drinking mild and bitter. Henry had come to rely increasingly on Nobby. Nobby had been in the house, he knew what he meant by "the front room," "me kitchen," or "them in the basement." He could be talked to frankly. There was no need to hold anything back, either what was in his mind, or the words which came naturally to his tongue. Not holding anything back had, since Clara entered his life, become an immense relief to Henry.

"You see, Nobby, Miss Clara don't want the relatives knowin' the Marquis kids is comin', on account of 'er feelin' 'e meant 'er to 'ave room for them as is in the will, which of course 'e never."

Nobby enjoyed both hearing the Hilton saga, and advising Henry. He nodded portentously.

"Too right 'e never."

Henry refreshed himself with a gulp of mild and bitter.

"So when I goes down an' sees what the postman brought us, 'Oh, ho,' I says, ''enery boy watch out for trouble.'"

Nobby moved his head so that he could speak into Henry's ear.

"'ow did you know 'o the letters come from?"

"Easy. I'd know 'em in the dark by the feel. Mr. George 'ilton sends a envelope with the address wrote on a typewriter and the name of 'is firm sort of pressed in like, on the back. The Reverend, 'e uses old envelopes with one of them labels stuck on. Lady Cole 'as lovely paper, big white envelopes so sharp and stiff you could cut yourself on 'em. Well, I thinks, may as well tip Miss Clara off so she don't get a shock like, so as I gives 'em to 'er I says, 'They've all wrote savin' Mrs. Levin'ton.'"

"What she say?"

Henry took a cigarette out of a packet in front of him, then, with his elbow, moved the packet towards Nobby.

"I didn't see 'er read 'em, but when I comes back for the breakfas' thin's she says, ' 'enery, I have had an answer to me prayers.' Then she tells me 'er brother George 'as written ever so nice a letter, sayin' 'e's been thinkin' 'er bein' tee-total and that, she wouldn't want to own a public, but wouldn't care for it to leave the family like, and 'ow 'e's willin' to take it off of 'er."

Nobby took a cigarette from Henry's packet.

"You think 'e's up to somethin'?"

"I'd take me oath 'e is. The old B 'ad 'im sized up, you ought to 'ave 'eard 'im lead off whenever 'e spoke of 'im. Created alarmin' 'e did."

Nobby lit his cigarette and smoked in silence for a while.

"If 'e's up to any funny business the ole lady did oughter tell the mouthpiece."

Henry pressed his elbow against Nobby's to show he was approaching the crux of the conversation.

"Mr. George 'ilton's not the only one what's after it. Lady Cole wrote that 'er old pot an' pan was wonderin' if 'e could 'elp, and she had said to 'im why not buy 'The Goat in Gaiters,' as she reckoned Miss Clara wouldn't be wantin' it, bein' 'as 'ow she was teetotal. She said 'as 'ow a public wasn't in 'er pot an' pan's line, but to 'elp Miss Clara 'e might take it on."

Nobby winked.

"Very nice of 'im I'm sure."

Henry returned the wink.

"Lovely of 'im. 'Course Miss Clara, she can't see 'arm in anythin', so it's no good me tellin' 'er, but Lady Cole never wrote that letter, she 'asn't the spirit to post a football coupon not without 'e told 'er she could,"

Nobby slapped the bar with the palm of his hand.

"I got it, 'enry boy. Someone's after it. No matter what they've wrote, they mean to sell it. Is the Reverend after it too?"

Henry dismissed Maurice's financial position with a jerk of his head.

"'im! 'e couldn't raise the price of a lick of paint on 'is front door."

Nobby felt he had got a grip on the situation.

"You tell Miss Clara to show them letters to the mouthpiece before she does anythin'. Don't let 'er as much as 'ave a look at 'The Goat in Gaiters' without 'e knows about it. It's a free 'ouse, you say, aren't so many of those goin'. I bet one of the big breweries wants it an' that Mr. 'ilton and Sir Cole know about it."

Henry ordered more mild and bitter for them both. He did not answer until they had both had a swallow from their refilled glasses. When he spoke it was in so low a voice that Nobby had to lean his ear almost against Henry's lips to hear.

"It's this way, Nobby. She's on about the dogs now. Do they like racin'? Do they live comfortable? Do they 'ave plenty to eat? Well, you know 'ow thin's are, so I'd fixed it with Perce we'd go on the Green Line to 'The Goat in Gaiters' first thin' Thursday, gettin' there round about openin' time, be quiet then, bars aren't never crowded openin' time of a mornin'. We could 'ave a bit of dinner there like as not, then we was takin' the Green Line back to 'The Dog and Pigeon,' that's no more than a step from where Perce 'angs

out, an 'ave a cuppa with them and see the dogs, all as nice
as nice. But if Mr. Willis knows about them letters I bet you
'e wants to drive us to Ashford."

Nobby whistled softly.

"You told Miss Clara you're fixin' to take 'er to Perce?"

"Yus. An' I told 'er Mrs. Perce was plannin' to give 'er a
cuppa and that."

Nobby scowled in a worried way at his beer.

"Does the mouthpiece know anythin' about dog racin'?"

"Maybe 'e don't, but I bet you the first thin' 'e asks Perce
is where does they race, meanin' The White City, Wembley,
or one of them flash tracks."

Nobby let out a long-drawn "Ah!" Then he had an idea.

"If Perce says Botchly Lane as casual as if 'e was sayin'
Wembley, the mouthpiece would just think it was a track
what 'e 'adn't 'eard of, wouldn't 'e?"

"Not Mr. Willis, 'e's all right but 'e's the busy sort, 'e'd
find out."

"Could they be raced on an Association track?"

"Not an' stop with Perce they couldn't. 'E'd get thrown
off anythin' but a flappin' track, 'e's been fined an' all, you
know, they say 'e did ought to have done a stretch, still 'e's
good to 'is dogs and 'e done well. But on a G.R.A. track
you got to fill in papers worse than a census, 'o was the
father, 'o was the mother, and there's a picture Perce says to
fill in so you know the colour and every blinkin' mark. Perce
'as dyed our last lot so often, and changed their names regular, 'e wouldn't know now what they was like to start with,
nor where they come from."

Nobby whistled.

"Can you keep the mouthpiece from wantin' to see 'em? I mean, 'e knows she's got 'em, and don't know nothin' about dogs."

"It'll be all right if I get 'er there first. All she cares about is to know they're 'appy, eatin' well, and that."

"Won't she want to see 'em run?"

"She might, but Perce says 'e'll fix it if she does that they 'ave a bit of what'll do 'em good, and she can watch 'em win, and pat 'em afterwards, and they'll be waggin' their blinkin' rudders, and 'e'll tell 'er 'ow they enjoys racin', and she won't move 'em then, no matter what Mr. Willis says; an' mind you, though 'e's a mouthpiece 'e's not a nark, it's just 'e wouldn't understand like."

Nobby looked doubtful.

"It's rough, you know, Botchly is."

"She won't think so. Perce says 'e'll fix it so Mrs. Perce brings people along to keep sayin' isn't it lovely to see the dogs enjoyin' of theirselves, and they'll be 'avin' cups of tea and actin' quiet, beside never 'avin' seen a race track she won't know any different."

"'ow did the old gentleman come to start with Perce?"

"'e didn't start with 'im, 'e started with 'orses with Perce's brother Alfie; sons they was, of one of 'is Jane Shores, proper sweet on 'er 'e must 'ave been, I reckon, for 'e'd never 'ear a word spoke against Alfie, nor Perce neither. Alfie's dead now, 'e was a bit of all right 'e was, and so's Perce. I reckon when the old B wrote in 'is wishes that Miss Clara was to see after the racin' dogs and 'orses 'e meant it, and 'e meant look after Perce and Mrs. Perce. They're all right, mind you, but it wouldn't do Perce any good if our dogs was took away, 'e needs the bees and 'oney see. If I can get Miss Clara down to Perce's place on 'er own, it'll be all right. Perce's place isn't so far from that mission where she works, and she gets on with them down there a treat, lovely to 'er she says they are."

It was the mention of the mission that gave Nobby his idea.

"I got it. Sunday! You tole me she goes to that mission of a Sunday. Well, what's nicer than you takin' 'er to Sunday tea after?"

Henry gazed respectfully at Nobby.

"You ain't 'alf a oner. 'Course that's the ticket, an' I won't need to say nothin' about not tellin' Mr. Willis, she never tells 'im nothin' about Sundays. I'll just say Sunday suits Mrs. Perce better."

"That's right, an' you get Mrs. Perce to talk to Miss Clara nice about bein' fond of the dogs an' that, an' she won't talk to no mouthpiece. What about the 'orses? Where do they 'ang out?"

Henry stubbed out his cigarette in the ash-tray.

"I fixed that, leastways I 'ope I 'ave. Alfie was all right. Mr. 'ilton 'ad four 'orses with 'im to start with, an' 'e always 'ad four 'orses right up to the time Alfie died. Mind you, they wasn't always the same 'orses, Alfie was always buyin' and sellin', but there was always four 'orses in the old B's name, and sometimes when Alfie'd done hisself a bitta good he passed a bit on, but mostly it was tips Alfie 'anded out. Wonderful tips 'e 'ad. I reckon the old B lost a lotta bees and honey when Alfie 'ooked it."

"But there are still four 'orses."

"Did oughter be. Alfie 'ad a son, proper shocker 'e is, you ought to 'ear 'is Uncle Perce on 'im. It's funny like, Nobby, when I was runnin' for the bookies, 'orses weren't nothin' to me but names wrote on bits of paper. After the war when the old geezer took me racin' it's all different like. You see the real 'orses, shinin' coats an' that, an' you wants 'em to win. You know 'ow it is outside the classics, if you know somethin' you can always make a bit; well, I got so that if I was at a race I didn't fancy winnin' when I knew there was a 'orse in the race could 'ave beaten mine if 'e'd been on 'is own."

Nobby made a reproving face.

"You don't want to get fanciful. Next time you 'ear somethin' good, if you can't bring yourself to 'ave a bit, you ring me, my conscience'll take it."

Henry grinned, but his mind was with Simon's horses.

"This son of Alfie's, Andy they calls 'im, was supposed to carry on same as 'is Dad. Alfie mighta done some funny thin's but 'e treated 'orses right, an' 'ad a proper place where they could muck around when they was finished with." Nobby raised his eyebrows. Henry nodded. "That's the short of it. You can get a fistful of long-tailed 'uns, now there's no meat, for some poor old 'orse what done you all right when 'e 'ad 'is health and strength. If I can work it we're goin' up to Andy's place when the kids come to stay, and Mr. Willis too. I'll give a lot to see Andy's face when 'e's asked where the four 'orses is."

Nobby had a horse he used for his log cart. He was fond of his horse, and treated him with the respect due to a loyal hard-working partner.

"Wouldn't mind bein' a fly on the wall when that so-an'-so knows Mr. Willis is Miss Clara's mouthpiece."

Henry nodded.

"Be a bit of all right that will. I tried to get the old B to do somethin', but 'e was old when Alfie went, and you know 'ow old people are. You know me, Nobby, I 'aven't often got it in for no one, but when I 'ave, I got it in proper."

"So you did ought to. 'e ought to 'ave the cat. You tippin' the mouthpiece off?"

Henry was shocked.

"Me a grass! Come off it! I reckon there won't be no need. Andy wrote to the old B soon after 'is father was took, sayin' 'e thought the four 'orses did oughter retire, that it was a lovely place what 'is father 'ad, where they could 'ave a beautiful old age. 'e wrote wonderful, I will say that, good enough for a Christmas card."

"Maybe, 'e'll say they're dead."

Henry swallowed some beer.

"Nor 'e can't neither, for I've the receipts all paid regular, the last one dated two days before the old geezer was took, an' they'll be in me pocket."

"What you told Miss Clara?"

"Showed 'er Andy's letter, she swallowed it 'a course, 'ook line and sinker, an' said it was jus' like 'er uncle to pay for old 'orses to 'ave a lovely old age an' didn't I think so, an' we mus' go an' see 'em some time an' thank the man for bein' so kind to 'em."

"You told 'er yet when you want 'er to go?"

Henry shook his head.

"No. I've enough on me plate right off. First there's fixin' Perce an' Mrs. Perce for Sunday. I'll take a chance on that, so Miss Clara can telephone Mr. Willis right off about takin' us to 'The Goat in Gaiters.' Then we've beds to buy for when the kids come, an' I'll 'ave to tidy me bedroom a bit, 'asn't 'ad a real turn out since I 'ad it. Then Miss Clara's got to be kep' out of the way, I'm sendin' 'er down to 'er mission, seein' Mr. George 'ilton, Lady Cole, an' the Reverend all wrote they would be comin' up."

Nobby finished his beer.

"I know 'e left you a 'undred nicker, but I reckon you'll earn it 'fore you're through, 'enry boy."

Henry also finished his beer. He looked thoughtfully into his empty glass.

"You said it, an' we 'aven't got properly started yet, you might say. When I know she means to 'ave a look at the lot I don't mind tellin' you, Nobby, I think of turnin' the job up."

Nobby signalled to the woman behind the bar.

"Nor I wouldn't blame you. Same again, Rosie."

* * * * *

Charles called on the Tuesday evening to make final arrangements for the trip to Ashford. Clara was out at the mission, but Henry, who had reached the front door expecting to see George, Alice or Maurice, greeted him rapturously.

"Only you! I made sure it was one of the relatives."

Charles had been looking for a chance to catch Henry alone. He followed him up to the kitchen.

"Don't let any of them in before she's seen the pub. She'll promise it to the lot and then there'll be hell to pay getting her out of it. If she decides to sell I'll write to Mr. Hilton and Sir Frederick, and I hope the price I ask shakes them. Couple of foxes trying to kid Miss Hilton they are trying to help. She needs a bodyguard, you know."

Henry was peeling potatoes for supper.

"Too right she does. I keep tellin' 'er she didn't ought to be allowed out. You know she can't get her tongue round a decent lie. That's why I pushed 'er off to 'er mission. We're expectin' the Reverend; 'e 'asn't wrote straight out what 'e wants, but I bet you a tanner 'e's got 'is eye on this place for 'is God-forbids to 'ang out in, 'cause 'e did say it was on account of them 'e wanted to see 'er. Well, you know Miss Clara don't want any of 'em knowin' the Marquis kids is comin', on account she thinks if anyone comes Mr. 'ilton meant it should be one of them in the will, which of course 'e never; but you mark my words, an' not wishin' to speak disrespectful, if 'is long nose gets in 'ere in two shakes of a duck's tail she'll 'ave told 'im all about the Marquis kids, she can't 'elp 'erself, tell anybody anythin' she would, fair gives me the sick it does."

Charles gave a sympathetic grunt, but his mind was not on Clara. Henry's mention of the Marquis children was the opening he had hoped for to raise a delicate subject. He sat on the kitchen table and lit a cigarette, while he pondered over a problem. What should he call Julie when speaking of her to Henry? It would be a good idea to establish something, he did not like to hear her lumped with Andrew as "The Marquis kids." Miss Marquis was right, but Henry might think it too formal. He would probably call her "miss" to her face, and Julie when speaking of her. He could not very well tell Henry what to call her, it was not as though she was a relation of Miss Hilton's. He decided to give Henry a lead and hope he would follow it.

"Letting Miss Julie have your room for a week is one thing, having relations park in it is another."

Henry did not pause in his potato peeling, but his mind was at the alert. What was this? *Miss* Julie. Mr. Willis could not have decided they were the old B's kids, could he?

"Miss Clara was willin' to 'ave 'er in along of 'er, but at her age you get set in your ways. Of course Julie," Henry corrected himself, "*Miss* Julie will share Miss Clara's bathroom an' that, Andrew can wash in 'ere an' use the stairs lavatory, same as I do. 'Course my room isn't much . . ."

Charles could not believe his luck. Henry was saying the very words he wanted to hear.

"Does your room want doing up?"

Henry could not believe his luck. He gazed stolidly at the potato in his hand. Not by the flick of an eyelash did he show the relief he felt at that question. His remark to Nobby about his room needing a turn-out was gross understatement. Daily he was expecting Clara to ask if she could look at it, and it was only reasonable that she should with the girl expected, and her knowing what the front room had been like. If Simon had been alive he would have asked for the money and had it cleaned and painted, but since his death money had been tight. He had not dreamt of Charles coming to the rescue.

"'asn't 'ad nothin' done for years, the paint an' that is a

bit off."

That was all Charles needed. In a moment he was pouring out to Henry what was in his mind. There was not much money of Miss Hilton's about, but Henry would understand there was no need to bother her about cost. He knew a man who would fix everything, paints, carpets, the whole boiling. Feeling he was holding Henry's interest, Charles forgot that he had been planning the decorations for Julie's room for days, whereas Henry had only just heard of the scheme.

"I've a feeling for pink and blue, duck-egg blue they call it. What d'you think of the idea?"

Henry could not hold back a startled "S'trewth." Pink and duck-egg blue! He could hear Nobby on that: "Never knew you was one of those, 'enry boy." Then thoughts of himself were swept away by thoughts of Charles. Pink and blue! No need to bother Miss Hilton about the cost! What was Mr. Willis up to? Julie better look out for herself, proper bird in a gilded cage she was going to be. No one could hide his thoughts better than Henry.

"Pink an' blue would be cheerful like."

Julie had not been out of Charles's mind since he had met her. She had been so much a part of his thoughts that he did not realise that while to him she had become a close friend, to Clara and Henry she was still a girl with whom on one occasion they had eaten tea. Charles was not given to analysing his feelings; he had come across introspective types in the army, and had thought them unhealthy. He appreciated, without sorting things out, that Julie was not the kind of girl he usually fell for. His choice, until he met her, had been for the sophisticated and smart, who knew their way around. He did not look further ahead than Julie's stay in London, and then only in terms of the restaurants where she would eat, the plays he would take her to see, the room in which she would sleep; it was never his way to plan ahead, he had found that for him love affairs came about naturally, or not at all; no plotting, just an urge on both sides at the right moment. With so much of his time spent mentally with her, the Julie he saw himself escorting around London was mainly invented. He remembered certain things about her which delighted him: her gauche way of blurting out what came into her head, her fingers, like some frightened bird he had caught, her brown eyes. He forgot her dyed hair, her probably limited wardrobe, her lack of knowledge of the world outside the circus, and, giving life to the creature he had invented, shepherded an outspoken, still timid, but well-dressed, sophisticated Julie around the most amusing London he knew.

Henry, who during tea at the circus had said little, had the more time to register impressions. He had taken a fancy to both Julie and Andrew, but he had seen them as they were, and the more Charles talked the more puzzled he became. Charles, after so many days of thinking of Julie, was delighted to speak of her, and who better to talk about her to than Henry, who had met her and knew what a charmer she was. Henry, to hide his thoughts, shuttered his face and stared with a disobliging expression at the potato he was peeling. Poor Mr. Willis, he had got it badly. Pink and blue bedroom! Night clubs! Theatres! Dancing at the Savoy! The poor kid wouldn't have the clothes for going to the sort of places Mr. Willis liked. It was a shame really, somebody ought to tell him. It never crossed Henry's mind that the somebody might be himself, that would mean poking his nose into something which was not his business, one of the deadly sins. He was glad when he heard Clara at the front door, for it bothered him to hear Charles, whom he liked, talking so foolishly.

"There's Miss Clara. You'll 'ave to say somethin' about the painter comin' an' that, but I'll send 'er to 'er mission on the days 'e's workin'."

Clara came slowly and rather wearily up the stairs. She was finding visiting the mission and keeping up with her friends there, while living in Kensington, tiring, but her eyes beamed through her pince-nez when she saw Charles.

"How very nice of you to call. Is it all right about Thursday?"

Charles gently pushed Clara into the chair by the kitchen table.

"What's Henry been doing to you? Starving you? You look terribly tired, you shouldn't flog up and down to that dreary mission."

Henry had moved to the stove. He turned to have a look at Clara.

"She does look a bit rough."

Clara smiled at them both.

"What nonsense! I'm not a bit tired, and my mission is not dreary."

Charles sat on the table beside her.

"If you weren't teetotal I should order you a drink."

"But I am. This afternoon at our mothers' meeting we were singing one of the dear old temperance hymns. 'Hark!

The temperance bells are ringing. Joyous music fills the air; Strength and hope their tones are bringing—To the homes where dwelt despair.'"

Henry left the stove and came across to Clara.

"You wouldn't 'ave been singin' about no temperance bells if you'd 'eard what was bein' said on this doorstep not an hour before Mr. Willis come."

Charles noticed that Clara's kind blue eyes had for a second a hunted look. He had always had an affection for her, but now when, because of Julie, he was burgeoning with love for the whole world, he felt a son's fondness for her. He took one of her hands.

"Don't let your relations bother you. I'm here to look after your affairs, you know."

Clara had been slightly low-hearted. What did Maurice want? It was unkind not to help people, especially a brother, but the possessions dear Uncle Simon had given her were only hers in trust; she must try and be firm, and not mind if her family were cross with her. She looked up gratefully at Charles, dear boy, what a comfort he was.

"They don't worry me. It's just that I'm an old muddler, and there seem so many things to see to, and I do want to da what is right for everybody. I'm afraid my brothers and sisters may not quite understand. But I'm in the wrong, you know, Mr. Willis, I ought to remember 'that if you trust you don't worry, and if you worry you don't trust.'"

Charles gave her hand a pat.

"Of course you should. I do wish you would call me Charles."

"May I? I should like that very much. As a matter of fact

165

I had begun to think of you as Charles. Would you perhaps call me Aunt Clara, as my nephews and nieces and their children do?"

Charles, still holding Clara's hand, said he would be delighted. Then, seeing Clara looked less flustered, he turned to Henry.

"Now, let's have it. Who was it came this afternoon after 'The Goat in Gaiters?'"

"Wasn't about 'The Goat in Gaiters.' It was Mr. Levin'ton come."

Charles looked questioningly at Clara, trying to put a face to Paul, whom he had only seen on the day of the funeral.

"Your sister Sybil's husband?" Clara nodded. Charles turned back to Henry. "What did he want?"

To Henry Paul was funny, but he was a relative of Clara's and therefore before her must be spoken of with some politeness. Had Charles not talked of nothing but Julie and painting the room for her, he would have given him an imitation of Paul, and used vivid words to paint in the picture.

"'e come 'ere all casual like. 'I was jus' passin',' 'e says, you know 'ow 'e speaks, Miss Clara, as if 'is voice 'ad been oiled like, 'e says, 'e was wonderin', seein' what good port we 'ad at the will readin', if Mr. 'ilton 'ad left any wines and that. 'e said if there was, knowin' it would be no good to you like, 'e would take it off of you; 'e says 'e wouldn't think there was need to trouble Mr. Willis about it, that maybe I could fix it."

Charles was furious.

"The dirty dog."

Clara smiled.

"Nonsense, Charles dear. I'm sure he meant to be kind."

"So kind," said Henry, "'e offered me five nicker if I could fix it."

"What did you tell him?" Charles asked.

"Where 'e could put 'is five nicker." Seeing Clara was not looking Henry illustrated his statement.

Charles had explained to Clara about her wine; it was a subject about which now and again she had pondered.

"I certainly couldn't sell the wine, for that would be taking money for something I think wrong. I might give it away, after all it's no good to me, and if my brother-in-law would like it . . ." Clara broke off looking confused, "or perhaps it should be destroyed . . ."

Henry and Charles exchanged looks. Charles said:

"If I were you, Aunt Clara, I wouldn't do anything for the moment. Wait until you've gone into everything before you make up your mind to part with a thing. You see, there's no hurry and you might be sorry if you rush things."

Clara got up.

"I think you're right. Dear Charles, what would I do without you? I am so glad I have not to come to a decision about 'The Goat in Gaiters' on Thursday for, as you say, there's no hurry. I shall go and take my things off. I feel so much better for seeing you."

Charles watched Clara climb the stairs. He came back to the kitchen and made a face at Henry.

"Blast the relations! Looks properly upset, poor old lady. I'll see if I can persuade her to let me write to Mr. Hilton and Lady Cole, saying there's nothing doing about the pub."

Henry was back at the stove.

"Be a bit of all right if you could, and to the Reverend too. It's keepin' from 'em all that the Marquis kids is comin' that's upsettin' of 'er. If the Reverend comes 'ere she'll tell 'im, and then we'll 'ave the 'ole boilin' creatin'."

Charles turned to go.

"Too right we will, but if I've got the relations right, letters won't stop them, the thing to do is to prevent her seeing them."

Henry sighed.

"Seems 'ard with 'er 'avin' a nice 'ome an' all but it'll 'ave to be the mission, every bloomin' day. Nothin' else for it."

* * * * *

Orlando Lane proved to be off the Folkestone Road on the outskirts of Ashford. "The Goat in Gaiters" stood flush with the lane, bounded on one side by a garden surrounded by a holly hedge, and on the other by a field in which were chickens, two cows, a goat, and well-kept coops and sheds. It was a spicy morning with a nip of frost in the air; as Clara got out of the car she raised a pleased nose to the walnut-ish scent of decaying leaves, mixed with the tang of chrysanthemums from the garden. The inn was early Georgian; with the years not only had the brickwork mellowed but the building exuded contentment from the many who had found pleasure inside it. Clara peered over the hedge at the chickens and cows, then up at the holly berries glistening in the sunlight, then down at the solid worn bench under the window, and turned a puzzled face to Charles.

"This doesn't look a sinful place. If I didn't know what went on inside I would have said it was good; that bench seems asking old folk to come and rest in the sun."

Charles looked at the bench. In his mind's eye he could see Clara's old folk, mug in hand, enjoying their drinks, and breaking long contented pauses with a word on local affairs or politics. This little inn would not attract passing traffic. It would be mainly local people who used it; it probably had seldom seen the dismal sight on which the law insisted, of waiting children in the wet and wind, gazing at the well-lit windows through which came a burr of talk, broken by cascades of laughter. He wondered how old Simon had come by the property, and why anyone was after it; for all it was on the outskirts of Ashford it was a real little country pub off the beaten track, it was hard to imagine it doing much business, but this was an illusion for he was sure George Hilton was no fool, and Sir Frederick Cole was an exceedingly successful man. He took Clara's arm.

"Let's go inside and see what it's all about."

It wanted a few minutes to opening time. Bert Frossart, the licensee, was in his bar cleaning glasses, it was his wife Millie Frossart who let them in. Charles had warned the Frossarts to expect Clara, but there was no need for a warning, there had never been a moment in her married life, save when her children were being born and she had been forced to allow relations or strangers to see to her home, when it had not been ready for inspection day or night. Millie was nearly seventy and her eyes did not see as clearly as they had done, but they saw clearly enough to sum up Clara. She sent Charles and Henry to the bar, and after Clara had washed and tidied settled her down in her parlour to drink tea.

Clara looked round the parlour. The window looked out on to the garden, where a large ginger cat lay in a patch of sunlight, sheltered from the wind by bronze chrysanthemums. The room was plushily furnished but cosy, the firelight glinting on family photographs, vases of pampas grass, a black marble clock, china and glass collected over the years, and, on a table in the window, a large Bible lying on a crocheted mat. She felt at ease with Millie Frossart and knew she would not be misunderstood if she spoke what came into her mind.

"How nice this is. Do you know, I'm so surprised. You see, I've signed the pledge, and I thought all public-houses were horrid. I've never been in one before."

Millie was not surprised at this. She was the daughter of a publican, as well as the wife and business partner of one, and knew that the Clara type, teetotal or not, never came into inns. They might have a drink in the lounge of an hotel, but if they looked like Clara, even there they were self-conscious, and asked nervously whether the glass of sherry, or small gin and lime, would go to their heads.

"There's publics and publics, very nice house this is, Bert wouldn't allow nothing else. We've worked here fifty years, you know, my father was here before Bert; we were married from here, we'll be sorry to leave."

Clara was troubled. Charles had made her promise to make no hurried decision to sell, but sell she had been convinced she must; yet fifty years was a long time; could it be right to turn old people out of their home even if it was a home where, regrettably, drink was sold?

"Of course I can't say yet what I shall decide, but I hope, even if I sell, you will be able to stay, that's what my uncle intended, it was in his wishes; he said he hoped I would arrange that the even tenor of life and sociability at 'The Goat in Gaiters' would go on, not only during my lifetime but after I'm dead, and he was such a dear, kind old man that, even though I think drinking is wrong, I should not like to disappoint him."

Millie, as she picked up her teacup, looked thoughtfully at Clara. Until the war Simon had frequently stayed in Ashford, and had spent his evenings at "The Goat in Gaiters." Millie had, when talking of their landlord with Bert, used many words to describe him, but dear, and kind, had not been two of them. If, however, Clara felt he had been these things, Millie was not going to spoil the picture by speaking ill of the dead.

"Whether you sell or not Bert and me will be giving up soon. You see, we've been disappointed. We had four boys. Our eldest, Percy," she pointed to where an enlarged photograph of a sailor was hanging, "he was drowned in 1916. Then Albert," with a quiet nod as though to a living son Millie pointed out a photograph of a boy dressed in army uniform, "he was in the army. Gassed he was. He lived with us after the war, and we thought maybe he would marry and settle with us, but the gas ate his lungs away, he died in 1921. Cyril," she smiled at a photograph on the mantelpiece, "he wasn't the settling sort. He went to Australia in 1920, he's married now, farming he is, but he never does the same thing for long." Millie got up and fetched a photograph in a silver frame from the table on which was the Bible. It was of a choirboy. "That's my Tom. He was what they call an afterthought. That's the photo I like best of him, lovely voice he had."

The room was now, for Clara, full of Millie's sons. She asked simply, but with pity shining from her:

"What happened to Tom?"

Millie took the photograph from Clara and put it back beside the Bible.

"With our other boys gone, Bert and me set a lot of store by Tom. He was always on about aeroplanes. Funny really, when you think of all the places he could have been killed, his bomber came down not far from here. Coming back from Germany it was, must have been hit, for it went to pieces sudden-like over a wood. The gentleman that owns the wood has put up ever such a lovely cross. When Tom went Bert said that settled it, we'd give up, it was no good going on with no one to follow-like. We reckoned old Mr. Hilton wouldn't last long and we'd finish when he died."

"Where will you go? This place has always been your home, it must have such memories for you."

Millie nodded, no need to answer that. The rooms still rang with the shouts of her boys. Each object she touched was alive with memories.

"We are still trying for a place near here. You see we're known and it's easy to get over to where Tom was killed, and put flowers by the cross."

Clara longed to say "Don't hurry. I shan't sell until you

have found a home." But there were her temperance vows, she had not yet seen the place where drinking took place. She got up, and asked to be shown the bar.

Bert, Charles, and Henry had a round of beer on the house before the bar opened. Bert had a face on which wrinkles had been deeply scored by laughter and sorrow. In a few moments Charles had pulled from him his intention to leave and the reason, and had learned that at the moment the right cottage had not turned up. Looking round, Charles could see how well everything, in spite of Bert's age, was kept.

"Could you stay on for a time if things worked that way?"

Bert's eyes glowed.

"Glad to, sir. You see, it's not only me and the missus, there's Gert and Daisy, the cows, we've chickens, a goat, and Ginger my wife's cat, and all our stuff. You know I'm seventy-four in June, and the missus is near seventy, and of course we're slowin' up. We'd never have left if we could have helped it. We always said, when Tom was alive that was, that they'd only get us out feet first. I shouldn't wonder if it won't be near enough true. I don't reckon we'll go on long when we leave, nor we wouldn't wish it."

Charles accepted this, Bert was not the sort who retired. He gestured with his glass in the direction in which he had seen Millie lead Clara.

"Miss Hilton may sell, because she's teetotal, but the old boy left a wish this place should go on as it is, and she looks upon any wish of his as sacred."

Henry saw Bert found this hard to believe.

"That's right, that is. Looks at 'is photo two or three times a day, she does, and says, "'enery, 'is wishes is a sacred trust.'"

Bert laughed until his laughter wrinkles became valleys. With a sweep of his tankard he drew Charles and Henry closer to him.

"Sacred trust! You ought to have seen him before the war. We hadn't a double room, so . . ."

The bar was open by the time Clara saw it. It was, she noticed, a surprisingly pleasant place, copper mugs and copper pans were hung round the walls. There was a vase of chrysanthemums on the bar, and the bottles, which surely should have had an evil look, caught by the sun, reminded her of a toy kaleidoscope she had loved as a child. Those who frequented public-houses should surely, as temperance hymns had taught her, look fallen: "Yield not to temptation, for yielding is sin," but nothing could have looked less fallen than the drinkers. There was Henry, his beer forgotten, staring out of a window up the lane. There was Charles, in spite of the mug in his hand, looking not only not-fallen, but almost uplifted in the way people looked uplifted in a church. There were two old men telling Sam some story, from which she gathered, though she could not entirely follow the story, that both were church bell-ringers. The only other visitor in the bar was a quiet, well-dressed man drinking what seemed to Clara water out of a small wine glass. Bert broke off his conversation to greet Clara, and to ask her what she would drink.

Charles came to the rescue.

"I don't expect you want anything just now, do you, Aunt Clara?"

Clara explained she had just had a cup of tea. The man drinking out of the small wine-glass moved up the bar to stand beside her.

"You're like my wife, she says there's nothing to touch tea."

Clara beamed. This was really very pleasant, and so unlike what she had been led to expect. She had to share her pleasure.

"It is so nice here, Mr. Frossart." Clara turned to her next-door neighbour. "I have never been in a public-house before, I'm teetotal, but a dear old uncle has left this one to me, so of course I had to see what it was like. I thought I should be a real fish out of water, you know, like 'Dare to be a Daniel! Dare to stand alone! Dare to have a purpose firm! Dare to make it known,' but it's not a bit like that, is it? Why, look at you drinking water. Now you really are being a Daniel, right in the lion's den, so to speak."

Henry had swung round at Clara's first words. There she went again. Quoting hymns in a public-house! She wasn't fit to be trusted for a minute.

"You come over 'ere, an' 'ave a nice sit down, Miss Clara, it's ever so pretty lookin' out."

Only Henry was disconcerted by Clara. Charles regarded her with amusement and affection. Mr. Frossart beamed and said it was the first time he had ever heard The Old Goat called a lion's den. The bell-ringers stopped talking and gazed at Clara with respect. The man with the small wine-glass told Clara that quotation put him in mind of his boyhood, it was fine to hear the old words again, for his poor old Dad had been a great chapel-goer.

175

Clara leaned against the bar and heard about the chapel, every detail of poor old Dad's end, and of his funeral, and the words carved on the marble slab covering his grave. At the end of the recital she felt almost like a relation of Dad's.

"And what do you do?"

The man knew his answer would please. He produced it proudly.

"Sell Bibles."

Clara could have sung.

"Do you! How splendid of you! I am sure I was guided to choose to-day to come here, so that I should meet you. You know, I was sure it was my duty to sell this place, but now I am less certain. If you who give your life to Bibles, can come here, it can't be a wicked place. I'm such a muddled old thing . . ."

Henry had been hovering behind Clara. He had seen the man's glass pushed forward twice, and twice seen it refilled. He knew at a glance Clara had landed on a real soaker. A few more people had come into the bar, and all were listening, and to him it seemed Miss Clara was making a show of herself. He took her firmly by the elbow.

"You come along of me, your dinner's ready."

Mr. Frossart waited until Clara was out of earshot, then he voiced the opinion of all in the bar.

"A real nice lady."

* * * * *

Henry, wearing one of Simon's overcoats and his old bowler, collected Clara outside her mission. The weather had turned bitterly cold, so Clara had decided it was time to wear her fur coat. This was of sealskin, it had belonged to her mother and had been bought at the beginning of the century so had a period air; but it was warm, and it was comfortable and so it had not crossed her mind to have it re-modelled. Henry and Clara might look to some an unusual couple, but as they walked towards their tram stop for the "Dog and Pigeon" there were neither smiles nor giggles; round the mission Clara's clothes had long since been accepted as part of "Miss Clara," "Lady Clara" or "our lady."

Clara had been refreshed by the children's service she had attended, and would have liked to tell Henry about it. Henry, apart from the fact that he did not want hymns re-cited to him, was rehearsing in his mind what Perce was to say to Clara. It would not be an easy afternoon for Clara was so convinced of the rightness of anything arranged by Simon it was hard to prepare her for the way the Perces lived. Jolting along on the tram Henry had tried several openings, but Clara dismissed them.

"You don't understand, Henry. In my work I've been used to visiting all manner of homes. If my uncle, dear old man, chose this place for his greyhounds I am sure he had very good reasons."

"What I was meanin' was Perce's set-up might seem a bit rough to you like."

"As long as the dogs are happy and well fed I shall be quite satisfied."

To Henry the journey to Perce's home might, as he had told Nobby, be only a step, for he had always used generic terms for large areas of London: "up West," "out Barking way." Perce's home and the mission were neighbours only in that they were both S.E. Clara panted beside Henry through a jigsaw of squalid little streets, under low railway arches and across bomb sites. Thinking of a tired body or tired feet was not only a sin, but made the tiredness worse. As she plodded along she attempted to keep her mind off herself, and her faith bright, not only in the ways of God but in the spot to which He had guided Simon to keep his dogs, by recalling how splendidly right Simon's arrangements, that she had so far seen, had proved to be.

"It may seem rather a long walk, Henry, but there is sure to be a reason. Look at those dear people, the Borthwicks, bringing Julie and Andrew up splendidly. I've not yet decided about 'The Goat in Gaiters,' but if there must be public-houses how merciful there are kind folk like the Frossarts to live in them."

Clara's words took Henry's mind off the coming visit to Perce. Must be a bit of all right having a pub. 'Specially a pub like "The Goat in Gaiters." Plenty of company, and your own hens and cows and that, and a nice field to keep them in. Clara was distressed to find that her thoughts refused to go where she sent them, but returned obstinately to her body. Constant service given to the bodies of others had caused her to ignore her own, but now it refused to be ignored. She had been tired recently; this would not have troubled her had it not meant it slowed up her thoughts and actions. It was, she supposed, only to be expected that she should be tired: there were the long journeys to and from the mission, and there were responsibilities which, wrong though she knew it to be to worry, worried her. So difficult to reconcile the rules of life by which she had lived with the various properties she had been left. How could you keep your temperance vows and yet own a "Goat in Gaiters?" How reconcile your duty to God who, it was understood, disapproved of gambling, and your duty to a dear old uncle, who had entrusted to you not only racing dogs and race horses, but something called "Gamblers' Luck Limited?" The missioner at the mission, dear good man though she had always found him to be, had been a little unhelpful when asked for advice. He had talked about the responsibility of riches, and had quoted the Bible: "Render therefore unto Cæsar the things which be Cæsar's, and unto God the things which be God's." But when she had asked him to define which of Uncle Simon's property should be considered God's, and which Cæsar's, he had seemed to suggest that if any profits there might be came to the mission then all her property, no matter how unlikely, belonged to God, whereas, if the profits went elsewhere, everything belonged to Cæsar. It was most confusing. It must, Clara supposed, be worry which made her, who all her life had slept soundly, now spend much of her nights awake. If it had not been that lack of sleep was making her muddle-headed she would not have minded her wakeful nights, for they gave her an opportunity to study Simon's face in the family group. She drew great comfort from looking at Simon's face; he seemed, with his twinkling eyes, so alive, as if he were on the verge of nodding to her and saying, "Don't distress yourself, I'm sure you are doing your best."

Clara tried not to let Henry see she was breathless and

tired. It was so good of him to give up his Sunday afternoon for this visit to her dogs, but finally she had to ask him to slow down.

"A little slower, Henry, I'm rather a fat old thing, you know."

Henry looked at Clara, and was dismayed, for she had turned a greyish colour.

"You look a bit rough, are you all right?"

Clara managed to laugh.

"Of course I am, but you were hurrying rather, and I'm not as young as I was."

Henry put a hand under Clara's arm.

"Just another coupl'a streets and across a bomb site and there we are. You lean on me."

Clara was glad of Henry's hand, but it shocked her that she should need it, for always before when hands were needed hers had been the ones to support.

"I must be eating too much. You feed me too well, Henry."

"You don't eat no more'n a sparrer; anyway I reckon you're thinner than what you was before the old gentleman was took."

"Nonsense. But if I am it's all the travelling we do. The day at the circus and the day at Ashford. I'm usually such a stay-at-home old thing."

"You didn't ought to do too much, there's no 'urry."

Clara stopped.

"Oh, but Henry, there is. Did you hear that hymn we sung at the end of our service this afternoon? 'Forward! Be our watchword, Steps and voices joined; Seek the things before us, Not a look behind.'"

Henry urged Clara on.

"'ymns is all right in their proper place, but you don't want to take them too serious. What's the 'urry? You seen the Marquis kids, an' fixed up them comin' to stay. You seen 'The Goat in Gaiters.' You're seein' the dogs . . ."

"But I have not seen my horses, nor Gamblers' Luck Limited, and I've not seen Mrs. Gladys Smith."

Henry saw this was his opportunity to put over his plan for visiting the horses.

"I been thinkin' of the 'orses. It was Perce's brother Alfie what used to keep 'em, you know, but Alfie's dead now, and 'is son Andy carries on like. It come to me Mr. Willis might run us up to give 'em the once over when the kids is stayin'."

"Oh, I don't think I ought to trouble Mr. Willis, he's been more than kind as it is."

Henry directed Clara towards a large bomb site. He replied soberly, giving no hint of how funny he considered her answer to be.

"No 'arm in tellin' 'im we're goin'. 'e needn't offer if 'e don't feel like it."

Clara stopped walking. She gazed across the bomb site.

"Do we have to cross that? Isn't there a road?"

Henry could see how bleak the surroundings to the Perces' home appeared to Clara.

"Road! Never 'ave roads along side of where racin' dogs 'angs out. Quiet's what they need. Perce and Mrs. Perce thinks no end of this place. Lovely walks the dogs get and no one narkin' round."

Clara was ashamed of herself. How distressing for Henry to think she queried Simon's choice of a home for his dogs.

"I'm just an ignorant old thing, I'm afraid sometimes you must lose patience with me." She had not sufficient energy to cross the bomb site without a rest. Unwilling to explain this she returned to the subject of her property. "Have you ever seen Gamblers' Luck being played, Henry? Mr. Willis tells me it's a kind of game."

Henry knew that the money Simon had put into Gamblers' Luck Limited had been a lucky investment. It had been at the Derby that Simon had first fallen in with the showman who had put up the idea. Simon, with Henry, had arrived early on the racecourse and Simon had said they would go over and see what was doing at the fair. Henry, who could throw a nice dart, had been collecting cigarettes by this means, at the moment when Simon and the showman got together, and so had missed the conversation during which Gamblers' Luck was born. He knew old Simon had been pleased with himself, for he had chuckled at intervals all that day, and in the following weeks, whenever he had attended a conference with the showman, had returned in remarkably good form. A year later Simon had travelled around watching Gamblers' Luck working, and he had taken Henry with him. Henry thought nothing of Gamblers' Luck as entertainment, but now that the question was asked he saw that Clara must be made to approve of it, as without her shares she might be short of money. As they picked their way round the remains of houses, rubble, and rubbish, he felt for words in which to make Clara see her property in a favourable light.

"Well, Miss Clara, it's a kid's game really. There's two great wheels see. On one there's pictures of birds, and on the other flowers. You get a ticket, and on it's wrote the name of a bird, and the name of a flower. Robin Rose or Daisy Thrush. Well, presently the wheel starts to go round and there's lights inside so you can see the pictures, and when the wheels stop the one what 'as the right bird opposite of the right flower gets a prize."

"It sounds a very pretty game," Clara panted. "The children would so enjoy it at the mission. What are the prizes?"

Henry thought back into the past. He remembered fine prizes by the standards of fairs in nineteen forty-seven, but he also remembered that whenever the crowd was big enough for the showman to risk it, no one held the winning ticket, though the crowd was made to believe that they did. If that was going on now, and there was no reason to suppose it was not since it had been part of the original plan, Miss Clara must be kept from noticing it; maybe the Marquis kids could help.

"All sorts. Dolls and that. I tell you what, the kids would enjoy it. I'll 'ave a look round and find where it's showin'. It's always workin' somewhere."

Clara was used to seeing appalling living conditions, but the Perces' house was a shock to her. It had, with the rest of the street of which it had been a part, been condemned for over thirty years. It was bug-ridden, damp and, when the Thames rose, infested by sewer rats. Of all the houses in an insanitary street the Perces' had been the frailest, ricketiest and foulest. In the impoverished nineteen-thirties when authority had decided that, however hard the times, the street must go, the Perces' house, the last in the row, had seemed to remain standing merely by being attached to its neighbour. Just as demolition work was about to start the war had broken out, and in nineteen-forty a land mine did the demolition work; but in the strange way of blast the Perces' house was by-passed, and left standing alone in a wilderness of ruins. Even in nineteen-forty, with homes growing scarcer nightly, the house would have been allowed to fall of its own accord had not Perce and Mrs. Perce been in residence, and, seeing what had been an overcrowded area unsuitable for exercising dogs, in a night become an open space, admirable for their purpose, had refused to move. The house had therefore been shored up and, though authority frequently sighed over it, was allowed to stand since nobody could suggest alternative accommodation for the Perces with their dogs.

The Perces saw Clara and Henry picking their way across the ruins and went out to meet them. There was little to choose between Clara and Mrs. Perce in shape, and, cleanliness aside, a great similarity in dress. Instead of Clara's sealskin coat Mrs. Perce wore what had been a coat of black velvet, its pile was now matted and had an appearance of growing in two directions. Clara, under her coat, wore a roomy maroon-coloured dress trimmed with coral braid, Mrs. Perce an equally roomy dress of green cloth trimmed with jet beading. On Clara's head was a hat of shapeless black felt trimmed with a piece of velvet. Mrs. Perce had a similar hat trimmed with violets.

Clara used a little lavender water on her handkerchief when at the mission, for it was usual for her nose to meet unpleasant smells. In greeting Mrs. Perce she was glad of her handkerchief, for the smell exuded from Mrs. Perce's clothes was formidable. Perce was a pot-bellied man who, in spite of shabby town clothes, had the air of a country man. It was easy, by closing the eyes, to re-dress him in the dateless, earth-coloured garments of a farm labourer. Both Perces shouted a boisterous welcome; the shouting was necessary for they had to make themselves heard above loud barkings of dogs. Greetings over, Mrs. Perce looked in friendly concern at Clara.

"You're tired out, ducks, and no wonder; quite a step from 'The Dog and Pigeon' and crossing the bomb site doesn't 'alf make you feel your feet."

Perce gave Clara's ribs a friendly nudge with his elbow.

"May be 'ard on the feet, but what I say is it's an ill wind: what done nobody a bit of good. The times I said to Mrs. Perce what we needs is a proper place for the dogs to exercise, for I used to have to take 'em walkin' for miles, then what 'appens? 'itler drops a bomb, blows the 'ole place sky-'igh and there's the place for our dogs, just where I wanted it. Might say it was an answer to prayer re'lly."

Mrs. Perce laid a dirty hand on Clara's arm.

"You come in, I got the kettle boilin', better 'ave a sit down before you see the dogs."

Clara was tired, but she had come to see her dogs, and was not shirking her duty.

"It's very considerate of you, but I think I should see the dogs now before it's quite dark." Clara turned to Perce. "Henry tells me your mother was a friend of my dear old uncle's."

Perce had not been briefed only by Henry as to what

should be said to Clara, but rehearsed by Mrs. Perce. He swallowed nervously, trying to recall exactly what he ought to reply. Henry prompted him.

"I was tellin' Miss Clara Mr. 'ilton was like a father to you and Alfie, that's right, isn't it?"

Mrs. Perce was quicker on the uptake than Perce. Her meetings with her mother-in-law had mainly been in the police courts, where she had gone in place of Perce to pay her fines for soliciting, or for being drunk and incapable. Poor Marie, when she had known her, could have been nobody's fancy, but both Perce and Alfie could vaguely remember the good days when she had been pretty, and there was always money about. They remembered how Mr. Hilton would arrive suddenly at the comfortable little suburban house where they had lived, his pockets bulging with presents, a bottle of wine under each arm. His arrival meant they were almost immediately sent to bed, but both recalled there were compensations, how they went to sleep replete with sweets, clutching expensive toys. Neither Perce nor Alfie remembered what had happened next. Other men came to the house, and their mother was frequently drunk, and later took to street walking, but both knew that Simon had no part in their changed conditions, but had remained fond of their mother and a friend to her sons. Through Simon, Perce and Alfie had spent their summers in the country, which was the beginning of Alfie's interest in horses and, later, Perce's in dogs, and it was Simon who had started them on their careers. Mrs. Perce had, in the past, discussed with both Alfie and Perce the possibility of their being Simon's sons, but neither had believed it. Their theory was that their mother, though a hopeless bad lot, had been a charmer when young and that Simon, though probably well aware of what she was and what she would become, had genuinely loved her. As far as they knew she had treated him abominably, but he had been given real affection by both of them. "You don't want to tell Miss Clara no more than what you must about your Ma, Perce," Henry had said. "She's dead and gone now, and there's no need Miss Clara should be upset 'earing what she was; proper turned up she'd be, seein' what a store she sets by the old B, callin' 'is wishes sacred and that. All you needs to say is your Ma was a friend of 'is and tell 'er 'ow you remembers 'is bringin' you presents and that." To recall these words Mrs. Perce gave Perce a nudge as she spoke.

"Go on, Perce, you tell Miss 'ilton of the time 'e brought you a little engine." She turned to Clara. "Always talkin' of it 'e is, and so did 'is brother Alfie, 'o's gone now p'or soul."

Clara looked thoughtfully at Perce. From his age it seemed more likely that he was a son of Simon's than that Simon had fathered the Marquis children. But had that been so, surely it would have been mentioned in his wishes. She felt Perce was ill-at-ease, and this distressed her, for it was not what Simon had intended. Probably, poor man, he did not realise that she was accustomed to hearing of nasty things, and had guessed that his mother and her uncle had been too intimate.

"I think, sad though it may be, we must accept that your dear mother and my uncle lived as man and wife."

The Perces were profoundly shocked. Mrs. Perce said frigidly:

"That's as may be. Now, if you follow Perce we'll show

you the dogs."

While patting innumerable barking, bouncing dogs Clara puzzled what she had said to upset the Perces. Never having seen Marie, especially the latter-day Marie, who was still painfully visible in the memories of the Perces, she could not know how her suggestion that Marie had lived with Simon as his wife scandalised them. Whatever his faults Simon had been a real gentleman, as his niece should know, and though he might have had a friend he was not the sort to lower himself by living with her. Clara, while attempting to catch the names of each dog as it was introduced, came to the conclusion that Henry was to blame, for he had definitely hinted that Uncle Simon had loved Perce's mother. Of course Henry had not said in so many words what he meant by the word "love," but what he believed the situation to have been was implicit in his manner. If Henry's supposition were correct, it was clear the Perces either knew nothing about it, or wished to know nothing about it. Clara, giving an extra pat to each dog as an aid to soothing ruffled feelings, decided that probably Perce's mother's liaison with Uncle Simon, if it had occurred, was the one slip in an otherwise blameless life. Respectability, Clara had noticed, was especially highly valued by such people as the Perces, it was not taken for granted as it was in some other sections of the community. If you were respectable you talked about it, and at a hint that anyone doubted your word there was certainly a shouting match, and sometimes a fight. What a distressing thing that she should have said what she had; no wonder the Perces were offended, they must have felt she was insulting the memory of their dead.

Henry watched Clara with troubled eyes. What a way to talk! Lived as man and wife! She wasn't safe to be let out, really she wasn't. If she wasn't quoting hymns she was saying things that should never be said. It was all right for him to speak to Perce and Mrs. Perce of the old gent as the old B. They had known him well and knew nothing disrespectful was meant, but for Miss Clara, the old man's niece, to say that about him wasn't nice at all.

It was Clara's habit to carry a notebook in her bag, for in her mission work it was often needed. She now produced the book, and a pencil.

"I really must learn my dogs' names. What did you say this one is called?"

There was a pause during which Perce's eyes telegraphed a message to Henry. Henry read the message aright. He laid a finger on Clara's notebook.

"You've no cause to trouble writin' their names down, Miss Clara. Time she's seen 'em once or twice she'll know 'em as if they was livin' with 'er, that's right, isn't it, Perce?"

Mrs. Perce edged nearer to Clara.

"That's right what 'enery says."

Clara peered through her pince-nez at the kennels, in each of which were four dogs, and Perce was holding several more by leads.

"I'm afraid I shall be rather slow at learning their names. I know you'll think this very ignorant of me, Mr. Perce, but to me many of them look alike."

Perce forgot that Clara had shocked him, and saw why Henry was fond of her. Nicely spoken lady she was. He had a reputation second to none for altering a dog's appearance.

It was said in his world that when he had the job of making one dog look the image of another he could even alter the colour of the eyes. Pride in his craft, and a wish to make Henry's Miss Clara feel one of the family, made him forget his instructions and speak ta her as Simon's niece.

"They are alike. When I done with 'em their own mother wouldn't know 'em."

Clara had written "Number one pale yellowish dog" in her book, and was waiting, pencil poised, for the name. Now she stared in bewilderment at Perce.

"How do you mean, when you've done with them?"

Mrs. Perce dug her elbow fiercely into Perce's back. Henry cleared his throat while he thought what to reply. Perce realised he had blundered and laboriously, his eyes shifting from Clara to Mrs. Perce, attempted to fumble back to safety.

"A'course they likes you to send the dog what you've entered to run in a race, but s'posin' that dog was ill, or that, you sends another what looks like it . . ."

Mrs. Perce gave Henry a glance describing what she would later say to Perce. Then she turned to Clara.

"'e's only 'avin' you on, Miss 'ilton. Perce wouldn't do nothin' like that. There's not a more regular man, nor more respected in the business, is there, 'enery?"

Clara saw the Perces were nervous, and that this was caused by something to do with the dogs. Henry had im-pressed on her that the Perces were not only fond of the dogs but needed them for their livelihood. It might not be that she could feel it right to keep racing dogs on which

190

people gambled, that must wait until she had seen them racing, but at once she must make it clear to the Perces that they would be looked after.

"Please don't think I have come to-day to interfere in any way. I feel convinced everything you do for the dogs is right, Mr. Perce. Apart from the fact that I'm sure that is how you would treat them in any case, it's certain my dear old uncle would allow nothing else. He left wishes, you know, and one of them was that his racing dogs and his four race horses should have consideration and kindness and be well looked after for the remainder of their lives."

Perce and Mrs. Perce looked at each other. What had she said? It was certain her dear old uncle would allow nothing else! She couldn't be talking about Mr. Hilton. Mrs. Perce was the first to see how needless all the worrying they had done had been. This lady would make no trouble. You could take her to a hundred tracks and no matter what was going on she wouldn't notice anything funny. It was likely they could get her to carry on just as the old man had carried on, even to buying a new dog when needed. She put her arm through Clara's.

"You come in to tea now, ducks, and Perce'll show you photos what he's had took of the dogs. And you'll want to know what they 'as to eat; it'll surprise you, shouldn't wonder if you'd fancy a plate of what they 'as yourself."

* * * * *

On the journey to London Julie and Andrew felt trapped. They were wild creatures visiting the tamed. How did the tamed behave? Had they their own code of manners? How did you find out how they lived? The children's discomfort was accentuated because Bess, stolidly disregarding their apathy, had insisted that they should be properly dressed for their visit. Andrew's wardrobe had been easy; those men attached to Borthwick's whose opinion Bess considered worth listening to had agreed that you could go anywhere in a nice blue suit, tidy overcoat and a hat. Julie's clothes had been more difficult. Bess had struggled to recall what the smarter women in their audiences wore, but could remember only much the same clothes she wore herself, but looking different, due, she supposed, to her size. There was, that season with Borthwick's, a lady high school rider universally considered a classy, yet refined dresser, and it was on her advice that Julie's wardrobe was planned. Bess had insisted on Julie drawing out of the Post Office what seemed an extravagant sum. When Julie had tried to point this out Bess had silenced her with an imperious hand. "This is money well laid out. I am not saying it will ever be called for, but if anything should go wrong this Miss Hilton would stand by you. Staying in her house you should be dressed so that she can take a pride in you." As a result, for the London journey, the children wore new clothes. Actually they were not so different from the clothes they usually wore, but, because they had been bought to wear in the world of the tamed, they felt more like casings than clothes.

Andrew, never truly alive except when on a trapeze, felt right when dressed for the ring, and the grey flannel or corduroy slacks, and the pullovers or shirts with which he covered his body between practices or performances, were to him no more than dressing-gowns, put on when not working. The blue suit, the new shirt and tie, and the blue overcoat—he had no intention of wearing the hat—would not have bothered him unduly had he worn them on the circus lot; he would have thought them cumbersome, but they would still have been to him but a covering worn when not in his ring clothes. It was having no practice dress in his luggage, and the feeling that he was being carried away, not only from his practice clothes but from his trapezes, that made the new suit and overcoat so terrifying. What did you do when there was no place in which to work? He hid it, but he was quivering with fright; would this land of the "theys" disembowel him?

At any other time new clothes gave Julie pleasure, but on this occasion she disliked them. She had never stayed as a visitor, and neither had the lady high school rider. That old Miss Hilton would not know about clothes, but Mr. Charles Willis would. Between Julie's small breasts was a letter. Nobody, not even Andrew, knew she had received it. It had happened that she was in charge of the office when the postman brought it. It was a most surprising letter; Julie had not known what to make of it, but had hurriedly tucked it out of sight for, funny sort of letter though it might be, it was for her, and that other eyes should read it, and that it should be passed round, and commented on, was unthinkable. Charles had written in gay spirits. He told her that she must not think she was coming to London to do what she liked, she was coming to do what he liked, and he would be round to see her the night she arrived with arrangements in triplicate for Operation Julie Marquis. He hoped that Aunt

Clara would let him take her out the night she arrived, they would have a bite somewhere and they might dance a bit afterwards. Would she please answer and say she would like to spend her first evening with him, for himself he thought it a good idea. He signed himself "Charles." Julie had not answered the letter, for she had no idea how to. Was he really planning to take her out to dinner, or was he making fun of her? Why did he sign himself "Charles?" When she moved the letter felt stiff and made the faintest crackle. The feel of the letter and the crackle had given Julie the queerest sensation, the sort of feeling she had just before she and Andrew went into the ring for their act, a mixture of being uplifted yet scared. Now that the train was rushing her towards the writer the uplifted feeling was gone and only fear remained. Suppose Mr. Charles Willis meant what was in the letter, how did a girl like herself know what to wear and how to behave? She knew nothing, she was sure to make terrible mistakes, and then Mr. Charles Willis would be ashamed. How did you learn how people like Mr. Charles Willis behaved? No girl in any magazine she had read, or film she had seen, was as ignorant as she was. She had seen one film where the heroine was a circus girl like herself, even a trapeze artist, but she had not been like any circus artist she had met. After the show the girl in the film had gone to restaurants and out dancing with the hero, wearing beautiful frocks, furs and jewels. The film had not shown where the girl lived, but it must have been a big place or there would have been no room for her wardrobe, and her life must have been quite different from the life of ordinary circus people, for she never seemed to have to wash, iron, cook and do the shopping, as well as repair clothes for the act. Could it be that Mr. Charles Willis had seen that film, and thought she was like that girl? Was that why he wrote about taking her out? Was he supposing she was arriving with smart clothes, furs and jewels? Was that why he, a gentleman like he was, signed himself just "Charles" to a circus girl he had met the once?

Clara and Henry were on the platform. A look at them both should have set Julie's and Andrew's minds at rest. It was a cold morning and Clara had on the sealskin coat which at any other time they would have recognised as a relic, which Bess would scorn. Henry would not have dressed up to meet the children, for he had placed them rightly, but since he was escorting Clara he wore Simon's old bowler. Had they crossed the ring with the clowns and augustes the audience would have seen them as figures of fun, and they would have laughed, and in the ordinary way Julie and Andrew would have smiled, but to-day there was nothing remotely funny about them, they were keepers opening the door of a cage.

As the taxi drove towards Gorpas Road only Henry was completely happy. To him the children's scared eyes, and monosyllabic replies to Miss Clara's questions were wholly understandable. "Poor little B's," he thought, "they aren't 'alf in a state comin' to stay, nor I don't wonder neither, I wouldn't care for stayin' with strangers meself." He eyed Julie thoughtfully. Nice little bit she looked, maybe Mr. Willis was on to something good. But if Mr. Willis thought she was a brass, he had got another think coming. That dyed hair could fool you for a moment, but if you looked at those brown eyes you could see she was innocent as a baby. "Shame re'lly, somebody did ought to tip her off."

Clara had been looking forward to the arrival of the children. She felt that at last she was carrying out a part of a wish of Simon's. She had hoped the children were looking forward to a week in London, most children would, but she could see that this was not the case with Julie and Andrew. She noticed their frightened eyes and nervous, hesitant replies, and as she told them that they must treat her home as their own, and do anything they fancied while they were with her, her mind was seeking a reason for their fear, and, thanks to her mission training, she came near to finding it. She had seen that same scared, almost furtive look, before; it meant that there was uncertainty as to the reason for her visit, and anxiety lest she pried into things that were not her concern. Julie and Andrew had not been told the wording of the will, and she had been advised they should not know it, but, not knowing it, they must be wondering why a silly old thing like herself wished them to visit her, if perhaps she had some demand to make of them. Visiting for the mission, when she came across those who were scared of her, she had found it best to talk of trivialities until fear of her abated, so she tried this method with Julie and Andrew.

"Such kind people Mr. and Mrs. Perce; quite soon some of the dogs will be racing and Henry is going to take me to see them do it. My uncle wanted me to look after them but racing is gambling and I feel gambling wrong. I shall decide what to do after I have seen them race. Quite a problem, my old uncle was such a dear man, and would have had nothing to do with anything wrong, but, of course, people hold different views about gambling . . ."

Clara's monologue came to an abrupt end when the taxi turned into Gorpas Road. Henry, riding with his back to the driver, had turned to make sure he found the house. At sight of the house he tapped on the glass and stopped the taxi.

"Miss Clara, the Reverend and his missus are on our doorstep." On Henry's order the taxi turned and drove into the next street, where it again stopped. Henry felt some explanation should be given to the children. "The Reverend is Miss Clara's brother."

Clara tried to feel what it was right she should do. Since Maurice and Doris were there ought she not to be honest, and drive up to the house and introduce Julie and Andrew to them? Was that not what God would wish? Was that not why at this moment He had sent Maurice and Doris to the house?

"I think, Henry, we should go home. I know I had thought it better my brother should not know about our visitors, but as he and my sister-in-law have come to-day I think I must accept they were guided to do so."

Henry thought quickly. Miss Clara was a shocker to move when she started on her guidance talk. But his orders had been clear. Mr. Willis had said he would write himself to all the relatives, but letters would not keep them off, and it was up to Henry to see that Clara and the relatives did not meet until she had decided what to do with her property, Mr. Willis wouldn't half create if he found out he had not only let the Reverend meet Miss Clara but the Marquis kids. There was only one way to talk to Miss Clara when she was taken religious.

"You couldn't be guided to go there now, Miss Clara, not seein' the promise you give Mr. Willis."

On hearing Charles's name Julie moved, so that she could feel the letter between her breasts. Clara felt the movement and turned to Julie.

"It's so difficult, dear, Alison and Marjorie are nieces, but you and Andrew are a sacred trust."

Julie had expected not to understand the world of the "theys," but what was now going on was more confusing than even her worst fears. She and Andrew a sacred trust! What talk was that? She was spared the trouble of even a monosyllabic reply. The taxi driver, who, having assessed his fares as the sort who would tip poorly, turned and asked in a surly voice if they had made up their minds where they wanted to go.

"What's your 'urry, mate? Someone after you?" Henry leaned across to Clara. "You take the kids to a nice little place and 'ave a cuppa till the Reverend's gone. I'll 'ang around and let you know when you can come 'ome."

If Henry had only advised tea and not mentioned hanging about, Clara might have agreed, but his last words settled the matter, Maurice was a brother. How horrid to allow somebody to hang about in order to warn you when a brother had left your doorstep.

"No, Henry, that would be very unkind. Tell the driver to go back to the house."

Henry tapped Clara's knee with a firm first finger.

"No, you don't. I got me orders from Mr. Willis, 'e said nothin' was to be told to the relatives until you 'ad decided what was right."

It was by accident that Henry landed on the word "right" but it changed Clara's mind.

"Dear Mr. Willis, he's so considerate, perhaps I should do as he advised." She opened the taxi door and got out. She beamed at Julie, Andrew and Henry. "You dear people have something to eat and, when you have finished, telephone to me and I will let you know if you can come home." She saw Henry rising to get out. "No, stay where you are, Henry. You needn't be anxious about me, I shall say nothing about the spare room."

Henry gave the driver instructions, then spoke gloomily towards Clara's loaf-like shape disappearing round the corner.

"Don't be anxious! Don't make me laugh! By the time you're 'alf-way up the stairs you'll 'ave told 'em 'o's 'ere, and the next thin' we knows we'll 'ave the 'ole boilin' scratchin' round like cats round a dustbin."

Charles's letters had prevented George and Frederick making further moves to acquire "The Goat in Gaiters." George might call Charles a young jackanapes, but he knew and respected the firm of Willis and Willis. Any property they were keeping an eye on would not be sold cheaply. Frederick might talk to Alice about monkey business, but he never underrated an opponent or wasted his valuable time. Willis and Willis were formidable opponents, and it would be time wasted trying to fool them as to the value of "The Goat in Gaiters." Both men were secretly annoyed that the letters they had caused to be sent to Clara should have been seen by the firm of Willis and Willis, and both, since they could not speak their minds to Willis and Willis, spoke them to their wives. When it came to mind-speaking Vera could do as well, and better, than George, who was hindered from letting himself go by his legal training, which had taught him to use words with caution. He had not said half what he intended to say when Vera broke in. She was surprised George should have been such an idiot as to underrate young Willis. She had seen at a glance that he was the sort to keep his talons on Clara's possessions, and if there were any pickings to be had, it was certain Willis and Willis would get them. As she thought of pickings going to the already prosperous Willis family, while none came to the needy children and grandchildren of Simon's eldest nephew, Vera felt such an uprush of rage that her face became bloated and blotched. George might accept such a state of affairs, but she was not going to. Old Clara was not to wallow in comfort while Ronnie and Ethel, Rita and poor Tim, Freda and Basil, not to mention little Pansy, Peter, Derek, Poppet, Noel and now baby Priscilla Annette, had to manage, not only without luxuries, but, too often, without what really amounted to necessities. It was not as if George was a rich and successful man like Frederick, able, even if he didn't do it, to give his family everything they wanted. George's family knew there was little help possible because he was incapable of earning more than he was doing. If it were the last thing she arranged she would see old Clara did something to help the children during her lifetime, though it would not be much, for she must live frugally so that, after her death, there would be a comfortable sum to divide. George might believe that nonsense about dogs, horses and that gambling thing not bringing in much, but she was not fooled. Uncle Simon had lived very cosily, hadn't he? Was there any reason why less income should be pouring in on old Clara? George interrupted there to murmur the words "death duties." Vera, carried away by rage, brushed death duties aside as if they did not exist. If George were weak enough to lie down under what had happened she was not, she would see justice done.

George knew Vera in a temper too well to make a suggestion while the temper was with her, but when the storm had died down he reintroduced the subject of Clara's income. Vera was, of course, right, it was an unfair will, but nothing would come of getting angry, anger, even when it was justified, was not an aid to clear thinking. They must play their cards carefully. The children were not the only needy members of the family, there were Alison and Marjorie. If there were a lot of money to come, which there never was nowadays with death duties screwing the last penny out of estates, it would be only fair that after Clara's death as many as possible of her relatives should benefit. There would not be, however, much money and therefore the long-sighted thing for Clara to do would be to leave what there was in trust for the youngest of her relatives. If the money were left in trust for Pansy, Peter, Derek, Poppet, Noel and Priscilla Annette, and Clara did not live too long beyond her three score years and ten, quite respectable sums would accrue by the time the children came of age. It was unlikely, as things were at present, with that young Willis hanging around, that Clara would come to him for advice, therefore the proper thing to do would be to get Clara's interest focused on the children. Priscilla Annette was not yet christened. Clara must be asked to be godmother, and at the christening a fuss must be made of her. She had never been made a fuss of, she would enjoy it. They must, too, plan Christmas. All the children together, a Christmas tree, little presents from the children to Clara, that sort of thing. Nothing should be forced, everything should seem perfectly natural, which indeed it was. He would write to Freda to-morrow instructing her to write to Clara about being godmother, and outlining the sort of letter that would go down well.

Frederick was not interrupted as he spoke his mind to Alice, for, with bowed head, she allowed herself to be blamed for having written the letter to Clara—for having brought her daughters up so badly that one had married a wrong-un and the other snivelled around, remembering a husband who had been killed instead of making the best of herself while she still had the looks, and so finding a second man with enough money to look after her and her children—for having most deceitfully led him to understand that she was her uncle's heir—and for doing nothing, now that Clara had all there was, to make herself so invaluable to her sister that when a will was made what was left went in the right direction. Frederick paused there for Alice to reply, and when instead she stood silent, with meekly drooping head, he shouted, his voice full of temper caused by knowing the blamed is not to blame, "Well, are you doing anything? Do you ever trouble to see your sister?" Alice did not point out that she had but taken down the letter Frederick had dictated, that the upbringing of the girls, as far as schools were concerned, had been his business, that she had begged Ann to delay her marriage to Cyril, whom she had never liked, it was he who had told her to stop croaking, he did not want unmarried daughters on his hands if she did. Instead, she pointed out, in the tone of one who accepts that she is a fool, that Clara was only two years older than she was, very strong, and likely to outlive her. Frederick resented the idea of losing property, especially a wife. Alice was his, there could be no thought of her dying, until he himself had died, and had therefore no further use for her. She was, he told her, an idiot; had he said anything about leaving anything to her? Of course not. When he spoke of the right direction he was naturally referring to Ursula, Gordon and Frank. If Alice were so rotten a mother she could not bring up a couple of daughters to have a bit of horse sense, the least she could do was to see her grandchildren were provided for. There was little enough money on her side of the family, but such as there was it was her duty to see came eventually where it had been promised. He added that she had better keep an eye on her brother George, or the old skinflint would beat her to it. Alice said meekly, "Yes, Frederick," but when he had gone from the room she looked up with an expression that was not only not meek but defiant. This was an order that need not be obeyed, for the giver of the order was most unlikely to be present when the result was known. She would see Clara, but what they talked about would be her own and Clara's affair. For Clara was strong and Clara led a quiet, healthy life, whereas Frederick had high blood pressure, and should neither excite himself nor over-work, both of which he did daily.

When Clara, a little out of breath, arrived at her front door, she was received with relief by Maurice and Doris.

They had especially chosen a morning visit, having decided Henry would be at home doing the housework, and if Clara were out, they would insist on coming in and waiting. Clara had answered Maurice's letter with a vague rambling one in which she said she was busy at the moment, but later it would be lovely to see Maurice. Doris would have ignored that letter, but there was one also from Charles. It was a carefully-worded affair suggesting it was written in friendliness, so that Miss Hilton's family need not be anxious about her affairs. It stated that on his advice Miss Hilton was coming to no quick decision about selling any of her property. Although it did not say so there was a hint that Clara's welfare in every direction was being guarded by Willis and Willis. Doris was slightly awed by lawyers. She and Maurice had few dealings with them. She read and re-read Charles's letter, wondering what was behind it. Maurice's letter to Clara had not mentioned property. He had said he had something to discuss. There was not a hint he wanted Henry out of the flat and Alison and Marjorie in it. In any case was Henry property? Because of Charles's letter the visit to Clara was put off, not that Maurice and Doris admitted it was put off, it was being too busy that prevented them going to London. They would have waited for some real excuse for their visit to Clara had their hands not been forced. Marjorie's job was coming to an end. The doctor she was assisting had married, and his wife was to take over her work. This would not have mattered, for Marjorie had immediately had an offer to do the same work at an increased wage for another doctor, but Marjorie had become difficult. She said she had no intention of spending her life drifting from doctor to doctor, it was a dead-end occupation; when times were hard she would be dispensed with and a sister, elderly cousin or wife would fill her place in exchange for food and a bed. She did not want her parents to do anything, she would in fact far rather they did not. She would find work, no matter what, which made it possible for her to train to be a masseuse. Maurice was pained. Daughters, until they married, should remain in the nest, or in nests borrowed for them by their parents. When he mentioned this to Marjorie he had said, "I am sure you will leave this to Mummie and me to decide," and then gently, "We know our fifth commandment, don't we?" Marjorie had replied, "Well, if you are going to start on The Bible how about Ye fathers, provoke not your children to wrath?" Maurice was too pained to answer that, and instead wrestled on his knees with the problem of daughters who were undutiful. "I wouldn't mind for myself, God, but I am a priest. Because of that my words should be heeded by all daughters, especially my own." When Maurice emerged subdued and creased from wrestling, Doris for once was impatient when he told her what, he understood, the line he should take should be, and refused to listen to much of his disjointed statement, breaking in finally with "Nonsense." Though Maurice's face showed him to be shocked and grieved at the use of such a word during so solemn a conversation, Doris paid no heed. If Maurice thought it was vouchsafed to him that he was to change Marjorie's mind by showing how deep his love was, and how much a daughter had power to hurt her father, she was afraid the vouchsafing was coming from below instead of above. Marjorie, as he ought to know, was the last type of girl to be influenced by that sort of treatment, it was in fact likely to drive her out of the house. There was only one way to deal with Marjorie and that was to present a sensible alternative. Marjorie was singularly lacking in social sense, as surely Maurice had noticed. Had he not heard both she and Alison say they did not care what work they did, provided it was honest and well paid? Marjorie would do exactly as she threatened if they could not suggest a better plan. Maurice must face the possibility of Marjorie taking on the job of a charlady if the hours left her free for her training as a masseuse, and there was sufficient money in it to keep her. How would he feel when it got round the family his daughter was a charlady? Nor would it stop at Marjorie, he could be sure of that, the next minute Alison would join her. They would lose both girls, and Maurice would be surprised to find what that meant to him. She would like to know who else was going to run the youth groups and the scouts and all the rest of it. If, however, he succeeded in making Clara see how improper it looked her having Henry in her house, and how much more suitable two nieces would be, and as well he talked her into paying the fees for Marjorie's massage lessons, and Alison's secretarial training, everything could come right. They need not lose the girls entirely, Clara could send them home for week-ends and that would mean they could keep an eye on their parish work.

Maurice liked support for his actions. He disliked feeling responsible for what he might say or do. The fear of being pounced on by his rural dean, or, worse still, reprimanded by his bishop, of appearing ridiculous in the eyes of his parishioners, of being sneered at by his family, was lessened when he felt he was acting on advice from on high. It was therefore an unwilling Maurice that Doris brought to Clara's doorstep, in fact he would have refused to visit Clara until he had received at least a celestial hint that this was the right moment, but Doris, with an urge to do something, was not a Doris to be gainsaid. She came from a suburban home where everything was sacrificed on a fire built of what the neighbours would think. Since her marriage to Maurice she had worried less what the neighbours thought, for the neighbours were parishioners and should pattern their behaviour on what was done in the vicarage; but she cared terribly what Maurice's family thought. Her own family's views mattered nothing, for she had married into a higher class, and it was theirs only to listen humbly when told how life was lived in the Hilton world. Every inflection was guarded, every word chosen so that they never knew that Maurice's relations actually looked down on Maurice because he was poor; it was a fear that stalked her that one day her family would learn the truth, and the glossy picture she had painted of Maurice the family counsellor, Maurice to whom all turned, would dissolve never to be repainted. Her upbringing had taught her that eyes were always peering from behind curtains, so nothing you did was unobserved. If Marjorie carried out her threat of finding work in London, and, as was only too likely, it was demeaning work, somebody would see, somebody would whisper, and then the dreaded moment would arrive, her family would find out what the Hiltons, so wickedly, thought of Maurice.

Maurice was delighted when repeated rings produced no

Henry. It seemed that without his interference the visit was not to take place. Gratefully he glanced skywards. It was when mentally he was framing thanks for unexpected ill-deserved help, that Clara arrived.

Because she knew she had tried to avoid meeting Maurice and Doris, and because there was something to hide, Clara tried to feel exceptionally affectionate.

"You dear things. I had no idea you were coming. I hope you haven't been waiting long."

Doris, because it was urgent she should feel so, tried to sound fond in her greeting, but she had not forgiven Clara for her behaviour to Maurice on the drive back from Simon's funeral, nor for having left herself and Maurice to hold the position of the poor members of the family on their own, so her effort was not successful.

"Good-morning, Clara. We had hoped to find you in. Maurice and I are naturally unused to standing on doorsteps."

Clara had been fiddling with her key in the lock. She stopped in surprise.

"Aren't you? How very odd. I really do the same sort of work as Maurice and I spend hours on doorsteps."

The door was open and they climbed the stairs. Doris's lips were pressed in a thin line. What impertinence! The same sort of work as Maurice! Had the business they were on not been so important she would have spoken her mind. To keep herself from that temptation she changed the subject.

"Where's Henry?"

Clara made the steepness of the stairs an excuse for not answering immediately. Where indeed was Henry? There could never be an occasion when it was right to lie.

"Such steep stairs, aren't they? You're both thin, but I'm such a fat old thing, they make me out of breath. Where is Henry? Oh, he's out doing something for me." She reached the top of the stairs and, with a feeling of triumph, threw open the drawing-room door. That was a good answer. It was perfectly true; if she was careful they need not feel she was hiding anything, the children's luggage was not here, Henry's and Andrew's camp beds were not yet put up, there should be nothing to give away her little secret.

Doris looked round the drawing-room. Henry had built up the fire before he left for the station, and it was now blazing behind the guard. The room had not much furniture for there had not been much worth keeping after moth and mice had been nourished on it. There were still no curtains, and to many the room would have seemed empty and bleak. But to Doris a huge room with a parquet floor, and a vast, though dusty, chandelier, were grand, and the blazing fire looked rich. She managed to stifle the upsurging of jealousy that it was Clara who had been given such luxury and looked round for something to start the conversation rolling in the right direction. Her eye caught sight of a long cobweb in a corner.

"This room must make a lot of work."

Clara's eyes beamed happily from behind her pince-nez. It was a pity so much had rotted away, but how fortunate there was nothing left to attract moths, for Henry, dear man though he was, would be unlikely to keep them at bay.

"Not really, there's not much furniture now so Henry can manage nicely."

Doris looked at Maurice. Henry had been brought not only into the conversation, he was now the centre of it. This was the moment for Maurice to say what he had come to say. Maurice accepted the message, and tried to send one back asking Doris to be patient, these things could not be rushed. It was a difficult message to send without words, and Doris did not receive it. All she saw was Maurice looking depressed, almost, only it was not a description to be applied to a husband, especially a husband who was a clergyman, hang-dog. She saw she must keep the conversation hovering round Henry.

"Don't you wish Henry was a woman? Men are never as thorough as we are, are they?"

Clara thought fondly of Henry.

"I wouldn't change Henry for anybody. I can so understand what he meant to Uncle Simon. Henry's not a servant, he's a dear friend."

Doris gave Maurice a prodding look. He really must say something now. Maurice licked his lips. How he longed for advice, just the faintest hint; he felt incompetent to handle this situation without guidance.

"The position has changed, Clara. Uncle Simon was a man, you are a woman."

"I don't see what difference that makes. He was a wonderful friend to the dear old man, and now he's being a wonderful friend to me."

Maurice used a tone he found effective when he wished to make parishioners consider their actions.

"Are you quite happy with only yourself and Henry in the flat?"

Clara paused before she answered. She must be careful to speak generally, for this week she and Henry would not be alone, and it would be lying to pretend that they were.

"Very happy. I think I may say happier than I have ever been. It was delightful at the mission, and of course I was glad to do all I could for Father and Mother, but having a place of your own is a great treat. I often look at the group taken at the birthday luncheon, and I hope the dear old man is able to see how happy he has made me."

Maurice and Doris thought of their copies of the family group, and felt a need to see the contented smile leave Clara's face. Maurice leant forward.

"Clara, Henry should not live here. It is not a suitable arrangement."

Clara was puzzled. Why had Maurice said that? Henry's was quite a nice little room, she believed. She never went into it, it was his property, willed to him by Simon. Maurice could not know she had allowed him to lend it to Julie, and that all he had this week was a camp bed, which of course would not be a suitable arrangement for long.

"I think Henry's quite happy. As a matter of fact the room has been done up recently. You were thinking that perhaps he should have Uncle Simon's room?"

Doris saw that Maurice was going to shilly-shally.

"Maurice thinks, and so do I, that you should have a woman or women in the flat. Henry could come in every day of course to do the work, but he should live out."

Maurice nodded.

"That is what I wished to talk to you about, Clara. I know you wouldn't dismiss Henry, so we have a suggestion to make."

Clara had no idea what they were talking about. She knew with certainty, in the matter of Henry at least, that she was carrying out Simon's wishes, so the opinion of Maurice, Doris or anyone else meant nothing to her. When you knew you were doing right there was no wavering. As well her mind was not with Maurice and Doris. How long were they going to stay? Julie and Andrew must think it curious that they had to sit in a tea-shop instead of coming to the flat. She smiled vaguely at Maurice, while wondering how, without hurting his feelings, to persuade him to go.

"Yes, Maurice dear?"

Maurice, pushed to it by a look from Doris, spoke more firmly.

"We think our girls should live with you. A most suitable arrangement."

Doris pressed the suggestion.

"They could sleep in Henry's room."

Clara's wandering attention was caught. Oh dear, how tiresome! This was just the sort of plan she had feared one of the family would suggest. It was out of the question of course. It would not be right. The flat was only hers in trust for others. It would not be easy to make the family see this; families felt, quite naturally, they should come first, and so they should when it was personal property, but this was not personal property, it was property belonging rightly not only to the human beings given into her care but to the animals as well.

"It would work splendidly," Doris said, "for Marjorie wants to train as a masseuse, and Alison to take a secretarial course. They could share the room . . ."

It was on those last words that Clara saw, as if the thought were flashed to her, how, without hurting Maurice and Doris, she could refuse to take in Marjorie and Alison. She had not seen Henry's room since the time when news came that Peterson had been killed, and she had gone into it to pack his belongings to send to his mother. It had been, at that time, crowded, having both Peterson's and Henry's possessions in it, and she distinctly recalled saying to Henry that he must be glad Peterson's box was being moved out, as there was no room for it. If there was no room for a box there could be no room for a second bed. To-day it would not be an impertinence to go into Henry's room, for it was at this moment nobody's room, for Henry had vacated it, and Julie not yet moved in. She got up.

"I'm afraid that plan wouldn't work. It's a tiny room, only just room for Henry, dear man."

Climbing the stairs behind Clara, Maurice and Doris exchanged looks. Doris's look was encouraging, it said, "Don't worry, I'm sure I can find space for the second bed." Maurice's look was unhappy. He was thankful the talk about Henry was behind him, but he could not feel it had had the effect it should have had. Had Clara followed what he was saying? Of course she was a sister, and sisters were apt to remember only a brother was speaking, and forget they were also listening to a clergyman. Even so she surely should have been a little confused and embarrassed.

Clara opened Henry's door and, sure that her memory had not failed her, stood back to let Maurice and Doris look in.

Maurice and Doris looked, and as they looked their eyes became glazed. Charles's decorators had made a charming job of the little room, so charming that though Clara did not know it, Henry had not slept in it since, partly because he felt silly in it, and partly because he was scared of messing it up, and was happier on a camp bed in the drawing-room. The walls were pale duck-egg blue, the ceiling a darker shade of the same colour. The curtains, and the hangings round the bed and dressing-table, were a delicate pink, as were the carpet and the satin eiderdown. By the bed and in front of the low glass-topped, many-mirrored dressing-table were white rugs. As a finishing touch that morning a florist had delivered an egg-shell blue vase filled with pink carnations, which Henry, on Charles's instructions, had placed on the dressing-table.

Clara, getting no word from Maurice or Doris, looked over their shoulders. She was charmed with what she saw. Dear Henry, how kind to make his room look so nice for Julie. And it was a small room, there was no room for a second bed. Then she saw the flowers and was humbled. What a good man Henry was. Why had she not thought of some welcoming flowers? So nicely arranged too, and such a pretty vase. Without self-consciousness she spoke her thoughts.

"Dear, dear Henry."

Maurice moved a step so that he came between Clara and Doris. Doris must not be contaminated. His voice trembled.

"The less you say the better, Clara. You have grieved and shocked me more than I can say. We must leave her, Doris."

* * * * *

214

Over cups of tea and buns in an A.B.C. the root of a friendship between Henry and the children was planted. Henry
saw the children were bewildered. "P'or little B's" he
thought, "why wouldn't they be? Miss Clara tellin' them she
can't wait to 'ave 'em in the flat, and the moment they gets
near the place, round goes the taxi, off Miss Clara 'ops, and
they finds theirselves sittin' in 'ere along of me." While or-
dering the tea and buns, Henry came to the conclusion there
was no reason why the children should not hear about the
Hilton family, and, with the exception of the reference to
themselves, about the old B's will.

Henry's talk soothed Andrew. Often on the circus ground
he listened to the tent hands talking. They were a mixed lot,
the uptilted lilt of Wales, the burred warmth of Scotland, the
lovely cadences of Ireland, broken by the nasal twang of
cockney England. Listening to Henry he felt less afraid and
less of an alien, for Henry brought the circus into the A.B.C.,
it was a sound link, almost as home-like as a roar from
Popeye. Henry, with the unconscious sensitiveness of his
type, had been aware that Andrew was scared, and knew
when he felt easier. Not until he was sure of this did he speak
to him directly.

"You're kippin' along of me. Julie's sleepin' in my room,
done up posh it's been, so of a night time we're puttin' a
coupl'a beds for us in the front room."

Henry did not know what this statement would mean to
Andrew. When Andrew had been too young for the ring
there had been nights when he had been allowed to travel
ahead with the tentmen, and had joined in the discussion of
where they should "kip." There would be, of course, the days

to live through, but to hear his nights were to be spent kipping with this Henry, with whom he already felt easy, was such a relief it freed his mind from the present, and it drifted like a homing pigeon to his work. There was that dive, he still was not satisfied with his line, there was a stiffening of his muscles.

Julie saw that Andrew had left them. She was resigned to this habit, but Henry was not and might think it rude. She nudged his elbow and directed his eyes to Andrew.

"It's a thing he does. Do you think this Miss Clara Hilton will understand? It's his work, he works in his head."

"She did oughter. She does it 'erself. I tells 'er something we did oughter do, and it seems all right like, and the nex' thin' she's 'ad a look at the old gentleman's photo and she takes a religious turn. Shockin' religious turns she 'as, quotin' 'ymns and that, and it all starts inside of 'er 'ead. Then down she comes to me and whatever it is we fixed she wants to change. 'I sees it different now 'enry,' she says. I reckon young Andrew sees thin's but 'is is work, which is more 'ealthy like."

"What sort of things does this Miss Clara Hilton do?"

Henry, with the slightest jerk of his head indicated to Julie that he was taking her into his confidence.

"She's got silly ideas about what was left 'er, always wantin' to do good instead of leavin' thin's be. I was wantin' you and young Andrew to 'elp me over somethin'. The old man left 'er some bees and 'oney in a thin' called 'Gamblers' Luck Limited.' It's one of them games they 'ave at fairs. Would you know where she could see it workin'?"

Julie kicked Andrew's ankle to bring him back to the table.

"This Miss Clara Hilton has a thing called 'Gamblers' Luck Limited.' Do we know anyone who works that?"

There were few circuses on the road, but many fairs, the same grounds were rented by both. Often when Borthwick's pulled in on a Sunday the caravans of the showmen owning last week's fair had not moved off, and in this way circus artists had friends amongst fair people. Naturally talk turned on the amount of money there seemed to be about, and in this way the children knew the names of many fair attractions. Andrew turned these over in his mind.

"Is it a ball game?"

Henry explained about the revolving wheels, and the pictures of birds and flowers.

"People buys tickets with the name of a bird and a flower wrote on. When the wheels stop the one what 'as the right bird and flower did oughter get a prize. But from what I see the thin' weren't on the level. It was fixed where the wheels stopped an' no one 'ad the ticket."

The children were shocked. In their experience showmen were honest to a degree, not only by inclination, but of necessity, returning as they did to the same grounds year after year.

"This Mr. Simon Hilton took you to bad places," said Andrew, "no showman we know would allow that. It's cheating."

Julie backed Andrew.

"It's true. Showmen mostly belong to a guild. They some-times have a novelty with them that isn't theirs, and perhaps there's a sharing of profits, but even so everything is under control of the showman, and he wouldn't allow that kind of thing."

Henry shrugged his shoulders.

"I can only speak as I find. The old . . ." he corrected himself, "Mr. Simon 'ilton I should say, was part owner of this thin' and we goes all over lookin' at it, and what I told you I see with me own 'meat pies.'"

Julie and Andrew stared at each other. It was Julie who saw a possible explanation.

"It must have been amusement arcades you went to. We don't know those, but I believe at such places sometimes you rent space for your amusement, anything could happen where there's no boss."

Henry understood that.

"That's more the ticket. I daresay it's run regular with a proper show, but it's one of those affairs you can twist when you want to. Do you know a regular fair comin' near enough to London you could write to, and see if they 'ad it workin' for Miss Clara to see?"

Julie and Andrew found it hard to believe there could be such ignorance. Born to the world of travelling circuses, the seasons when they travelled were as clearly indicated as the seasons of the year. You did not hunt the hedges for nuts in April, and you did not look for fairs on showgrounds in November. They tried, in putting Henry right, not to sound scornful, but Henry knew they thought him a fool.

"All right, all right. So I didn't know. So what? Keep your 'air on, it's the first time I knew there was 'arm in askin'." Henry saw the children were ashamed. "That's all right. No need to get in a state. But you see I was reckonin' on your 'elp. We got to find this 'Gamblers' Luck Limited' and we got to find it workin' nice, so she doesn't get thinkin' she didn't oughter keep the shares, see?"

Julie felt the letter between her breasts.

"Wouldn't this Mr. Charles Willis find where it's to be seen?"

Henry lit a cigarette before he answered. It was funny about these kids. He didn't know quite where to place them. His inclination was to class them with himself. Living the way they did they probably felt as he did about the law. You had to keep the right side of it, but that didn't mean you pushed things under its nose. He answered with caution.

"Mr. Willis is a very nice gent, couldn't want nicer, but a course in a way 'e's the same as a busy . . ."

Sam had sent Julie and Andrew to school regularly, as the law required. Sam was strict and neither had appeared in the ring, nor even walked in the parade until they were twelve; but only Julie and Andrew were his immediate concern. If a family travelled with them, he did not always demand to see certificates to show the children were old enough for a licence, nor was he constantly nagging at parents if a week or so's schooling was missed. He prided himself that police were more than welcome to visit his circus, and they could look into everything for they would find nothing wrong with Borthwick's. Nevertheless there was uneasiness when police were looking round, and relief when they were gone. Julie's pleasure in her letter was dimmed.

"Is that what he is?"

"Not a real busy, nor a flatty, 'e's a mouthpiece."

"Why did he come to visit us with this Miss Clara Hilton?" Julie demanded.

"'cause it's 'im what sees to what was left Miss Clara by the old gent."

Andrew saw what was troubling Henry.

"You wouldn't like him to find 'Gamblers' Luck Limited' in case it was played wrong, and then there's trouble for the showman."

Henry nodded.

"I 'ate a grass."

On the matter of informers the three were in complete agreement. Sam and Bess might know or suspect a great deal wrong with some other showman's set-up, or something about one of their own staff or artists, but provided it was not cruelty to a child or animal, they avoided where possible going to the police. Understanding Henry's reluctance to call in Charles Willis they turned their minds to their friends amongst the showmen, and soon remembered one who wintered at Mitcham. It was when they told Henry this that the week in London almost ceased to frighten Andrew and became a week brimming with possibilities. "Mitcham," Henry said, "you an' me might pop along there tomorrer, young Andrew, and if there's anythin' goin' or comin' you might fancy to do, you only got to put a name to it. Miss Clara wants you to do what you like."

Might fancy to do. Andrew had a press cutting in his breast pocket. It was not a cutting he had thought anyone must see but himself. Above all Julie must not read it. He had only brought it on the chance of a miracle, of escaping for a few hours, and now there was no need for a miracle. This Henry could see the cutting and he would understand and arrange everything.

Henry looked at the clock.

"Reckon Miss Clara did oughter 'ave got rid of the Reverend. You take one case Andrew, and I'll take the other, and we'll find a telephone box."

Clara's voice was full of happiness as she told how splendidly the visit had passed off. Once Henry stopped her and made her repeat a sentence. When he came out of the box he was grinning.

"Come on, kids. Miss Clara 'asn't 'alf put her foot in it. She's not fit to be on her own, straight she isn't. The Reverend wants 'is God-forbids to stay along of us same as I thought 'e did, and what does Miss Clara do? Instead of sayin' 'no' sharp and plain, she shows 'em my bedroom."

"Why was that putting her foot in it?" Julie asked.

Henry looked at her, laughter in his eyes.

"Of course you 'aven't seen it. Mr. Willis 'ad it fixed special for you. All pale blue and pink it is. An' there's flowers for you on the dressing-table. What d'you suppose the Reverend and his missus thinks when they're shown a room fixed that way, and is told it's been fixed special for me?"

Henry's description of Maurice and Doris had been racy but accurate. Neither Julie nor Andrew could visualise the bedroom, but they belonged to the circus world, where most augustes had in their wardrobes, clothes, usually underclothes, which when seen would raise the easy laugh the public always gave the suggestion, that a man was a homosexual. What Maurice and Doris must have thought hung unspoken between them. Then they looked at Henry and began to laugh. The suitcases were put down on the pavement and the three leant against an area railing tears dripping down their cheeks. As the gust of laughter died a newer and funnier possibility struck Henry, and a new gale of merriment shook him. At last he mopped his eyes and picked up Julie's suitcase.

"Come on. We must get 'ome or Gawd knows what else Miss Clara may 'ave got up to. I can't wait to tell my friend Nobby this one, 'e'll die laughin', straight 'e will."

Full of the warmth of the shared joke the three hurried towards Gorpas Road.

* * * * *

To Clara it seemed that to the children their visit slipped quietly and happily by. She wished she could feel that they were growing to know her better, so that they were certain that she was a friend to whom they could always turn. It was, however, understandable that they were shy with her. Hesitatingly they managed to call her Aunt Clara, as the nieces and nephews did, but it was merely a change of words, it did not mean they felt less formal with her. Indeed why should they? The nieces and nephews had known her since they were babies, and were used to her being a frumpy round-about aunt, to Julie and Andrew she must seem a dull, silly old thing, whom the name Miss Hilton fitted better than Aunt Clara. She wished the children were at home more than they were, but considered it natural that they were always out. Did she not say to them whenever she saw them, that her home was their home and they must use it as they liked, she ought to be glad she told herself, that they took her at her word. Dear Charles was being so kind, giving Julie such a nice time, and Henry was splendid about taking Andrew out, it was very naughty of her to feel lonely. It was seeing them so full of plans, often running out without remembering to say goodbye, or coming in without telling her what they had been up to, that made her feel what a dull old thing she was. She had planned not to go to the mission while Julie and Andrew were with her, but after two days spent almost entirely alone, without saying anything, she returned to her mission work.

To Andrew the visit to Clara seemed the opposite of quiet. Each day shimmered as if every hour exploded excitements like fireworks against a night sky. The trip to Mitcham and the easy "kipping" in the front room gave him a friend. Henry had admired Andrew on a trapeze, and was as proud of him as if he were a young relative. He had never had anyone to be proud of before. He had been proud of the old B in his way, but that was pride in his carryings-on rather than in his achievements. Henry looked forward to telling Nobby about Andrew, and at some time taking him to see him perform. The boy was not a bit like he had been at his age, nor like any boy he had ever known. In his tolerant way Henry accepted him exactly as he was, dreaming, full of startling knowledge, or innocent as a baby. He made Henry feel protective, he would have laughed at himself if he had known that was how he felt, but it was the truth. It was on the way back from Mitcham that Henry saw the press cutting. It had been a successful visit. The showman had never had anyone working "Gamblers' Luck Limited" for him, it was a nice job, he said, but it needed to draw a big crowd, and so was unsuited to small fair grounds. He had an idea where it might be working, he would let Andrew know in a couple of days. He had then told Andrew to go and find his wife, and had taken Henry to a nearby pub where, over glasses of mild and bitter, they discussed horse racing. Henry had never met show people before, and he was impressed. He had not missed the respect shown the showman by the girl in the bar, nor by those who dropped in, nor the air of authority which exuded from him. It was on the top of a homeward-bound bus, while ruminating over these things, and shaping the way he would speak of them to Nobby, that Henry saw Andrew take the press cutting from his pocket.

"I saw this in a paper two weeks ago. It says The Flying Fishes are in London because Anton, he's the eldest, has a broken ankle and is in hospital."

"An' 'o might The Flyin' Fishes be when they're at 'ome?" Henry wagged a finger at Andrew, who was looking scornful. "Don't come the acid with me, young feller, if it was the name of a 'orse or a grey'ound I'd know it which you wouldn't."

Andrew had been dismayed by Henry's ignorance, but already in one day he was grasping that he must expect ignorance in the world of the "theys," and that ignorance did not make a person dislikeable.

"They just happen to be the greatest trapeze artists in the world, that's all. They're an American combine. Their publicity hand-out is that they're a sister and two brothers but they aren't. The girl Alicia is American, and I think they're all Americans now, but Antonio, that's Anton, was born in Italy and the other man, Albert they call him, in Sweden."

"'ow d'you know all that?"

Andrew wriggled with impatience.

"Everybody knows about them. It's like saying how do you know that Walt Disney made Donald Duck."

"Everybody don't know, I don't know for one, and I'd lay half-a-bar nor wouldn't nobody else on this bus. Anyway what's these Flyin' Fish mean to you?"

"They're here for the Christmas circus, but without Anton they can't work for Albert is the catcher . . ."

Henry stopped him.

"Look 'ere, I take it you wants me to 'elp you. Well I can't if I don't know what you're jawin' about. Now tell me quiet-like, with no fancy talk, what you're after."

It took time, for every term Andrew used was unfamiliar to Henry. But gradually he got a dim idea of an aerial act. He understood, for he had seen it, that in Andrew's act with Julie he did the flying and Julie such catching as there was. In a great act like the Flying Fishes, the catcher had much more to do, but what he had to do depended on who was working the act with him. In The Flying Fishes aerial act all three were stars, and an act could have been arranged for Alicia and Albert only, but they did not want to work a double act while Anton was away, for their fame was built as a trio, and they would not be out of the ordinary as a duo. If they could find a substitute for Anton they would work this Christmas, if they could not they were cancelling their contract and resting until Anton was well.

Once Henry understood, Andrew had an ally. Henry

learnt there would be no opposition from the Borthwicks if Andrew worked for somebody else, as they did not use him in the winter except on feeding and caring for the animals, and on odd jobs, and if The Flying Fishes took him he would come back to Borthwick's with special publicity, which would be useful to Uncle Sam.

"If that's right," Henry asked, "what's this 'ush 'ush business?"

Andrew hesitated. It was new to him to have a confidant. Then the cockney warmth shining from Henry's soul broke down his reserve.

"It's Julie. She hasn't the gift as I have. Her father wasn't an acrobat, but she and I must work as a duo for there isn't any other work for her, I mean not in our line and she wouldn't be happy in other work. There's a contract with these big circuses that the next summer season, perhaps more, after the Christmas you've worked for them you must tent with that circus. If The Flying Fishes take me, and Anton needed a longer rest I would have to tent with them, instead of with Borthwick's. If Julie knew she'd say it's all right, I mustn't lose the chance for that, but it wouldn't be all right for Julie. If you have been part of a good act it's terrible to be nothing, you get everything put on you nobody else wants to do. So if I can see this Anton, he's the boss, I must tell him it would only be for Christmas, otherwise I can't do it."

"Fancy yourself don't you? Why should these Flyin' Fish want a nipper like you?"

"Because I'm good."

The answer came with such absolute assurance, allied to lack of vanity, that Henry was silenced. Understatement was his birthright, and normally he would have flashed back a retort to cover his embarrassment at such shameless bragging, but this time he could not, he did not know why and sheered off from the inexplicable.

"When did you see that piece in the paper? Reckon they may have got someone by now."

"I don't think they have. Only on Sunday I read a list of the acts engaged and they weren't on it."

"You say this Anton's in 'orspital?"

"It's called The Orthopaedic." Andrew struggled with the difficult word.

"Was you plannin' 'e should see what you can do? Was you thinkin' of 'angin' a trapeze up in the ward?"

Andrew giggled. Then he explained that like any other work, aerial trapeze work had its own jargon, which could only be understood by those in the profession.

"If I can get to see Anton he'll hear what I can do and then he can arrange for Albert and Alicia to try me out."

Henry, though accepting he was up against a quality in Andrew he did not understand, was not prepared for too much big talk.

"'ark at you! The way you goes on, you'd think all you had to do was to whistle and there was a trapeze 'angin' from every lamp-post. Would this Anton see you if you wrote?"

They had reached the root of the matter.

"I write badly, I wouldn't be able to say on paper what I can do. Do you think you could manage I could see him without asking?"

The rheumatic heart of his childhood had familiarised

Henry in the ways of hospitals. He remembered countless visiting days. No one had noticed who came in or went out.

"Nothin' easier. Just give me time to find out which is the visitin' days and you're in."

Julie could not at first feel at ease with Charles. She could not know how much she had been in his thoughts, and how well, in his imagination, they knew each other. She suffered from a recurring fear that he was only taking her out as a joke. Each time she became relaxed and was enjoying herself, Charles would remark that she was a scream, or laugh affectionately at what to him was her endearing naïvety, and at once, crimson-cheeked she had jerked back into her shell. Charles could feel when she was happy with him and when she was not, but re-meeting her he fell so in love he was past reasoned thinking about anything that concerned her. There had been a note with the flowers in her bedroom, saying he would call for her at half-past six that evening, and he would not have time to change. The lady high school rider had told Julie that if a gentleman asked her out, and said he wasn't wearing evening dress, you couldn't go wrong in a nice black dress under your coat. Charles did not know that night about the lady high school rider, but without knowing it he backed her taste. The utility copy of a model chosen for Julie suited her beautifully. It outlined her figure and toned down her brassy hair. The lady high school rider had told Julie that by changing accessories you could make the same dress look different each time you wore it. For these changes Julie had a sash with roses attached, for one occasion, and matching green beads, earrings, and chiffon handkerchief for another. It was chance she left these adornments for another night, and so Charles first saw her as he had dreamed she would look. In his eagerness to have her to himself he took her to a quiet but first-class restaurant, and on to dance at one of the simpler places. It was Julie's first view of restaurant life. She had been up to London for the day with Bess and Sam, and constantly passed through it, but she had never imagined the London Charles knew. She looked round at the other diners, and up at the hovering maître d'hôtel, her brown eyes wide. When Charles had to order the dinner Julie could only shake her head and shrink into herself as the string of strange words fell round her. Charles watching her melted as if he were butter in the sun. She wasn't real. His usual methods with girls were unthinkable when dealing with Julie. He who never thought of himself at all, was filled with the strangest longings. That he was back in uniform, so that he could fight for her. That he could scatter flowers over the carpet for her to walk on. That there was something that she wanted that he alone could obtain for her. As the meal progressed his need to touch her, to feel his arms round her slim body, hurt, so he hustled her through the sweet course and, refusing coffee for them both, out into his car. But when they were alone, her complete unawareness of how he felt, and unawareness of how any man alone with her might feel, made the thought of holding her in his arms seem gross. He did gasp as he shut the car door, "Oh, Julie!" But there had not been a glimmer of understanding in her reply. She had been fascinated by the commissionaire, who had helped her into the car. As Charles spoke her name she turned politely, her enormous brown eyes larger than usual, due to the excitement of the evening, and replied sedately,

"Yes, Charles?" To keep his hands busy, and his mind off his desires, Charles started the car, muttering "I was only going to say shall we go and dance a bit?"

Charles had arranged things so that he was free from work during Julie's visit. He had told his father he would be looking after somebody for Clara. He let it be understood the somebody was a niece of Clara's he was helping to entertain. His father was surprised that Charles should take time off for such a purpose, for from what he had heard Clara's nieces were likely to be a dull lot. But Charles was the only boy in the family, the other Willises having produced daughters, and there was openly expressed hope that Charles would marry soon and produce sons. His father hoped this more fervently than anyone, but as he pointed out to his brothers, as long as the girls gave Charles what he wanted without marrying him, it was unlikely that Charles, income tax being what it was, would saddle himself with a wife. A dull daughter-in-law would be a misfortune, but any daughter-in-law would be acceptable if she got straight down to having a family, so he told Charles it would be quite all right if they didn't see him for a week, and he would telephone if anything that needed him cropped up. Charles was therefore free to serve Julie from breakfast-time until she insisted on going home to bed. His car was in Gorpas Road by nine each morning, and each morning he had an excuse for his early arrival, to which each morning Henry gravely listened.

Henry, companioning Andrew, was unable at first to envisage a Julie with whom Charles was in love. That Charles was after her, he could accept, but that a gentleman, such as he was, could be thinking of her seriously did not, to begin with, cross his mind. Then the way Charles shot up the stairs, almost as soon as he had opened the door to him, and the look in his eyes made him change his ideas. His views on Charles's feelings he kept to himself, the only outward expression he gave them was a long surprised whistle. As the days passed he added to the whistle a sympathetic shake of his head, a shake which said it was shocking what love could do to you. There was Mr. Willis, who only a short while back had been as nice and sensible a gentleman as you could wish to meet, turned in two or three days into as near as made no difference a deaf mute who could do nothing but gaze at his girl, and hurry her out of the house. Because of Charles's habit of hurrying Julie where he could have her to himself, Henry, seeing the end of the children's visit in sight, realised he must pin Charles down to a day to visit Clara's horses, so on the fourth morning when Charles was inventing a new reason for calling at nine o'clock, he cut him short.

"That's all right, sir. Miss Julie's just puttin' on 'er tit-for. Would it be all right for us to go to see the 'orses Monday?"

Charles had been about to bound up the stairs. He paused in mid-bound as it were and gaped at Henry, his expression that of one coming round from an anaesthetic, still unable to focus the eyes, or take in what was said.

"Horses! What horses?"

Henry was patient. Slowly, as if explaining something to an imbecile, he reminded Charles that he had promised Clara that while the children were with her he would drive them to see her four horses. When Charles grasped what he was being told he was dismayed.

"Oh I say, Henry! Did I? What a frightful waste of a day. Miss Julie would be bored stiff. She sees enough old crocks in the circus. I tell you what, I'll stand a hire car, you and Andrew take Miss Hilton to see them."

Henry clung to his plan. His feelings about Andy were strong. During the years he had been with Simon, Alfie and Perce, and their dealings with the horses and dogs, and their red-hot tips, had been the woof, threading the dull warp of life in Gorpas Road. When the old man had been strong enough they had once or twice visited Alfie's stables. They were not much to look at, for Alfie's ideas on the way to live had been on a level with Perce's, but the horses were well cared for, and Henry had often watched Alfie lean on the gate into his field, and call an old horse, and see him fondle him, and give him a piece of sugar or slice of apple, while he reminded Simon of the horse's history. It was usually a rather shady history, but neither Simon nor Alfie minded about that, and the conversation usually finished with Alfie saying that he reckoned the old horse had earned his bit of comfort now his racing days were done. When an old horse had been his at some time or another, or when he had earned him money, Simon paid what he called the old-age pension. For Henry those days at Alfie's stables, with buttercups in the fields, for their visits were mostly in the summer, had remained clear in his memory. Watching Andy, or the stable lad, exercising the horses. Seeing a foal; though rearing foals was not in Alfie's line, there had been on one occasion a very young one trembling on spindly legs. Always there were Alfie and Simon standing by the shabby loose boxes, and in memory Henry's nostrils filled with the mixed scents of Alfie's filthy pipe, Simon's cigar, flowers, and ill-kept stables. His ears still carried Alfie's confidential cockney twang as he confided to Simon plans he was laying to fix things so that they made money on a horse, interrupted by Simon's clipped words, and for background a horse stamping, birds singing, sometimes it had been a cuckoo. Every mind carries its pipe dream, Henry's was to be an Alfie. He knew it was only a pipe dream, yet he knew how it would feel to lean on your own gate, calling up your own horses. So when through Perce he heard suspicions of what Andy was up to, it was not only his real love of horses which made him angry, but in putting his father's place to wrong usage, Andy had destroyed a dream. At Charles' words this anger seethed up.

"No you don't, Mr. Willis. A promise is a promise. Miss Clara's not one to ask favours, but she 'asn't seen much of the kids and she'll enjoy the day out."

Charles looked gloomy.

"It's miles. It'll take all day."

Henry saw Charles was yielding, so he spoke soothingly.

"T'aint miles, only Essex. She did oughter see 'em. You know I got the receipts, the old gentleman paid regular for their keep, 'e paid the last cheque two days before 'e was took."

For a moment Charles' mind was off Julie, and on Clara's affairs.

"That's right. I must see those. It's just their keep, isn't it? They're not racing any more?"

"That's right. Alfie 'ad the 'orses, but 'e was took not so long before the old gentleman went. 'is son Andy carries on. I got the letter what 'e wrote the old gentleman, you must read that, lovely it is, all about the place 'e 'as where the 'orses can 'ave a beautiful old age. 'is father 'ad old 'orses, nice field for 'em an' all, but I reckon from what this Andy wrote in 'is letter 'e thinks 'e's done better."

The children had arrived on a Wednesday, and they were going back to the Borthwicks on the following Wednesday. It was already Saturday. It seemed to Charles deplorable waste of the last day but one. Still, it was clear from what Henry had said, and the look on his face, that there was no getting out of it.

"You better get those papers for me. I'll look them over before Monday."

Charles had turned to climb the stairs. A knowing grin spread across Henry's face. That ought to fix Andy. Then an idea struck him, which would please Charles and be a help to Andrew. He whistled through his teeth, and when in answer Charles turned, he drew him back to him with a jerk of his head.

"I don't think Miss Clara would mind if the kids, Miss Julie and Andrew I mean, was to stay a coupl'a days extra."

Charles smiled fatuously at Henry. It was as if he had become his fairy godmother.

"I say! Well, that is an idea. I mean, what about your room?"

Henry grinned more broadly.

"Now, Mr. Willis, you can't think I'd sleep in there." Henry wished Charles was not desperate to see Julie, or he would have told him about Maurice and Doris's visit. "I reckon we'll keep that nice for Miss Julie, I'm quite satisfied kippin' in the front room."

Charles took out his note case, and put five pounds in Henry's pocket.

"You're a pal. I'll see Miss Hilton and fix up about Monday."

* * * * *

It was a silent party that drove to Essex, for each had matters on which to brood.

Julie and Charles might have been alone in the car. Julie was not yet in love with Charles, but trembling on the rim of love. Her exceptionally strict upbringing under Bess had kept her from exploring the qualities with which her mother's blood had endowed her. From somewhere she had inherited a puritanical strain, which, backed by Bess's training, had kept her from even mild adventurings in sensual matters. Now Charles's love, though he had not yet kissed her properly, was surging over her in waves, each wave seeming to uncover a new unexplored Julie. Sitting beside him in the car she was as conscious of his nearness as he of hers; desire ran between them so strongly it could almost be seen. The difference between the two was that Charles knew what he wanted, and Julie did not. Charles had not yet sorted out his thoughts, but it was growing on him that he wanted Julie not for occasional love but for always. He knew there must be difficulties, but he was too bemused to list them, they must wait until later. There was the trouble

235

of his being the only boy in the family, some day he supposed he would be head of the firm. There would probably be a lot of cackle from the uncles and his father, but none of that mattered in the present, where all he could concentrate on was Julie.

Henry's mind darted to and fro like a bird picking up crumbs. He knew what the two in front were feeling, and they had his sympathy. Shame to feel like that when you had three people with you, one of them Miss Clara. To Henry the days were passing too quickly. Even with the two extra days which had been arranged that the children should stay there seemed little time left, and, as he put it to himself, he wouldn't half feel a draught when young Andrew had gone. It had taken Andrew's visit to make Henry conscious that his life was dull. It was not that there had been much doing towards the end of the old man's life, but he had not noticed it; there were still tips coming in, with the chance they gave of winning a bit, and the old man had needed so much looking after there was no time to think of anything but him. But Miss Clara was different. He was fond of her, you couldn't help it somehow, but now that he had been given a taste of a fuller life he wondered if he could stick going on with her. There was Gamblers' Luck, which he and Andrew were taking her to see, there was Botchley to fix for her to watch the dogs race, but that was the lot, unless you counted Mrs. Smith. It looked as if in a week or two he would have nothing to do but wait for Miss Clara to come home from her mission. During Andrew's stay he had met people and seen things that were new to him. That afternoon at the hospital had been something to remember. He had kept out of it at first, just giving Andrew a push to join the party round the bed. All three Flying Fishes had been there, for Alicia and Albert were visiting Anton. It had been odd to Henry to see Andrew, such a shy lad, suddenly full of talk, and to watch the way The Flying Fishes listened to him. When it came to making an appointment for Andrew to go to the gymnasium where they practised they had called Henry in. It was to him Anton gave directions, explaining the time and the place, taking it for granted he would have Andrew on the spot at the right minute. It had been something different talking to acrobats, and seeing them practise had been a real treat. Watching Andrew and Julie in the ring had been nothing to it. In the gymnasium the trapezes were not so far away, and though he did not understand a word he heard, he had felt he belonged. The two Flying Fishes and Andrew wore practice clothes, and while they were working Henry stood by, holding towels and dressing-gowns, and between work-outs they joined him, and discussed the programme they would do at Christmas. Henry appreciated that if Andrew joined The Flying Fishes there was nothing for him to worry about, he would be sure to live in the flat, and Henry could see himself going a lot to the circus, maybe taking old Nobby along. But would Andrew join The Flying Fishes? It was funny how stubborn he could be. If only he would talk it over with Julie; it was only fair to give her a chance to speak for herself. From what Henry had seen of her, which was not much, she was fond of Andrew, and would be the last one to stand in his way. He might have fought against his belief in keeping yourself to yourself, and not poking your nose in where it was not wanted, and spoken to Julie himself, had he not arranged this trip to see Andy. He kept reminding himself if he was right about Andy, Andy would deserve anything that might come to him. He was not going to tell Mr. Willis anything, but if Mr. Willis saw things for himself it was not his fault. But telling himself things did not silence Henry's conscience, which nagged at him. He was defying the code of behaviour by which he lived. If Andy thought he was a grass he was not so far out. He was uncomfortable enough as it was, and had no intention of making himself feel worse by putting his nose into Andrew's business.

Clara's mind had been with her fellow workers at the mission. They had been glad she had not taken the week's holiday, there were so many little jobs which she enjoyed doing, but which when she was away others seemed to find a burden. There was a great shortage of money at the mission. As soon as she had seen everything and everybody she must have a talk with Charles, and see what could be spared without those entrusted to her suffering. Thinking of the important talk she must have with Charles, Clara looked at him. He had half turned to smile at Julie. Henry was sitting next to her, she touched his arm, and, because Andrew was on his other side, spoke in a whisper.

"Henry, do you know, I think Mr. Willis likes our little Julie."

Henry glanced at Andrew. His red head lolled against the car window, he was completely cut off from them, absorbed by his aerial world, he and Miss Clara could talk of anything and he would not hear one word. As for the two in front, they would not notice if everybody fell out of the car. His difficulty was how to answer. It was not safe saying much to Miss Clara, or the next thing would be she would sing a hymn about love to Mr. Willis. He wore what, had Simon been there, he would have called his "damn disobligin'" expression.

"Mr. Willis is ever so nice a gentleman."

Clara missed Henry's expression and his tone of voice, for her eyes were on Julie. It was not her custom to discuss unannounced love affairs, she considered it both impertinent and ill-bred, but to her Julie was a child, and the thought which had come to her, though pleasure-giving, had no more substance than a fairy tale.

"Oh, Henry, wouldn't it be delightful if those two could grow fond of each other? It's just what dear old Mr. Hilton would have wished, isn't it?"

Henry could hear a ghostly rolling chuckle, from which was wheezed out Simon's comment on that. The comment, though only heard in his imagination, made him damp under the collar. His tone was both embarrassed and full of disapproval.

"That's as may be, we don't want to go fillin' our loafs with what aren't none of our business. As for the old gent, there's no sayin' what 'e might 'ave thought for 'e never set 'is pies on Miss Julie, not since she was a baby, that is, if then."

Clara accepted without query that the subject of Charles and Julie was closed. It had been very silly of her to have spoken of it. After all, the children had only known each other a day or two, Henry could not realise she had been speaking of what was no more than a silly old woman's daydream, so she had probably offended his taste. She should have remembered that courtships in his world, if they occurred at all, followed complicated but well understood rules, walking-out becoming in course of time steady-company, a state which she feared too often did not become marriage until a baby was expected. It was very stupid of her to have forgotten this and Henry had every right to feel shocked. She really was becoming a very blundering old thing. Pondering on herself in this way brought back to Clara other blunderings. She remembered last week, when she had so selfishly felt out of things because she saw so little of the children. There had been too many days recently when she forgot to count her blessings. And what blessings they were. Her comfortable home. The companionship of dear Henry, and splendid Charles. These drives in a car; why a few months ago riding in a motor-car was such a treat, and now it was always happening. So much arranged for her, the lovely day at Ashford, and the day at the circus, and now this beautiful day. She looked out of the window; the red berries in the hedges, the white trails of traveller's joy, the bare trees against the delicate winter sky, and suddenly it seemed her cup was too full. She turned to Henry, her eyes behind her pince-nez swimming with tears.

"Henry, I have so very much to be thankful for. Do you know, I believe the dear old man knows that." Clara paused, and it seemed to her that glory filled the car. "He does know, Henry. He's here in the car with us."

From the moment he saw the tears Henry, as later he told Nobby, knew Miss Clara was working up for one of her religious turns; but what she said he was not prepared for.

The old B in the car! Going where they were going, and seeing what he guessed Andy was up to, as he described to Nobby, "properly turned him over." To throw off the feeling of awe, accompanied by a cold sensation down his spine, Henry joked.

"Don't know where 'e'd sit. Like sardines as it is."

Clara was by now sure Simon was with her. She was uplifted beyond hurt from a joke.

"Not as we remember him, just his soul." Clara clasped her hands. "Help me to remember this day, Henry. I'm getting spoilt by kindness and comfort. I forget that except when we drove to the funeral I never went even in a taxi, I mean, why should I? The whole point of asking me to meet the children and take them across London was that it saved taxis, for we could go by bus."

Henry had no idea what Clara was talking about, but he was convinced, whatever it was, she should not be allowed to go on. This was the worst turn he had seen her have, even worse than the attack she had that time in the cemetery, when she had told him the old man had picked his own text for his tombstone. He considered telling Charles to stop somewhere, so they could give her a cup of tea, but he turned the idea down, no need for everyone to know she was not herself. He spoke firmly.

"You 'ave a nice bit of shut-eye. We'll be there in two shakes of a lamb's tail, and after we'll 'ave our dinners."

Clara closed her eyes; it was good to hold the glory to her, the certainty of being guided, of Simon being pleased. Henry, thankful to have quietened her, returned to his uneasy conscience. Andrew, who had heard nothing, flew from a trapeze to be caught by Albert. Charles's left hand was off the wheel, his fingers had found Julie's, both fell into a trancelike state. Then suddenly they turned a corner and ahead of them was the lane leading to Andy's stables.

At first sight the place was much as Henry remembered it, it was when they came in sight of the house that he had his first surprise. In Alfie's day the house, which had once been a farm, had been shabby; it was usual to see broken hinges on the doors, and it was years since it had been painted. The garden, or what had been a garden, was a tangle of weeds, shrubs and rubbish. Now the house had been done up, there was vivid green paint everywhere, muslin curtains in the windows, and the garden was evidently looked after for it was tidy, and though at that minute there was little to see, there were wintry remains of what, a few weeks before, must have been a fine show of flowers. Henry, his eyes goggling, directed Charles.

"The stables is at the back like."

Now they had arrived Charles managed partially to detach his mind from Julie.

"Thought you said it was a bit rough and ready. Looks like a stately home to me."

A lorry stood in the stable yard. In it, trembling, stood four old horses, a fifth, squealing with terror, was being whipped into finding standing space where no reasonable standing space existed. Andy, very smart in what he took to be a country gentleman's clothes, was shouting:

"Get in, you brute." Crack went his whip. He roared at the driver. "Come on, you, give us a 'and." The driver joined Andy, together they tried to force the horses forward so that they could close the lorry. Neither man had seen the car, so Julie took them by surprise. For a moment she had been too horrified to move, then she was out of the car. Andy had thrown down his whip to have both hands free. Julie picked it up and cracked the handle down on Andy's head.

"You beast you! You filthy beast! You louse!"

Charles soon convinced Andy who they were, and had him first blustering, then shilly-shallying, and finally cringing. Charles demanded to see Clara's horses, and when it was clear there were no horses, asked where the telephone was, as he wished to ring the Police Station. Andy, seeing the game was up, was about to lead the way to the house, when Clara stopped him.

"Do I understand my horses aren't here?" Andy growled that he had said so, hadn't he? "Then where are they?"

Andy looked at Charles who half shook his head, there was no need for Clara to know the details. Julie, however, was not so squeamish.

"They've been killed, Aunt Clara."

"Killed!" Clara's voice trembled. "On purpose, do you mean, Julie?"

Julie nodded.

"He buys up horses and sells them to slaughter-houses. Men like him make lots of money doing that."

Clara looked again at Andy. She was used to sinful people, it was understanding them which was difficult. This man had killed her uncle's horses, horses entrusted to her care. But why? Then a horrid thought struck her.

"When did you kill them? I mean, was it recently?"

Henry saw what was in Clara's mind.

I reckon Andy killed 'em off just as soon as 'is Dad was took, knowin' the old gent was gettin' on like and wouldn't be down to see 'em. They was done for long afore 'e thought of givin' 'em to you."

Andy scowled at Henry.

"Proper nark you are. What you want to bring 'im 'ere for?" He jerked his head towards Charles. "Dad was always good to you. Anyway, people've got to eat, 'aven't they?"

"Eat!" The word came from Clara in a gasp. It was not that she did not know that horse meat was for sale, but it had not struck her that anyone could be so wicked as to sell Simon's horses for food. "Do you mean you sold Mr. Hilton's horses to eat?"

Andy could see no point in being cross-examined.

"I said so, 'aven't I?" He turned to Charles. "If you want to telephone, come on."

Clara pointed to the horses which Henry, Julie and Andrew were fondling.

"Are you selling those to be eaten?" Andy gave an assenting growl. Clara turned to Charles. "I don't want you to call the police, dear. If I can have these five poor dears instead of my four I shall be quite satisfied."

* * * * *

Doris discovered swelling with righteous anger was wasted swelling, unless there were those to watch the swelling, and, on hearing what caused it, start to swell too. Maurice, in the matter of swelling, was not a satisfactory companion, too soon righteous anger was swamped by fear. He spent much time on his knees pointing out that though he had been disappointed by the will, he had not complained, which, considering what he had understood was to happen to make up for the smallness of his stipend, he well might have done. That he was in no way responsible for Clara's actions. It was of course disgraceful that she should have a man in her flat, and that she should keep him in such a bedroom suggested unspeakable things, but it was not right that he should suffer for his sister's sins. He implored that these points would be kept in the forefront of the celestial mind, otherwise a faithful servant might be ruined by gossip reaching, first his rural dean, then his archdeacon, and finally his bishop. It was after many days, during which Maurice wore continually the look of one wrestling, that Doris decided to take action, and to take it without Maurice. It would be delightful to be, for once, sought after. The merest hint and she would have the family begging to see her. Doris knew Maurice's family too well to rush her fences, the opportunity would come if she waited. It came in a letter from Vera, which asked if it were true that Marjorie's job was coming to an end, for if so she knew Freda would love to have her stay. It would be a nice change for Marjorie and a help to Freda, who found her hands rather full with baby Priscilla Annette, Poppet and Noel. Vera added that it was such a help in the family when there was someone free who enjoyed lending a hand in busy times, didn't Doris remember what a help Clara had been? In the ordinary way that letter would have infuriated Doris, with its suggestion that her Marjorie was to be the family drudge, but on this occasion it pleased her. She answered by return; it was a long letter describing the many offers of work Marjorie had received, and the possibility of her training in London, it finished with "in any case I don't think Maurice would care to risk Marjorie living the same sort of life as Clara, we don't want that sort of thing to happen twice, do we?" "That sort of thing" was underlined.

Vera received Doris's letter at the breakfast table. She skimmed through it in a bored way. The final sentence she read twice. She passed the letter to George.

"It's from Doris. Don't bother with it all. Read that last sentence."

George read and frowned. What the devil did Doris mean? What sort of thing? Vera half-heard George's fussy ruminatings. She had never thought anything of Doris, she was suburban and dreary, but she was shrewd. If she gossiped she had never done so about the family, for she would know she would soon be snubbed if she attempted it. That sentence suggested that she took it for granted she was merely remarking on something already known. What behaviour would seem to Doris so unseemly that Maurice would fear it breaking out again in Marjorie? It could not be anything to do with morals at Clara's age, so what? The answer came in a flash. Her crisp voice interrupted George's monologue.

"Drink." Vera was only interested in other Hiltons than her own if they could be of service in some way to her children. She brushed aside George's careful sentences about not jumping to hasty conclusions. "I'm not jumping to anything. But Clara's always been teetotal and when they take to it they're the worst. I suppose Henry started her off. I never trusted him from the first time we met him. If Clara's only drinking any odd bottle Uncle Simon left I don't think it matters, but if she's buying stuff she must be stopped. It's expensive and she should be made to think of the children, and I don't mind telling her so, I think it's my duty."

George pursed his lips. If that were the trouble, and he was not prepared to accept that it was, something must be done. Anyway, whatever it was that Clara was up to, it must be looked into, they could not have her disgracing the family. The question was how best to handle the matter; he must find an excuse to go and see her. It was then Vera thought of the telephone. If people drank she believed they usually did it in the evening. They would put a call through to Clara that night and see how she sounded.

Clara, Henry and Andrew were having supper of bread and cheese round the drawing-room fire. It was a miserable night, and they had settled down in the pleased apathy which follows heat and food after being out in the cold. Clara, her cup of tea in one hand and a plate of bread and cheese on her knee, beamed at Henry.

"A splendid evening. It's like passing milestones. You were quite right, Henry, in spite of its name it's a delightful game, everybody was enjoying themselves."

Andrew's friend, the showman, had discovered a fair to be held in an agricultural hall in aid of a Christmas charity, and that one of the attractions engaged was "Gamblers' Luck Limited." Henry had arranged with Andrew to drop a hint to the showman as to Clara's interest in the game, but that proved unnecessary, for Clara at once announced who she was. First she shook the showman by the hand, then, having explained about her shares, identified herself with "Gamblers' Luck Limited." When the barker tried to draw a crowd by warning them there were only a few tickets left to sell, though she shook her head at him, she beckoned the showman over and, while whispering it was wrong to tell lies, opened her purse and bought several tickets and distributed them amongst children, explaining to the crowd that it was only right she should do so as a dear old uncle had left her shares in the game. Only three times while she was there was a big enough crowd collected for the game to be played, but on each occasion she took a personal interest in the prize winner, and what was selected as a prize. Henry, at first nervous and embarrassed for her, was, before they left, reconciled for once to Clara's outspokenness. Of course she was making a bit of a show of herself, he could see people nudging and smiling, but there was no spitefulness in it. Anyone could see Miss Clara was a lady born, and thought having shares meant she was a partner in the whole outfit, prizes and all. Anyway no one could say she did not make things go, and the showman certainly thought so, for when they left he presented her with a shopping bag which she had pointed out to the prizewinners as an exceptionally good prize. It lay now on the table beside her. He eyed it admiringly.

"That bag's a smashin' job, isn't it, Andrew?"

The bag was a plastic affair in pale blue with a design of roses on it. Andrew, who for once was attending, grinned at it.

"Just the thing for you when you do the shopping."

Henry laughed. He knew Andrew was having a dig at the

joke attached to his bedroom. Clara joined in the laugh, not because she knew what the joke was but because she was happy. It was so pleasant by the fire with Henry and Andrew, almost like having a family of her own. Thinking this she remembered what was happening in the morning.

"Oh, dear! We shall miss you and Julie to-morrow, shan't we, Henry?"

There was the faintest pause while the query passed between Andrew and Henry as to whether this was the moment to drop a hint. Henry decided it was.

"I don't s'pose we seen the last of 'em, not by a long chalk, do you, Andrew-boy?" It was at this moment the telephone bell rang. Henry looked in surprise at the clock. What an hour to ring up! Then a thought struck him. Maybe, seeing it was Julie's last night, Mr. Willis had thought up something, in which case it was better he took the message than Miss Clara.

George, hearing Henry's voice, demanded in his most legal manner that Clara be brought to the phone. Henry, surprised at hearing George and not Charles, hesitated before answering that he would fetch her, which made George put his hand over the receiver and whisper to Vera, "May be something in it. Fellow didn't want to bring her."

Clara, who had been pulled from her warm contentment with a jolt by Henry's awed "It's the relatives, Miss Clara, Mr. 'ilton," arrived rather flustered to pick up the telephone.

"Well, George? This is a surprise. Where are you?"

George, his ear strained for slurred words or thickness in Clara's speech, said he was at home, where else should he be? That he and Vera had been thinking it was a long time since they had heard from her, and how was she?

Clara was puzzled. Many months passed as a rule when nobody asked after her, and then it was not asking after but a postcard hoping she could render some little service. Then a premonition came to her which made her search for something to talk about. It was one of the children. Vera wanted a bed for the night. She could so easily put up a bed in her bedroom. It would be unkind to refuse, but Henry had just suggested that Julie and Andrew would be coming again, so splendid if they were to look upon the flat as their own, just what Uncle Simon would wish. Because she felt her thoughts were unkind she spoke with extra warmth and eagerness. George and Vera must not know she did not want the family in her home, perhaps if she talked of other things the three minutes would be up and they would ring off.

"Oh, George, you remember 'The Goat in Gaiters'? You said you'd buy it, I may still sell it. I haven't decided anything but it's so lucky I hadn't sold it or else I wouldn't have had anywhere to put the horses."

At the other end of the phone George shook his head at Vera, to show he did not like what he was hearing.

"Horses! What horses?"

"The racehorses, only there aren't any. I mean there never were. Imagine, poor old things, they had been eaten. Uncle Simon would have been very angry, I'm glad he never knew. I believe Andy's father was a dear, good man very like Mr. Perce, his brother, who has the dogs, but though of course no one is wholly bad I'm afraid Andy is not satisfactory."

Henry, at the first mention of "The Goat in Gaiters," had

got up and gestured to Andrew to join him. They tiptoed into the hall. At the other end of the line George's face was very grave. He signalled to Vera to listen in, and held the receiver so that she could do so.

"Could you speak more slowly, Clara. I am having difficulty in following."

"Are you! Well, I was saying it was lucky I hadn't sold 'The Goat in Gaiters' for now the Frossarts, dear good people, are making a home for the five horses, in the field."

George spoke in the voice he used to quell excitement or hysteria in a client.

"If I understood you aright and Uncle Simon's four horses have been sent to a slaughter-house, then how can they be in the field of 'The Goat in Gaiters,' and how can there be five of them?"

Clara, thankful that George seemed interested, laughed.

"Not the first four of course. These are five new ones. There were five poor old things just going to a slaughter-house. Charles Willis wanted to send for the police, but I said 'no' I'd take those five instead. He was very cross with me, and made Andy pay me some money, not, of course, to me, Charles took it, and he has told The Society for the Prevention of Cruelty to Animals about him, and he's told the police and he thinks Andy won't dare travel horses in a cruel way again."

"Are you and Mr. Willis on such terms that you call him Charles?"

"Yes, and he calls me Aunt Clara, he's such a dear, and so kind. There is a hymn the children sing at the mission and I never hear it without thinking of him. 'Help the feeble ones along, cheer the faint and weak;' he does just that, dear boy."

Henry put his hand over his mouth to hold back his laughter. She was off again, but it was all right this time, he wished he could see Mr. George Hilton's face.

George's face was growing graver and graver. Clara's rambling story seemed to him to show clearly that she was breaking up in some way, and it might be that she was drinking. But what he disliked more were the references to Charles. Willis and Willis were a sound firm, but did they know what their young man was up to? Money was tight these days, and standards slipping, it was a possibility the young jackanapes was getting himself in with Clara so that he could skin her of anything there was. He felt there was no purpose in prolonging the conversation, some far more drastic action than a telephone conversation was needed. He said, much meaning in his voice:

"Good-night, Clara. Vera and I will be coming to see you."

Clara looked upon visits from her relatives as a permanent possibility. She feared them not because they would turn her from what she knew to be right, but because she disliked seeming unkind. Her family were so used to her being glad to be of service when she could, they could not be expected to understand she now had a family of her own who must come first. She told Henry and Andrew of George's final words, unconsciously imitating his emphasis, but she was not especially disturbed by them herself, it was to be hoped that when he and Vera did come it would be at a time Julie and Andrew were not there. Soon after the telephone conversation had finished she had put it from her mind, and, full of gratitude for a happy and successful evening, had gone to her room.

Henry watched her loaf-shaped back climb the stairs then he rejoined Andrew.

"You know what that means, young feller? That Mr. Mr. George 'ilton smells somethin', or 'is missus does and she's worse than 'e is." While they put up their beds Henry explained the dangers of the situation to Andrew. "You see what'll 'appen if they gets a foot in. Next thin' we know they'll be usin' us regular, and that puts the lid on your kippin' 'ere if you gets fixed with The Flying Fishes."

Andrew, accustomed to being planned for, had taken it for granted that if his working in the Christmas circus could be arranged, he would, as now, kip with Henry while Julie slept in Henry's room. The mere thought of living with strangers brought back the terrors which had haunted him before he had got used to Henry. Henry saw how Andrew felt, and now, knowing him, rightly interpreted his expression.

"No need to act up, it' 'asn't 'appened yet." He took a wheedling tone. "You know what I'd do? I'd catch Julie soon as she comes in. Fix it with 'er, and tell Miss Clara first thin', and then it's all okey doke. Mr. George 'ilton and 'is old strife and all the rest of the relatives can try all they knows, but it won't do no good, 'cause there won't be no room, see?"

Andrew saw, but persuading him was not so easy. He was sure he would not be able to get out of tenting with The Flying Fishes, and he knew there could be no job with them for Julie. There was a chance she could join the circus for the tenting season, but it would be to live with him only and do odd jobs, and for that she might as well be with Borthwick's; but Henry beat down his objections. He had learnt from Andrew what an advance professionally working with The Flying Fishes would be to him. Then there were Charles and Julie. He could see Charles's face when he heard Julie might be coming to live in the flat. Then there was Miss Clara. She would be no end pleased, and, though she would not see it that way, it would be one in the eye for the relatives. Lastly there was himself. It would make all the difference having the kids around, he could hardly wait to go up to old Nobby, show him a couple of passes for the circus, and watch his face when young Andrew got on his trapeze.

"Nark it. You go to sleep. I'll 'ave a smoke in me kitchen and wake you when Julie comes 'ome."

It was three in the morning before Julie came home. She had the translucent look of a fumbler in the mystery of love. The lady high school rider had stated that blue was sweetly pretty as well as classy for a young girl's first evening dress. So Julie had bought a utility frock in taffeta, the original model of which, though this was not known to the lady high school rider, had been outstanding for its simplicity of line. Julie had accessories which the lady high school rider had made her buy to disguise she had only one evening dress. She had not worn the disguises, for the first time she had put on the frock Charles had implored her to wear it every evening for the rest of her stay. The next time she wore it, because she was easier with Charles and had begun to grasp his ecstatic laughter was not at her, but at what she said, she told him about the lady high school rider. They were dancing at The Café de Paris at the time, and Charles's laughter rose above the orchestra and made the dancers turn to look at them. Henry had not seen the blue frock properly before, and now, watching Julie climb the stairs, he thought it a smashing job. Then his eyes left it and came to her face. She was standing on the top stair, half facing the kitchen, but she did not see him. She was trailing her coat in one hand; suddenly she dragged it to her face, while from her came hiccupping sobs. Henry forgot why he was waiting for her; he put his arm round her, led her to the kitchen, sat her down and closed the door.

"Now then. Now then. No need to create, 'enry's 'ere. Come on, ducks, cheer up. I won't 'alf give you a rollickin' if you don't stop it. Tell you what. I'll put on a drop of milk to 'ot. When you got that in you you'll feel better."

Still half crying, Julie drank her milk and, because Henry was so comforting a person, attempted to explain her tears. She and Charles had just said good-bye. Charles had said it wasn't really good-bye because he would be coming down to see her at the winter quarters, but it wouldn't be any good if he did, Aunt Bess and Uncle Sam wouldn't mean to but they'd spoil things. Charles had said it wasn't good-bye because she could come up to London often. But that wasn't true, Charles didn't know what a lot there was to do, he thought you could just go away when you liked and nobody would think it odd, but it wasn't like that at all.

Henry waited for a pause. Then he patted the shoulder nearest to him.

"You stop it, there ain't nothin' to cry about. You wait

until you 'ear what I've got to tell you. Ever 'ear of The Flyin' Fishes?"

Julie had been so absorbed in what she supposed were feelings unique to herself, that Henry's words had the effect of cold water on an hysteric. She came back to the kitchen breathless but entirely herself.

"Of course."

"I didn't oughter tell you this meself. I promised young Andrew 'e should, but 'e's 'avin' 'is bo-peep, and I reckon you wouldn't want 'im to see you all swelled up like that, would you? What you and me know is one thin', an' you don't need to say nothin' about we-know-what to young Andrew."

Julie took her handkerchief from her bag and scrubbed at her face.

"I can't think why I told you. Andrew mustn't know anything and, anyway, there's nothing to know. Do I look awful?"

"'nough to scare the crows. Now listen 'ere . . ."

When Henry had told her Andrew's news Julie's first reaction was sisterly irritation.

"Oh, he is stupid! Imagine him thinking I'd let him turn down a chance like that."

"'e thought there wouldn't be nothin' for you at Borthwick's if you didn't 'ave the act."

"There wouldn't, but that wouldn't matter. He couldn't go on working with me for ever. I'm not much good, you know. What made Andrew change his mind about telling me?"

Henry grinned. This was the pith of the story, the defeat

of the relatives, and Julie had not yet taken in what Andrew's working in London would mean. When she did happiness shone out of her as from a torch in a street without lights.

"Henry! Why we'll be here for months and months."

"Too right you will." Henry jerked his thumb towards the door. "Up you go now and get your loaf on your weepin' willows, and in the mornin' you let young Andrew tell you what I jus' told you. And don't you let on you've 'eard anythin' previous. Then after, you an' 'im can go and tell Miss Clara."

Julie picked up her coat and bag and moved towards the door. She had so much happiness she wanted to give some of it away. On a thought she turned back to Henry.

"You won't have to defend her from those Hiltons all alone now. You'll have Andrew and me to help you. Anyway, if we're here they can't be, can they?"

Henry's eyes twinkled.

"Not unless we turn the front room into a kip 'ouse, which isn't goin' to 'appen. You wait till I tell Mr. Willis what's fixed, 'e won't 'alf be pleased."

* * * * *

Henry was alone in the flat when Perce telephoned.

"That you, 'enry boy?"

Henry had been feeling a little hurt with Perce. It had seemed to him that since he was trying his best to fix things so that Perce kept the dogs, he might have sent him a tip or two in exchange. His feelings showed in his reply.

"'ullo, stranger."

Perce's voice was reproving.

"Now then, now then, 'enry boy, that's not like you, that isn't, you never been one to get sarky. I know 'ow you feels, you says to yourself I might 'ave put you on to somethin'." Henry was going to answer, but Perce went on. "An' I would 'ave, but thin's 'as been shockin' lately."

"Miss Clara sent your September bill straight to Mr. Willis."

"True enough, 'e sent a kite straight off. I'm on to somethin'. You told me the old gent left you a 'undred long-tailed uns." Henry made a cautious agreeing grunt. "Could you bring Miss 'ilton to Botchley second Saturday in December, and bring two or three classy-lookin' friends of 'ers?"

Henry got the scent. If Perce talked of bringing friends he was on to something very hot. There would not only be his hundred pounds to slip on.

"There's a coupl'a kids livin' 'ere . . . Reckon I could fix to bring 'em."

Perce's voice was doubtful.

"Kids! Got to be sharp to get this on. Can't do it till just afore the off, an' even then if they was to know you an' the kids was friends of mine it would be all U.P."

"'ave you forgotten Miss Clara? You can't keep 'er quiet. When she gets to Botchley the first thin' she does is to look for you and Mrs. Perce, an' when she sees you she says, "ow are you, Mr. and Mrs. Perce, 'an 'ow are the dear dogs?' An' don't think nobody'll 'ear for she speaks ever so plain, an' don't think nobody'll notice 'er, for she'll stand out at Botchley like a sore thumb."

Perce made clucking sounds.

"All right. All right. Me and Mrs. Perce wasn't born yesterday. I'll let you know what time the race is, see. Then you comes down just afore it, an' says you gone to look for me, an' you leaves Miss Clara in the car."

"What car? The only car what we got belongs to Mr. Willis."

"Strewth, don't bring 'im along. If there's trouble, an' there could be mind, you are innocent as an unborn baby, you was only puttin' on the cocks and 'ens for me, you never bet more than a oncer in yer life, an' the kids never 'ad a bet afore. If that mouthpiece is around it won't be so 'ot. That sort's so sharp it's a wonder they don't cut theirselves."

"Don't know where I'll get a car. Money's tight since the old B was took, and there won't be much until Miss Clara's fixed what to do about everythin'."

Perce laughed.

"Come off of it. If what I'm layin' on comes off the way I reckon it will, you won't need to worry to find a car. You can buy a garridge full of 'em, so I reckon you can oblige with the cost of 'irin' one for the afternoon."

"What price you reckon he'll start at?"

"Ten to one."

Henry whistled.

"Ten to one! A thousand nicker!"

"That's right. An' if what I'm workin' come along it's a cert for 'e can't be bumped nor nothin', for 'e'll be round the track an' past the post afore the other dogs 'as got goin'. The only thin' that worries me is 'ow to get the bees on afore anyone smells anythin'."

Henry thought of Nobby.

"I know a feller might come. Knows Botchley. I'll see if I can fix it. That dog won't 'alf 'ave to do a vanishin' act after."

Perce laughed.

"You trust me. The vanishin' lady ain't nothin' to it."

Henry had only just replaced the receiver when Julie came up the stairs carrying Clara's fairing shopping bag. Since she and Andrew had come to live in the flat as residents she had taken it for granted she would do her share of the housework. They had only been back three days and they had been three shy days for Julie. She could not see how she had been so silly as to talk to Henry about Charles. It was not as if there was anything really to talk about. When she was with him she clung to any subject to chatter about to escape even a look which would remind her that he had seen her cry, and knew what the tears were about. Now, though she had noticed nothing, she teased him about the telephone.

"Were you talking to your best girl?"

Henry knew how Julie felt, and knew she would get over it if he left her alone. He took the shopping bag from her.

"Better get on with the veg, 'adn't we?"

Julie was taking over most of the cooking. Henry was a shocking cook and she was a good one. Henry did not mind, for she was not too much in his kitchen. By six at the latest Charles was round to fetch her out and much of the rest of the day she was upstairs washing, ironing and mending.

While preparing vegetables for a stew Henry took Julie partly into his confidence.

"The old gent wouldn't 'ave liked Perce to go short, 'e reckoned to keep 'is fourteen dogs along of 'im, they don't bring Perce in much but it comes regular. Miss Clara 'as been to see the place an' was ever so satisfied. That was Perce telephonin' now. Miss Clara wants to see 'er dogs racin' and Perce was sayin' some of 'em would be out second Saturday afternoon in December."

Nothing was mentioned that Julie did not consider in relation to herself and Charles.

"Charles could come along too."

Henry appeared to be concentrating on the carrot he was scraping. His voice was casual.

"There's dog racin' and dog racin'. The old gent, 'e didn't go in for it in a flash way, 'e fancied little tracks. A track called Botchley Lane is where 'is dogs races mostly."

Julie laughed.

"It's all right, you can come clean. Most years the men who tent with us back dogs, and in the winter go to the tracks. I know the names."

Henry had not thought of that possibility. Julie and Andrew seemed such innocents.

"You two ever 'ad a bet?"

Julie sliced a turnip.

"Never, we wouldn't know how to."

Henry, saying mentally, "Thank Gawd for that," relaxed.

"Got to learn sometime. When we get to Botchley I'll show you both 'ow, but not with your own money, though, mind you, if you was to risk a bit it would do no 'arm. Sometimes Perce puts me on to somethin' good."

Julie nodded but she was thinking of the wasted afternoon.

"Charles will be all right. He could take us in his car. If

you think it's all right Aunt Clara's dogs being with Perce and racing at Botchley he won't interfere."

The right answer fell like a gift into Henry's brain.

"It's 'im I'm thinkin' of. You see, a gentleman like 'im didn't ought to be seen except on a regular track." Henry's words made Julie stop working. Her expression showed she was struggling against shyness, that she longed to speak but could not find the opening words. Henry sensed this was the moment to break down the little barrier which had grown between them since she had cried on his table. "What is it, ducks? You can tell old 'enry, can't you?"

Julie leant on the table, her eyes fixed on Henry's.

"Would you answer two questions truthfully?" Henry nodded. Julie took a breath as though she was gathering strength for a race, her words fell over each other. "Don't you think my hair looks shocking? I mean, a girl of the sort Charles usually goes with wouldn't have peroxided hair, would she? And would you know from how I speak where I come from?"

Henry tried to be tactful.

"It looks dyed, a course, and dyed 'air never looks the same as what natural does, it was all right for the circus but it'd look better natural now you aren't workin'. But there's nothin' you can do about it, so I wouldn't worry, I daresay 'e's got used to it by now."

"In other words it looks terrible, which is just what I thought. But I can change that. Now, what about the way I speak?"

Henry grinned.

"Since you ask me, you speak a bit B.B.C. So did Andrew when 'e first come, but 'e's dropped it now."

"Is it awful to speak B.B.C.?"

Henry looked in a puzzled way at the vegetables in front of him.

"It's all right if it comes natural, but it's terrible when it's put on like. You know I speak somethin' shockin', but it's natural, see. I don't think you can 'elp it, it's the way you been taught."

"But you'd know at once it was taught, and wasn't natural. I mean like the way Charles speaks is natural."

"Of course. The moment Mr. Willis opens 'is north and south you can 'ear where 'e belongs."

"And when I open mine you can hear where I belong?"

"You did oughter, but the funny thin' with you is you can't. I can with Andrew mind, 'e speaks nice a course when you 'ear 'im against me, but you don't need one ear let alone two, to know it ain't what 'e was born with. Now you, though you don't speak no different to what Andrew does, seem different somehow. I reckon your old man was class. Andrew says your Mum said 'e was a marquis. Shouldn't wonder if it was true."

Shyly Julie looked at the table.

"I wish it was true, if it was I could learn to be the sort of girl that Charles knows, couldn't I?"

Henry picked up his knife.

"You an' me won't 'alf catch it if we don't get on. Miss Clara don't get nothin' but a sandwich at that mission."

"I wish she needn't go every day. Must she? I think she

gets tired. She doesn't look as well as that time you came to see the show."

"No wonder. Look at the weather, 'nough to give you the sick, and then the journey. Takes 'er an hour each way." He broke off and stared at Julie. "D'you know what? You could 'elp to keep 'er at 'ome. I got an idea see."

At tea time when Clara came home Julie was waiting for her. She took off Clara's voluminous coat, and helped her off with the galoshes she wore when it was damp, and settled her in a chair by the drawing-room fire. Clara felt the constriction in her throat which came to her when she received an unexpected kindness.

"Julie, you spoil me. I'm quite unused to being looked after, usually I'm looking after other people."

Julie sat on the floor at Clara's feet.

"Henry's getting your tea ready. I wanted to ask you something."

Clara smiled. This was what she had hoped would happen some day. Little Julie treating her as an understanding old aunt, just as the nieces did.

"Yes, dear?"

It was not easy for Julie. She was not yet comfortable with Clara, who was still a "they," the workings of whose mind she had not penetrated. But Clara was an experienced listener, accustomed to give her whole mind to the pourer-out of troubles, sifting what she heard as the stream flowed by her ears. She had thought about the children's voices, wondering why they had been taught to speak in that way, and had been comforted to notice they were not as terrible as those put-on voices sometimes were. She was touched and humbled to hear that Julie had just spoken to Henry about hers. Dear Henry, what a good man he was, so full of understanding, it was no wonder Julie chose him to come to with her worries. As the stream of words eddied by, Clara's sifting brought to the surface the reason behind what Julie was saying. At the mission she was constantly hearing confessions from girls, or about girls, from worried mothers. Whatever they had done the motive was almost invariably the same, a wish to please some man. Clara had heard of shop-lifting and stealing for make-up and clothes. She knew of homes in which there was near civil war over latchkeys. Of cases of petty pilfering for permanent waves. Now she added a new want to her collection of girlish needs: an educated accent. Dear little Julie, she was growing fond of Charles! How splendid if she had been right that day they went to see the horses, and Charles was growing fond of Julie.

"You mustn't think," said Julie, "that I'm speaking against Aunt Bess, she's wonderful to us, but meeting you, and others like you I can't help noticing, can I? How do I get to talk like you do?"

How indeed! Clara tried to remember who, if anybody, had told her how words were pronounced.

"I don't think there's much to learn, dear. Now and again there's a little slip, but we can soon put that right, it's just the way you shape the words. I'm such a muddled old thing, I doubt if I'm the person to help you, perhaps somebody who teaches elocution . . ."

Julie's interruption shot out.

"No. It must be you or nobody."

Clara's ear held the pronunciation of "you."

"I don't get much time, but I'll see what I can do. I learnt to sing as a girl, not that I could, but girls did then, it was part of our education, you know, and I remember vowel sounds were important. We might find a few minutes every day to practise those."

"Not a few minutes please, I'd like to get quite right, and that'll take time. Couldn't you stay at home a bit and teach me?"

On the words "stay at home" Clara's heart lifted. Home! And Julie had said it. It would be delightful to stay at home, not to have to make that exhausting journey, not to be expected at the mission every day, but would it be right? Wouldn't it be a giving in to temptation? It was so easy to persuade herself that it was as much, and even more, her duty to stay at home sitting by a warm fire teaching Julie, as to drag herself to South London.

"It would be delightful dear, nothing I should like better, but would it be right? I must think it over and let you know."

"I don't see why you bother about that old mission, it's a nasty journey and makes you tired."

Clara patted Julie's cheek.

"Naughty girl. It's a splendid little mission, such good people work there, and the folk I help are such dears. I don't say I may not decide to stay away for a time to help you if I can, you are a sacred trust, but I can't decide in a hurry. Remember the hymn, dear, 'In this world of darkness we must shine—You in your small corner, and I in mine.'"

Clara spent the evening pondering over Julie's request, and before she went to bed she found the answer. Andrew,

266

who was tired after a day's hard practice at the gymnasium, had started to put up his bed the moment Clara left the drawing-room, so she found Henry, who was filling her hot-water bottle, alone in the kitchen.

"Henry, I have decided not to go to the mission for the time being. I shall telephone the missioner to-morrow, he will be cross for there's such a lot to do as we get towards Christmas, but I must do what I feel right, and what I know dear Mr. Hilton would wish."

Henry side-tracked talk of Simon.

"You goin' to teach Julie to speak nice?"

Clara sat on the kitchen chair.

"If I can. I really think she should have professional help, but she seems against the idea, so I'll start her anyway. I thought we would read out loud, a classic, you know."

Henry did not know, and he thought pityingly of Julie. The poor little so-and-so hadn't half let herself in for something. But he was glad to hear Clara was not going to the mission.

"That'll be a bit of all right. What say I bring you your breakfast in bed just to celebrate like?"

Clara laughed at the idea.

"Of course not. I wouldn't eat in bed unless I were ill. I'm only staying at home to help Julie, you mustn't make a sluggard of me." She looked fondly and humbly at Henry. "You are a dear man. You are so good with the children. I doubt if Julie would have spoken to me about her little trouble if she had not spoken to you first. What a pity you never married and had children of your own."

It was years since Henry had thought of Gertie.

"I near did once. I wasn't much more'n a nipper when I first set me pies on 'er. Smashin' she looked. Red 'air she 'ad same as Andrew. Ginger I called 'er."

"Why didn't you marry her?"

It did not strike Henry how miraculously time could heal. He did not remember the demented boy who thought of killing himself.

"She died, sudden like, of the 'flu."

"And you never thought of marrying anyone else?"

Faced with that question Henry's subconscious brought to light that a red-headed forever young and lovely ghost made flesh and blood girls seem coarse. Embarrassed he found a laugh.

"Not me. I know when I'm well off. All I've got goes to me, see, if I'd married I might 'ave ten God-forbids, as well as a strife to keep. Besides, from what I seen, I'm well out of it. You ought to 'ear some of the jaw-me-deaths what fellers I know 'ave got spliced to. Now, there's your bottle. I'm slippin' out to see me friend."

Nobby gave Henry a welcoming jerk of his head.

"'ow's thin's? Another mild and bitter, Rosie."

While drinking Henry described the latest developments, except those that concerned Andrew. He was not spoiling the surprise he had for Nobby at Christmas. He told Nobby briefly about his talk with Julie and that they had succeeded in keeping Clara from her mission. Then, glancing round to see no one was within earshot, his mouth against Nobby's ear, he told him about the visit to Botchley Lane.

"Mind you, I don't know nothin' nor never will. Perce

268

keeps hisself to hisself, and quite right too, but if it's anythin' like a tip 'e give us once afore, it's a cert."

Nobby turned his mouth to Henry's ear.

"Nothin' ain't a cert in dog racin'."

Henry readjusted his position.

"If what I think is right this is. I don't know mind, not for certain, but Perce 'as got a pal what 'as a rest place for grey'ounds, lovely so I 'ear, smashin' grey'ounds goes there." Nobby moved excitedly. Henry laid a restraining hand on his arm. "'e can't do it often a course, but just now and again like. You know what they say about Perce, time 'e's fixed a dog nobody wouldn't know it."

Nobby nodded, he picked up his mug, swallowed some beer, smacked his lips, then drew Henry towards him.

"Is the dog from the rest place bein' done up to look like one of Miss 'ilton's?"

"Not as I know of. The idea's to get there just afore the race. We leaves Miss Clara in the car, an' you takes one of the kids an' me to the other, an' just afore the off we slip on all we can put our 'ands to, 'cludin' my 'undred what the old B left me."

Nobby clicked his tongue approvingly.

"An' very nice too. There aren't often more than four bookies at Botchley. If we all put our money on same time they won't get a chance to tip each other off. Mind you, they may turn nasty after. That might be awkward with Miss 'ilton wantin' to see 'ow nice grey'ound racin' is."

Henry lit a cigarette, with his elbow he moved his packet invitingly towards Nobby.

"Perce'll see to that. 'e knows Botchley same as you know

this pub. I reckon 'e'll fix it so there isn't no trial. A coupl'a dogs or that won't turn up for a race, an' the manager will put in one of Perce's what runs there regular 'o everybody knows, or thinks they does."

Nobby drew away from Henry and picked up his mug.

"Wonderful, isn't it, the brains some 'as?" He raised his glass. "'ere's to Perce."

Henry nodded and drank.

"An' to our afternoon at Botchley." He raised his voice. "Same again, Rosie."

* * * * *

George and Vera decided to keep their suspicions about Clara to themselves until they had seen Doris, and discovered what she knew and how she had found it out. Vera had said, "We don't want to make a who-ha about it, it would make her feel important. We must think of some occasion when we would meet anyway." The occasion they decided on was the christening of Priscilla Annette and at once Vera wrote to Freda.

Freda found caring for a new baby, as well as Poppet and Noel, tiring, and was not in the mood to be dictated to by her mother. Basil was never in the mood to be dictated to by his mother-in-law. Why, they questioned angrily, should they ask Uncle Maurice to take the christening? Nobody ever asked Uncle Maurice to take anything. It was their baby who was being baptised and they would have her baptised by somebody they chose, presumably their vicar. Uncle Maurice would spoil the party, and as for the idea of asking Aunt

Doris, it was crazy. Uncle Maurice and Aunt Doris were the sort of relations you hid from your friends, you didn't exhibit them at christenings. Why was there no need to ask Alison and Marjorie? They were the nicest of the cousins in spite of their awful father and mother. They were especially inflamed by Vera's last paragraph. "By the way, drop that idea of asking Aunt Clara to be a godmother. It is out of the question. I will explain later." Freda, like all Clara's nephews and nieces, was fond of her. It was not a fondness which they showed, for unless they met her she was out of their minds. She shared that place in their hearts kept for their childhood books and toys, the plot where they had made a garden, and the trees they had climbed to set up telegraph wires of string. Clara's cosy rounded figure in roomy dresses of plum, maroon or grey had always appeared in time of need. When that major catastrophe of childhood, the upsetting of the status quo, occurred, Clara's arrival had comforted and recreated security. When they were ill she had been the centre of their hazy world, wearing a large apron sitting by the bed reading aloud, and in the night her bulky outline, stooping over a coal scuttle, had come and gone as the fire flickered. In the way in which stubborn resistance is met by parents when they attempt to part with their children's treasures no longer apparently valued, so resistance sprang up at a hint of criticism of Aunt Clara. Drop asking Aunt Clara! They would certainly ask her, bless her. The plans for the christening of Priscilla Annette had, until that moment, hung fire; on the reception of Vera's letter everything was settled.

The letter Freda wrote to Clara was carefully worded, for

she and Basil were determined Clara should not think she was being asked to be a godmother because of her money. Freda's letter to her mother was firm. They would not have Uncle Maurice. The date of the christening and who should officiate was fixed. Clara had been asked to be one godmother and Alison the other.

Clara's letter from Freda arrived by the morning post. She was breakfasting alone, for Julie was not yet down after a late night, and Andrew had already left for the gymnasium. As she buttered the slice of burnt toast that Henry had made for her she gave the matter of the christening earnest thought. Freda's letter was charming, and whatever she decided the dear child must know she was pleased that she had been asked. It was particularly sweet of her to say the baby did not want christening presents, but that was nonsense, all babies should have christening presents, she would send the little pearl safety-pin she had been given at her own christening. But should she be a godmother? A godmother made vows on behalf of a baby, and ought to be there to see them carried out, so a great-aunt was not a good choice. It was an admirable idea to choose Alison, who was a splendid girl and would make a fine godmother, but should not Freda choose another of that generation for the second godmother?

When Henry came in to clear the breakfast he found Clara smiling apparently at nothing. He did not care for that. Too often in his experience too much smiling heralded one of her religious turns.

"What's up? Look like you'd won a football pool."

Clara continued to smile.

"That's naughty, Henry. You know I think gambling of any kind is wrong." She picked up Freda's letter. "My niece Freda has written to ask me to be godmother to the new baby."

Henry doubted the motives of any relative of Clara's.

"Oh! Does she say why?"

"I shall refuse. She says I'm not to give a christening present, but I shall of course. Miss Alison, my clergyman brother's girl, is being asked to be the other godmother. I was thinking, instead of posting my present, I should like to see Miss Alison and get her to take it with her, and some cakes and crackers for the christening tea as a treat for Poppet and Noel."

Henry paused in his table-clearing.

"When you say 'see' was you thinkin' she could come 'ere?"

"Yes. Andrew is sure to be out, and Julie won't mind going to her room; but I might tell Miss Alison about them. She's a dear girl and won't say anything unless I give her permission."

Henry looked severe.

"Before you do that, you'll ask Mr. Willis. You know 'ow it'll be, the moment they feels they're bein' done out of somethin', the 'ole boilin' will be 'ere, same as they was in the old gent's time. You don't want to start nothin' like that."

Clara did not like to hear Henry speak of her family in that way, but he was uneducated so did not appreciate he was being impertinent. She picked up her letter, and said gently but conclusively:

"I shall write to my niece now. Julie shall post it when she goes out to do the shopping."

Clara's attempts to teach Julie how English should be spoken succeeded by example rather than training. She could hear Julie's pinched vowels, and Julie could hear Clara's rounded ones, but there would have been no improvement if Julie had not noticed that, to show her how words should sound, Clara opened her mouth, while she, aiming at the same effect, kept hers half closed. Now that her mind was on educating herself Julie discovered speaking nicely was only a small part of all she needed to know. Spending so much time with Clara she picked up the knowledge that much that Bess had taught her she needed to forget. Words and expressions Bess had carefully instilled into herself and Andrew she now learned they never should have used. When alone she would mutter, "you can't say serviette, it's a napkin." "I mustn't ask anybody to pass the cruet. I must ask for mustard, pepper or salt." She had seen pain on Clara's face when in a teashop she had called the waitress "miss," and later Clara had said, "I know you would like me to tell you, dear. You say 'waitress,' never, never 'miss.'" Most difficult to overcome was the habit of murmuring "pardon." Bess had taken such trouble with that word. "Always say 'pardon,' nice manners cost nothing." Now to say pardon was wrong; no matter what happened, even if you knocked somebody over all you said was "sorry," at least that was all Charles seemed to think necessary. Some things she learnt she loved. She had been brought up to look on baths as luxuries, so it was a joy to discover in Clara's house they were considered necessities—"when do you like your bath, dear, morning or evening?"—and that it was usual even to have a second one if you were dressing to go out to dance. Each morning as she cooked her breakfast Julie discussed what she was learning with Henry, and usually, though sometimes he had caustic comments to make, especially about baths, which he thought unhealthy, he was interested. On the morning that Freda's letter arrived he was inattentive. Julie turned round from the stove where she was cooking bacon to look at him.

"What's up?"

Henry closed the door.

"The relatives is at us again."

By now Julie had learnt the names of most of Clara's family.

"Which of them?"

"Mrs. Pickerin'. She's one of Mr. George 'ilton's lot." Henry grinned reminiscently. "You did ought to 'ave 'eard the old gent about 'er kid. All on account of callin' 'er Poppet, created alarmin' 'e did. I can 'ear 'im as plain as if 'e was in this kitchen. 'Poppet! Damn disgustin'.' Well, now there's a baby come and Mrs. Pickerin' wants Miss Clara to be godmother."

"Isn't that nice for her?"

"Could be, could be not. Smells to me like Mr. George 'ilton and his missus is at the back of it, 'opin for somethin' for the baby."

"Why shouldn't the baby have something? Aunt Clara's got no children. Wouldn't it be nice for her to have a baby to be interested in?"

Henry came over to the stove and dropped his voice to a whisper.

"A baby'd be all right if it stopped there, but it won't. Miss Clara's funny about the old gent, I mean 'e wasn't like she thinks 'e was, she 'asn't no need to carry on about sacred trusts and that, but you know what she is, thinks a thin' did oughter be done, an' you can't stop 'er. You 'aven't seen one of 'er religious turns, chronic they are. I don't like what I've seen of the relatives, an' no more don't Mr. Willis, but relatives is relatives an' as' their rights, but they won't get rights nor nothin' else till Miss Clara's fixed thin's so everythin' what the old gent left 'er is satisfactory . . ."

"Like the horses?"

"That's the ticket, though, mind you, they was extra, seein' they weren't the ones what 'e left. But it's the same thin' to 'er; she's got to get the 'ole boilin' settled afore she can 'and out anythin' to the new baby, nor any of 'em. And that's why we don't want 'em nosin' round. I reckon this christenin's just a way for 'em to get climbin' our apples and pears."

Julie put her bacon on a plate and sat down at the table to eat it.

"I wonder if it would help if I told her that her uncle wasn't our father, or do you think she knows?"

"She knows, but that don't alter thin's, you was part of the trust, so to speak, an' you two's sort of fixed stayin' 'ere an' all, so we don't want no Miss Alison comin' an' upsettin' of 'er."

"Who's she?"

Henry repeated what Clara had told him.

"When you're with Mr. Willis to-night you 'ave a talk to 'im, 'e told me 'e expected me to keep the relatives off of 'er, but she 'as stubborn fits. Proper sarky she sounded when she was tellin' me about the letter. Put me in mind of the old gent when 'e was tellin' me to mind me own bloody business."

That evening Julie made Charles listen while she repeated what Henry had told her. It was not easy, for Charles never wanted to talk to her of anything that did not concern themselves. He liked to erect a screen of personal jokes and memories which shut them away from other diners and dancers. Since she had defended the old horses he often called her Saint Julia, and amused himself and her with supposed stories of her latest rescues. Her mantelpiece was full of china and glass animals, birds and insects, whose lives he pretended she had saved. To tear him from the intimate world that he treasured she had to show him that side of herself which Borthwick's Circus knew. The Julie who saw to it that she and Andrew had their full rights, from which no artist, however hard they tried, could push them.

"I want to hear how I rescued the sea-lion, Charles, but I won't listen until you've heard what I've got to tell you. Aunt Clara's being very good to us, and if we can help her it's up to Andrew and me to do it."

Charles reluctantly put a purple china sea-lion back in his pocket.

"All right. Let's have it."

In explaining Henry's fears and reporting that she had posted the letter to Alison, Julie told Charles more than she realised. He had not visualised her life in Gorpas Road. He saw her only as she appeared when he called to fetch her, and he had only known those parts of her day of which she told him. How she had visited the gymnasium to watch Andrew work, or something funny that a bus conductor had said. She had talked of "when I was ironing," or "I was mending something." He liked to think of her in the drawing-room or her pretty little bedroom, occupied making herself ready to go out with him. Now a new pattern was shaped. "I was cooking my breakfast when Henry said . . ." "Aunt Clara asked me to post the letter when I was out doing the shopping."

"Aunt Clara really means to see Alison Hilton, she showed me the little brooch she wants her to take . . ." "I think she'd be glad if this Alison Hilton knew about Andrew and me, she thinks hiding things is wrong, but Henry says she wants to get everything settled."

When she stopped talking Charles said:

"I thought Aunt Clara went to that comic mission every day. Doesn't she go any more?"

Julie tried not to sound as if there was anything to hide.

"Not for a bit she isn't. I think she's tired."

"What's the secrecy stuff? Is the old girl ill?"

"No, nothing like that." Julie felt she must tell a half truth, or he would drag the whole truth from her. "It's something she does for me. It's my secret, please don't try and find it out."

Charles was silent, his mind hunting for any possible service Clara could do Julie. It certainly could not be to do with clothes, the poor old girl did not know the first thing about them. It could not be housework or cooking, for he had long ago discovered that Clara was not fond of either. Julie's secret! Something she did not want him to know. Then he guessed. Subconsciously he had noticed her correcting herself. "Pard . . . I mean sorry." A struggle to remember there was an "a" in "really." That friends should not be described as ladies and gentlemen. He was deeply touched. He could see Clara and Julie working together. Nothing would have been said, but the labour would be for him. It humbled him to think of Julie struggling to fit herself for his world, while he did nothing towards making his world fit for her. He had been wallowing in his happiness, and to keep the bloom on it had avoided a family row. He leant across the table and laid a hand on Julie's.

"You're a darling, and I'm a lazy brute."

Julie was puzzled.

"Lazy about what?"

"Aunt Clara's doings. Poor old lady, everything ought to have been tidied up weeks ago. We can't see the road until it is."

Julie did not move her hand, but her fingers twitched with slight impatience.

"I don't see how clearing up her business is going to help, the relations will still bother her. If she tells this Miss Alison about Andrew and me, Henry says they'll all pounce on her. It's a shame she should be worried, because she's getting old and she's so sweet."

Resolution was growing in Charles. Clara must see all her property and come to a clear decision what she would keep and what she would sell, then, those things settled, he could face his father and the uncles without any repercussions there might be, affecting the old lady. As far as he was concerned he could go on advising her, if not as part of the firm, as one who hoped to be a new kind of relation.

"It'll help. You do what you can to get her to make up her mind about things. Get her to decide whether her conscience will let her keep the pub, and what she wants done with her greyhounds . . ."

"She's seeing them. Henry's arranging it."

"Good. Until she makes up her mind about things I can't arrange a sale or have any idea of her income."

"She's awfully glad to have you. She's always talking about it. If you weren't looking after her I don't know what she'd do."

Charles saw the not far distant blaze of a family row. He saw the uncles and his father in conference behind a closed door. He could imagine how quickly it would be decided that somebody else had better look after Miss Hilton's affairs to keep him from "that girl." None of it would matter. He would do exactly as he thought fit, but there was always the danger of a whiff of the conflagration reaching poor old Clara's nose; he wouldn't put it past one of the uncles writing to her. He squeezed Julie's hand before letting it go.

"Stop looking like a spaniel. I shall be around to look after her." He brought the sea-lion out of his pocket. "Now, Saint Julia, let me tell you how you saved the life of Sugar-Daddy the sea-lion."

* * * * *

Botchley Lane lay off the road to Tilbury. The Saturday of the race meeting turned out a wretched day, lowering skies, drifting rain, and an east wind. Perce, when he telephoned Henry about final arrangements, was jubilant.

"Couldn't 'ave 'ad a better day if I'd fixed it meself, 'enry boy. The bookies'll be so froze they won't think fast, an' it ain't fit for Miss 'ilton to get out of the car, an' so Mrs. Perce'll tell 'er. Couldn't want anythin' nicer, could you?"

The race track called itself Botchley Lane Stadium. It consisted of a soggy field round which ran a cinder track, a tottering building of rotting wood, from which peered blue faces selling totalisator tickets, a temporary counter made of beer cases, from behind which a trollop served tea in chipped cups which had first been rinsed in a bucket of dirty water, six traps, a winning post, a rickety loud speaker and a hare perched on a wire fan-shaped contraption, which was drawn by a hand winder.

All outings were treats to Clara so, in spite of the weather, she meant to enjoy herself. She had been told by Henry that the Perces had provided the car, which she thought extraordinarily thoughtful of them, and she was particularly touched when she learnt that Perce had telephoned to arrange that she should see the racing without leaving the car. She was delighted that Henry had included his friend Nobby in the party; she had not before met him, but she had not forgotten how helpful he had been in getting rid of the rubbish in the drawing-room. She had hoped since Julie was coming that Charles would be with them, but accepted Julie's explanation that Henry thought Charles would not mix well with Nobby and the Perces, and so she had not told him where they were going. On the way down Clara was the only talkative member of the party, everyone else had their minds on other things and answered her only in monosyllables. Henry kept touching the bulge in his pocket, which was his hundred pounds. It was all right having a gamble, but wasn't he a fool risking all he had on a dog? Perce was all right, but the weather was shocking, easy enough for any dog to skid at a bend. If he left off living with Miss Clara, that hundred would keep him going until he got fixed up in a new job. Julie was silent because she hated deceiving Charles. She had told him that she was going to watch Andrew working, and he had behaved like a sulky child because she had not allowed him to come too. She wished she knew what he was doing, so that she could imagine him doing it. Six o'clock, when he was fetching her to see a film and have dinner, seemed hours away. She hoped Aunt Clara would be pleased when she had seen the races, and decide definitely that she would not sell her dogs. Then she could tell Charles where they had been, he would still be cross he had not been allowed to come, but less cross when he knew she had helped Aunt Clara to make up her mind about one part of her property. Nobby sat beside the chauffeur, very conscious of his wad of notes. He hoped he would get a chance of a word with Henry before the race. It was awkward they couldn't speak to Perce, still, if Perce was up to what Henry thought he was up to, it was obvious they couldn't, it would spoil their chances of getting a good price if they were seen with him before the race. He must try and find out if Henry was still going the limit in spite of the weather. Andrew was silent from anxiety. For once he was not mentally on a trapeze, but going over in his head the instructions Henry had given him. Knowing how vague he was, Henry had been careful to impress on him how important the bet laying was. "Don't let me catch you dreamin', you keep your mind on the fac' you're seein' after a quarter of all old 'enry 'as in the world."

A muddy lane led to the entrance to Botchley, and from the side of it Mrs. Perce stepped out and stopped the car. She was wearing an army-surplus mackintosh over her velvet coat. On her head was a triangle of rubber from which, like seaweed, hung dripping hanks of hair. She hung in at the car window.

"Out you get, all of you. You'll like to get close up, but I know a place where the car can stand and me an' Miss 'ilton can see the race lovely, without gettin' our feet wet."

The smell exuding from Mrs. Perce's clothes when dry was formidable, but the smell exuding from them when wet was unique in its powerfulness. Clara had her lavender-scented handkerchief out before Mrs. Perce's head was half inside the car window. The others were less fortunate. As they walked up the lane Nobby remarked to Julie "Pongs a bit, don't she?"

Mrs. Perce directed the driver to drive into the entrance to the stadium and there to turn.

"You want to face the right way to get off, you may be glad to get away quick." She felt this might not sound well so added, "On account of it bein' so wet."

Clara peered through the rain-splashed windows, and her heart sank. Had dear old Uncle Simon ever seen his dogs race on a wet day? Surely it could not be kind to have them out in such weather. She pretended to blow her nose, for Attar of Mrs. Perce, in the small space of the car, took more getting used to than any scent she had met previously.

"Do you think it's kind to have the dogs out in such weather?"

Mrs. Perce laid a friendly hand on Clara's knees.

"Bless your kind 'eart, ducks, but they loves it. There's a race startin' any minute, you watch the dogs as they comes round, an' you'll soon see whether they're enjoyin' of their-selves or not."

In a few minutes the hare bounced round followed by six greyhounds. It was not a race in which the Perces were interested, but Mrs. Perce, seeing that the dogs seemed well trapped, that there was no accident and no fighting, decided to adopt them.

"What did I tell you? No one couldn't say they wasn't 'appy. I was only sayin' to Perce dinner time, it's a shame we couldn't 'ave the fourteen runnin'. It breaks me 'eart to leave any of 'em be'ind, they seems to know where we're goin' and they cries like children 'cause they ain't comin' too."

Clara, finding the presence of Mrs. Perce in spite of her lavender water, overpowering, opened the window. She peered through the rain at the people gathered round the bookmakers. In drab, water-logged clothes, they looked a dismal lot, in contrast the six dogs she had just seen run, seemed gaiety personified.

"The dogs looked as if they were enjoying themselves, but those poor people look wretched; do they have to come?"

Mrs. Perce thought quickly. It had been agreed that,

seeing what was planned, if possible Clara's mind should be kept from the subject of betting.

"Mostly they'll be here because they're fond of dogs. You know, it's funny 'ow you get about 'em, if it's a dog you got an interest in, you feel like 'e expects you to be there whenever 'e's runnin'.""

Clara knew from her mission work that people thought nothing of queueing all night, no matter what the weather, to see a football match, and presumed dog racing had the same sort of appeal. Having just seen a race she could not imagine why it should amuse anyone, but she could see for herself that it did, or was it the gambling angle? Too often, across kitchen tables, she had heard of losses on horses and dogs. She turned back to Mrs. Perce.

"There is one point that worries me. I think all gambling wrong. On the other hand my dear old uncle left his dogs in my care, or rather in your care, and it was his wish that they should always have care and consideration. If I could believe these people really came for an afternoon's enjoyment and not for gambling I should feel happier about owning dogs, but do they?"

Clara had a way of drawing the truth from those to whom she spoke. Mrs. Perce surprised herself by the truthfulness of her answer.

"A course they bets. You wouldn't alter that by not 'avin' dogs. Bettin's in the blood, if they didn't bet on dogs they'd do it on somethin' else. I seen people bet on which of a coupl'a bed bugs would walk quickest up a wall. Thin's still isn't too good, there's many families livin' all on top of each other like, and young couples sharin' a 'ouse with the girl's

people and more often than not the man don't take no interest in 'is job, an' you know 'ow it is to-day, you works
your guts out and they take 'alf of what you earn out of
your pay packet, an' that with prices risin' every day. I
reckon it's the bob on the 'orse or the dog what makes life
worth livin' for many."

"It's very sad if that's true."

"Lots of true thin's is sad, but that don't alter thin's. You
can't stop people 'avin' a bet, but you can see your dogs lives
comfortable, same as Mr. 'ilton wished." Mrs. Perce lowered
her voice so that the chauffeur would not hear what she said.
"You've seen 'ow Perce and me lives, 'omely, but we're good
to the dogs an' no one can't say no different; 'enry wrote us
about Andy. Nasty bit of work Andy is, an' me an' Perce is
glad 'e's bein' watched, an' glad to 'ear 'ow you saved five
p'or old crocks from Andy an' 'is like. But if you don't mind
me sayin' so, ducks, what 'appened to those 'orses did oughter be a lesson to you. Take the dogs away from me an' Perce
an' sell 'em, on account of someone riskin' a coupl'a shillings
on 'em, an' what might 'appen to the dogs?"

"Is it only a couple of shillings? I'm afraid these people
may risk more than they can afford."

Mrs. Perce saw Perce join the group of owners about to
lead their dogs round before the next race. She longed to
give him all her attention, but it was her business to set
Clara's mind at rest. She pointed to the tote windows, and
without a hint of the excitement rising within her, explained
that buying a ticket on a dog was not unlike buying a ticket
for a seat in a cinema, it was a set price, it cost two shillings.
She did not mention higher priced tickets or that anyone

bought more than one ticket. Clara was surprised and impressed.

"Only two shillings! Of course that doesn't affect the principle, but I'm glad they don't cost more."

Outside the entrance to the racecourse Henry had divided his forces. He took Andrew with him and put Julie in Nobby's care. The two parties were not to appear to know each other, and they had never met or heard of Perce. To Nobby Henry whispered that, sad though it was to waste the money, confidence was to be built up by foolish betting on the race before their race; if Nobby stood behind him he would hear which dog could not win, and therefore he and Julie should back it. In answer to Nobby's anxious query about the chances of their dog in this weather, Henry managed a confident wink, and raised his thumbs.

More money than anyone looking at the shabby down-at-heel crowd would suspect changed hands at Botchley Lane. Everybody who went knew that some dog was probably fixed to win, and their aim, either by eavesdropping or bribery, was to discover which dog it was to be. Perce, because of his reputation, seldom brought off a real coup, any dog of his was watched and backed if there was the faintest chance of a win. That afternoon was the triumph of his career. The rain made it difficult to see clearly, and the dog Perce was supposed to be running was one he usually put into a race only for the purpose of obstructing other dogs, in order that another of his should win. In this race he had only the one runner, which it was understood he had put in to oblige the owner of the track, as the bitch he had intended to run was in season.

The laying of the bets was so simple that, as Henry told Nobby after the race, it was almost a shame to take the money. The dog borrowed for the afternoon had been an open racer, and still was faster than any dog that raced at Botchley Lane. There was much swearing and angry shouting after the race, but there never was an inquiry held at Botchley Lane. If you risked your money there you were supposed to know what you were doing, and to put up with it when you were outsmarted; but Henry, having seen all the winnings collected, felt it was better they should leave. He gave Nobby a signal and, followed by angry shouts, the four walked towards the car. Henry jerked his head backwards at the shouters.

"You don't want to pay no attention to that lot," he told Julie. "Just common they are, an' can't take a beatin'."

Julie gave him a straight look.

"I don't know how that was worked, but I don't think the bookmaker who called me a crook was far out. I'm awfully glad Mr. Willis didn't come. I hope Aunt Clara doesn't let her dogs race here any more."

Henry was disappointed in her.

"Now don't take on. That race might 'ave been a bit off the straight, but all dog racin's that way, isn't it, Nobby? An' don't you go suggestin' Miss Clara takes 'er dogs away from Perce, for they're 'appy where they is. You don't want 'im sendin' 'em somewhere where they might be treated cruel, like Andy did the 'orses, do you?"

Clara had seen nothing unusual in the race. She smiled happily when they reached the car.

"Have you seen enough? I don't wonder, it's so very wet.

That last dog that won is one of mine, didn't he seem well and happy?"

Mrs. Perce clambered out of the car, and while the children and Nobby got in, she opened her large shabby bag, into which Henry pushed a bundle of notes. Clara leant out of the car window to say good-bye.

"Please remember me to dear Mr. Perce, and thank him for arranging the car and tell him that I've so enjoyed myself in spite of the rain. I'm glad I had that talk with you. It will certainly help me to make up my mind."

As the car drove away from Botchley Lane, Clara looked at her damp family.

"I'm afraid it wasn't much fun for you, dears."

Julie, pretending to settle more comfortably in her seat, managed to nudge Henry, who was sitting on the tip-up seat in front of her.

"You enjoyed yourself, didn't you, Henry? He had a little bet on that dog of yours, Aunt Clara, that won the last race."

Clara knew Henry betted now and again.

"Very naughty of him. I hear you buy a two shilling ticket. How much can you win for two shillings, Henry?"

In Henry's breast pocket was more money than he had ever owned before, but from his tone he might have won nothing.

"It all depends whether a dog's fancied or not, Miss Clara."

* * * * *

Freda, like all Vera and George's children, had a strong family feeling, so she disliked quarrelling with her mother. Vera, after she had got over Freda's firm letter, met her daughter half-way by partially explaining why she wished to meet Doris, and why she did not think Clara should be a godmother. She admitted that she had no real reason for saying there was no need to ask Alison and Marjorie, it was only that she had tried to arrange that Marjorie should help with the children and Priscilla Annette, and Doris had written rather a rude reply. Freda and Basil, apart from Freda's wish to put things right with her mother, were so charmed with the hints dropped they would not for anything have missed finding out what the fuss was about. They laughed until tears streamed down their cheeks at Vera's "We are rather troubled about your Aunt Clara, something not very nice may be happening there, and we have reason to think Aunt Doris knows something. You will understand we don't want to make too much of the affair and so, if we could meet Aunt Doris in the ordinary way at the christening, it would be such a help." Basil had an inventive mind, and described for Freda Clara street-walking in Cork Street, as proprietress of a night club which sold drugs as a side-line, and as a receiver of stolen goods. The joke of the parents suspecting dear, solid Aunt Clara of anything, and saying that Aunt Doris knew something, was too good to keep to themselves so Rita, Tim, Ronnie and Ethel were invited to the christening, and warned if they did not come they would miss a good laugh.

There was to be a party after the christening, so Vera asked Freda to arrange that Maurice and Doris came to the house well beforehand, so that they could have their talk. Freda, in return for a promise from her mother that she should be told everything, did as she was requested, and after the smallest exchange of greetings shut the four into the drawing-room.

Doris was triumphant. This was what she had waited for. Maurice was at last being treated as he deserved. The whole parish had been told that he was taking a family christening, and her parents that Maurice had been asked to select the day, because it was unthinkable he should not take the service. Maurice, though glad that his family were at last being guided to treat him with proper respect, was not happy about the guidance given to his daughters. He had told Alison clearly it was not his wish that she should see her Aunt Clara, and he had added, "Mummie and I have our reasons." Alison had stared at him and then laughed and said, "Don't be so silly," and that evening had told him that she had written to Aunt Clara to say she would call before the christening, and that Marjorie would be with her. Maurice, on his knees, repeated this conversation. He explained that though of course he realised it had been overheard on high, he thought it might have been overlooked. He drew attention to endless service given without reward, for nobody could describe his stipend as a reward, and also often without proper encouragement, for those put in authority over him, though perhaps gifted in other ways, were brusque and lacking in sympathy. He implored that as a sign that his work was properly noted in Heaven, Alison and Marjorie should become meek, and should show meekness by humbly begging forgiveness for having disobeyed his wishes, and Alison for the words, "Don't be so silly." But the day of the christening arrived, and though Maurice was pale from wrestling and his trouser legs creased with kneeling, the sign was not given, and Alison and Marjorie, refusing to notice that he was pained, ate a large breakfast, and immediately afterwards dashed off to catch a train, merely shouting, "See you at the church." So it was a subdued Maurice who sat beside Doris in the train, and Doris, aware of this, could have shaken him. Here, for the first time, they were important to the family, they had knowledge George and Vera wanted, this was the moment to assert themselves, to refuse to be snubbed and treated as poor relations, and Maurice had to choose this day of all days to look hang-dog. "Do forget what Alison said," Doris implored, "and give your mind to what we have to say about Clara." But Maurice looked more hang-dog than ever, and asked how that was possible when his darlings were in that polluted place.

Vera had to change her tone from kindly condescension to warm fondness for a favourite sister-in-law, before Doris allowed Maurice, with much prompting from herself, to speak of Henry's bedroom. When at last the story was told it was met with incredulity. "You can't mean you think Clara's silly about him in that way?" said Vera. "Redecorating a bedroom is not proof of undue affection," George explained. Doris, her cheeks aflame with the excitement of holding the floor, said that Maurice had not accurately described the room; it was all pink and blue, that a great deal of satin had been used, it was in fact the sort of room you would connect with a film star, rather than with a man servant.

Slowly George and Vera accepted what they were told. Neither mentioned drink, but both wondered if drink had its part in the story. George was unwilling to make a definite decision right away as to what should be done. It was, he said, unfortunately a not uncommon story. The world was full of men waiting to get hold of the money of silly ageing women, who were perhaps lonely. Obviously Henry must be got rid of, but it might not be easy. He would take advice and let them know what was decided.

On the excuse that they must come and see Poppet and Noel enjoying Aunt Clara's cake and crackers, Freda drew Basil, Ronnie, Ethel, Rita, Tim, Alison and Marjorie out of the party, and beckoned them into her bedroom. There, choking with laughter, she told them what she had learnt from her mother their elders suspected. She was made to repeat the story four times; by the end of the fourth none of them were standing, aching with laughter they were sprawled on the bed or the floor; at intervals one of them would gasp, "Aunt Clara and Henry!" and another spasm of laughter overcame them. It was in the middle of one of these spasms that the bedroom door opened and Vera came in, followed by George, Maurice and Doris. Vera struggled not to sound cross. The laughter had been heard by the guests, they had tried to say it was the children, but Poppet had spoilt that by coming in to show off a paper hat from a cracker. Really, they must pull themselves together and think of the guests. Maurice, looking more pained than ever, added that Alison should remember she was a godmother and this was a day to be treated seriously.

The arrival of the older generation killed the laughter, and gave Alison and Marjorie a chance to think about what they had been laughing, and to discover it was not funny. They told the truth together, scorn and revulsion growing with each word. They had met Julie, and described her. They told of Clara's gratitude that by looking after the Marquis children she was able to carry out at least one of Uncle Simon's requests. Of Henry, who had gladly given up his room to Julie, seeming to think nothing of taking to a camp bed in the drawing-room. They recounted what Clara had told them about the five old horses she had sent to the Frossarts. They repeated what she had said about dog racing, that gambling was wrong, but selling Uncle Simon's dogs to strangers seemed worse, and, though she was finding it hard to decide what was right, she had more or less decided they should stay with the Perces. They told of the design they had seen for Uncle Simon's gravestone, and how she believed Uncle Simon had chosen the words to be put on it. Finally, so carried away by indignation she was almost crying, Alison said:

"The words are 'Let your light so shine before men that they may see your good works . . .' I think those words are true of Aunt Clara, almost you can see a gold light shining from her. I should hate to think what coloured lights would shine out of all of you with your filthy minds."

George, Vera, Maurice and Doris were for a moment silenced. George was the first to rally. He told Alison she was talking a lot of nonsense, and, linking himself with Maurice, reminded them that, as Clara's brothers, it was their duty to see her nephews and nieces were treated fairly. Any money that Clara had inherited belonged after her death to her own family and not to any fly-by-nights mentioned in the will.

He was interrupted by Freda. She had been carried away by Alison and Marjorie's rage, and was determined to take her stand with them.

"Shut up, Father. If you bother Aunt Clara about her wretched money I shall go straight to her solicitors and tell them what you have been thinking about her. You wouldn't like that, would you?"

Clara, knowing nothing of what had taken place at the christening, was touched to the point of tears when two days later she received a large piece of christening cake, together with flowers sent with fondest love, from those of her nephews and nieces who were present.

Henry eyed the flowers and the cake with the deepest suspicion.

"They're up to something, that lot," he confided to Julie. "Cake and flowers don't come up our apples and pears unless something's expected."

* * * * *

Whenever Charles tried to persuade Clara to make a final decision about the disposal of her property he found her evasive. She agreed that she should get her affairs settled, but said she must not be hurried, she must be clear in her mind what was right. When Charles tried to pin her down to when she would get things settled, she avoided the question, saying gently, "Soon, Charles dear," and then with some vague excuse would wander away.

It was easy at Christmas to find excuses for delay. Clara

might not be going to the mission, but she had many old friends to visit there, and many parcels to pack and take to them. There was the excitement of the opening of the circus. Seeing Andrew and Julie with Borthwick's had been wonderful, but now that she really knew Andrew, that he was living in her flat, she felt the pride of an aunt in a brilliant nephew. Charles had bought the seats, and arranged they should be in twos, not near enough to make them one party but near enough for them to meet in the interval. Clara and Henry were across a gangway from Charles and Julie. Clara almost spoilt the performance for Henry. Wrapped in her sealskin coat, her eyes gleaming with childlike excitement from behind her pince-nez, she gazed round the arena, and in no time was in conversation with those in the seats next to her, those in front and those behind. She pointed out The Flying Fishes on the programme and more or less explained Andrew. "My dear uncle asked me to take an interest in the children, I don't really think he's related, you know, but that makes no difference. They are such dears. It's been so nice for me having them. If you lean forward you can see Julie." In vain Henry looked disapproving, and tried to draw Clara's attention to the ring. "That'll be where they comes on, Miss Clara. Look, you can see a 'orse waitin'." "Lovely pattern of sawdust, isn't it?" Clara was adding to the pleasure of her neighbours and, thinking only of this, refused to be silenced. "Such a treat for me. I've always been such an old stick-in-the-mud. I can hardly believe that I'm sitting in this lovely seat, and that one of the performers is my dear Andrew."

On another day the Borthwicks came up to see the circus

and had high tea in the flat beforehand. There was the Christmas visit with Henry to the cemetery to put a wreath of holly on Simon's grave. There was Christmas Day itself. Since she was a child Clara had given all of Christmas Day, not spent in church, to seeing that others enjoyed themselves. This year Julie, Andrew, Charles and Henry planned that she should have a happy day. When tired and cold, she puffed up the stairs on her return from early service, she was greeted by a lighted Christmas tree, parcels and cries of "A happy Christmas." It was, as Clara told Charles, such a surprise. "I'm not used to being made a fuss of. You must give me time to get over Christmas before I can put my mind to business."

There was a reason for Clara's dilatoriness that Charles did not know; Clara had tried several times to get Henry to take her to visit Mrs. Gladys Smith.

"I really must see her, Henry. After all, she ought to know that Mr. Hilton left a wish she should be adequately provided for."

Henry's comment was always the same.

"You don't want to go botherin' 'er. She's 'ad 'er 'undred pounds, I told you she's all right."

Clara knew there was some worry in Henry's mind in connection with Mrs. Gladys Smith. He said she was a person who did things her own way, but Clara felt he must know she did not wish to interfere. It might be there had been intimacy between Mrs. Gladys Smith and Uncle Simon, but even so it was past history now, and Henry should know her better than to think she would mention it, or even in her mind criticise the poor woman. In her bedroom she searched Simon's face in the family group. What would he wish? Henry was such a dear man, it was unlike him not to help; was it faithfulness to the old man's memory? In the end, after much thought, she decided to visit Mrs. Gladys Smith alone.

Clara did not write to advise Mrs. Gladys Smith she was calling, for Henry's statement that she was a woman who did things her own way suggested a door shut to visitors. Having decided that the visit must be paid, without a word to anybody, on a bitter afternoon in February, Clara went to Paddington.

Lipton Grove took a lot of finding. It was one of the maze of streets radiating from Paddington Station. No street could look pleasant that February afternoon, the sky was leaden with snow clouds, and a two days' old fall of snow mixed with soot was frozen over everything. Lipton Grove looked particularly depressing. The houses were Victorian, of the period when atrocious stained-glass was inserted over the front doors. When new the houses might have possessed an air of solidarity and respectability, but for years they had been neglected, and had come down, and now exuded a shady shabbiness. Clara, accustomed to shady shabbiness of streets and houses, recognised the quality, and felt a little anxious as she rang the bell of number one.

In the window on the left of the front door there were yellow lace curtains. As the bell jangled through the house these moved, and though Clara could see nobody, she felt eyes fixed on her. Presently steps came down the passage and the front door opened.

Gladys Smith must have been a blonde. Now, at seventy-odd her hair was yellow white, her wrinkled skin heavily made up, and she filled to bursting point the dusty velvet dress into which she was upholstered. Two points struck Clara. Mrs. Gladys Smith's eyes, which were the bluest eyes she had ever seen, and the behaviour of the front door, which appeared to have no fastenings, but merely swung open when touched. Mrs. Smith was clearly puzzled by Clara, so there was caution in her "Yes. What is it?"

Clara was too experienced an uninvited caller to move, that would give the effect of one intending to force their way in, and could lead to a foot being placed against the door. Quietly she stated her business.

"I'm Miss Clara Hilton. He left everything he had to me . . ."

Clara had to stop there, for Gladys let out a yelp, then, leaning against the wall for support, let out roar after roar of laughter. Between laughs she managed to gasp, "Excuse me, dearie." "You must think me rude, but I can't help myself." Each time she attempted to pull herself together another look at Clara's earnest face, rather blue with cold, at her pince-nez, her sealskin coat, and her loaf-shaped figure, and she was off again. "Oh, I am sorry, but you'll be the death of me, straight you will." At last she got control of herself, and taking Clara by the arm led her into her sitting-room, and settled her in an armchair by a blazing fire.

Gladys's life had been a fight to obtain and hold comfort, security and what to her were luxuries. Relations had whined and begged. Always there were grasping fingers trying to snatch. Often there were hands out for bribes. As a result her room bulged with what she had managed to obtain and hold. Cushions of worn velvet and taffetas, dolls on the divan, pictures festooned on the walls, with, in many cases, fans stuck over their frames, too many chairs, too many tables, too many rugs, too many mirrors, and too many ornaments.

"Forgive me, dearie. I was always one for a good laugh, and knowing your uncle as I knew him you can see it struck me all of heap when you said you were his niece."

Clara had not resented the laughter. It was regrettable that Mrs. Gladys Smith was what she was, or rather what she had been to Uncle Simon, but she had an infectious gaiety, which made it possible to imagine how, as a young woman, she might have charmed him.

"I don't wonder you laughed. Up to the end he was such a smart old man, and I'm such a dowdy creature." Clara held out an envelope. "I've brought the family group with me. It was taken on his eightieth birthday."

Gladys Smith looked at the photograph and made clucking noises.

"Proper old rip, wasn't he? Never think he was eighty, would you? Look at those eyes. You'd swear he was just going to laugh. 'Course I hadn't seen him for some years, but he hadn't changed much, it's a speaking likeness."

"Isn't it. I find that photograph a great help. You see, although he left everything to me, except legacies to you and Henry and other friends, it was only to take care of tilings for him. He scarcely knew me, I think he chose me because I was the unmarried one, and would have time to carry out his wishes. When I'm in doubt what he would have liked I look at that photograph and I seem to find the answer."

Gladys gave Clara a quick, thoughtful look. Then she jumped up.

"Whatever must you think of me? What'll you have, dearie, a cup of tea, or would you like something stronger? You've only got to put a name to it, it's all here."

Over cups of tea, and fancy biscuits out of an ornate tin, Clara told Gladys about the will. Henry should have been there to share Gladys's reaction. On first hearing what the property had consisted of, it had been all she could do not to laugh, but as Clara talked she ceased to be amused, and instead wished that Simon was not dead, so that she could give him a piece of her mind. He was a cruel old beast wanting his joke even when he was in his coffin.

"I think," Clara said, "I've got everything settled now. I've seen everything and everybody mentioned in the will. I've left you to the last I'm afraid. Very lazy it sounds, but I'd hoped Henry would bring me to call, as you knew him."

Gladys answered that only with a nod. She refilled Clara's cup, and lit a cigarette for herself.

"Let's hear how you've settled everything first, we'll come to me later. Your uncle was fond of Ruby Marquis, but there were so many. He never thought he was their father, you know."

Clara's eyes shone as she spoke of Julie and Andrew. She explained as best she was able how gifted Andrew was, and of his present position with The Flying Fishes. Gladys's interest was practical.

"Good. Then you've nothing to worry about where he's concerned. What about the girl?"

Clara looked into the fire. She was drawn to Gladys, should she confide in her?

"It's too early yet to be sure, but I think she's fond of young Charles Willis, the lawyer, and he of her."

"Would that work? They come out of different drawers, don't they?"

Clara looked embarrassed.

"I know, but I think if they really love each other it will be all right. Of course, Charles doesn't know this, but I went to see his father."

Gladys nearly let out a surprised whistle.

"You did! And told him, you mean?"

Clara nodded.

"Everything. He was charming, just the father I should expect Charles to have. He wouldn't stand in his son's way, I mean if he loves Julie."

The more Clara told her the more protective Gladys felt.

"What's Julie like? I mean, I remember Ruby, she was a good sort, but not the kind to marry a gentleman."

Clara struggled to describe Julie.

"She had dyed hair, but she's had it cut short now, and she's letting it go back to its natural brown. There were little faults of speech to correct, but they're getting better. You'd like her very much, she's straightforward, and I think she should make a splendid wife and mother."

Gladys dismissed Julie. She saw she would never get a true picture of her from Clara.

"What about the horses and dogs? I knew Marie, Alfie and Perce's mother. Poor thing, she was a terror at the end. But she must have been lovely once. You know, there was never anyone else your uncle loved but her; sometimes he'd talk to me about her, it changed him even to speak of her."

Clara gave Gladys a grateful smile.

"I'm glad you told me that. Henry had given me to understand he was fond of her, but what you've told me convinces me I'm right in leaving the greyhounds with Mr. and Mrs. Perce. They're very happy there; I think gambling wrong, but, as Mrs. Perce pointed out, I can't stop people betting by selling the dogs, but I can know they're happy if I leave them with the Perces, and I've seen them race and I know they enjoy that."

"Where do they race?"

"Botchley Lane it's called."

A startled "Botch . . ." slipped out before Gladys could hold it back. She hurriedly changed the subject.

"What about the horses?"

Clara explained about Andy.

"Of course I didn't think of anything at the time, except the old horses, but sending them to the Frossarts at 'The Goat in Gaiters' has helped me to decide about that. You see, I think drinking wrong, but 'The Goat in Gaiters' is a charming place, and the Frossarts are dears. We've had some old stables rebuilt and there's a field, and the horses seem happy and rested." Clara caught her breath. "Oh dear, I didn't mean to say that. If you see Henry don't tell him I went down to call on the Frossarts. Nobody knows. I went all by myself, just after Christmas. I let them think I was at a party at the mission where I used to live."

"Why shouldn't you go if you want to? It's none of Henry's business."

"He worries about me, dear man, and there was a little scheme that I had to discuss with the Frossarts privately."

Gladys, seeing Clara had finished her tea, moved the tea tray to another table.

"What about Gamblers' Luck?"

"I'm keeping that. It seems a harmless game, and it brings in a little money which will be a help."

"That's the lot then."

"Yes. Except you."

Gladys went to the window and drew the curtains.

"I'm all right."

"That's what Henry says. But Uncle Simon wished you should be adequately provided for. Do you pay rent for this place?"

Gladys finished with the curtains and crossed to the divan and beat up the cushions.

"Now and again I did, but it went back into the house, so to speak, repairs and that. I wrote about things to your uncle and Henry came along and we fixed things together."

It was obvious Gladys did not want to discuss business. Clara wished it was not her duty to force her to.

"Do you use all the house, or let part of it?"

"There are four rooms let."

The warm-hearted Gladys of a few minutes before was gone, there was no friendliness left in the room. Clara did not know what the trouble was, but she could feel she was upsetting Gladys, whom it was her duty to see adequately provided for.

"Don't think I've come to interfere. I just want to know

how things are. Please come back to your chair. I want to tell you something. Nobody else knows."

Suddenly Gladys knew what Clara was going to tell her, and knew she had known it subconsciously since she came into the house. She moved towards her, full of warmth and kindness.

"That you've got to get things settled. That's it, isn't it?"

"Yes. But nobody knows. I'm so fortunate, I suffer very little and it's so much pleasanter to live your ordinary life as long as possible. I was told I should have an operation, but it was just the time of Uncle Simon's eightieth birthday, so of course I had to wait for that, and then just as I was planning to go to hospital he died. I've been much too busy since for anything like that."

"Are you going to have it now?"

"Soon. I've told Mr. and Mrs. Borthwick, and they're asking Julie to come down for a day or two to help them. I shouldn't like her to be bothered."

"It might be all right."

"That's not the impression I get from the doctors. I wouldn't be operated on, but it may allow me to live normally for a time, I understand without it I shall shortly be a complete invalid. That's why I have to bother you. If I should die I thought of leaving you this house for your life-time."

The door opened and a shrill voice shouted from the passage.

"Cheerio, Gladdie dear. Lovely weather for it, I don't think."

Gladys opened the door wider.

"Come in, Dorrie. I'd like you to meet Miss Hilton."

When the front door had slammed behind Dorrie, she still seemed to be in the room. There was no mistaking Dome's profession. It was in her walk, in her unwillingness to speak to a woman not of her world. Clara struggled to appear matter of fact. Not to sound appalled.

"Did my uncle know?"

Gladys did not hesitate, though she could still hear Simon saying, "I'm countin' on those hussies of yours keepin' me in me old age." The old man might be dead, she might kill any chance she still had of being left the house, but "never split on a pal" had been her rule for living.

"Not him, dearie. Is it likely?"

Clara considered Dorrie quite dispassionately.

"She's not at all young, is she?"

Gladys pulled her chair nearer the fire, so her legs could feel the comforting heat.

"No. Neither are the other three. It's a terrible life when you're getting on." She moved her head to indicate the window. "It's snowing again. I never did care for railway stations at the best of times; you try hanging about outside one on a night like this. Often it's a waste of time, but they don't give in. They've got guts, I'll say that."

"Couldn't they do some . . ." Clara fumbled for a suitable way of expressing her meaning, "some other work?"

"What?"

Clara turned her mind to the mission. What was it girls of that sort did?

"Laundry work?"

"Not them. They're not the domesticated sort. The only

time they've got down to anything for long is when they've made mail bags for His Majesty."

"But they can't go on doing, what they do, for much longer, can they?"

A weary look passed over Gladys's face. She had often asked herself that question. "The girls" as she called them, were supposed to pay, and supposed to feed themselves, and officially she had no idea on what they lived. Actually there were many weeks when no rent was forthcoming and sometimes she provided a meal. A sudden dislike of discussing the problem of "the girls" swept over her. All her life she had laughed at problems. Laughter was the way to treat worries, to send them scurrying like rats into dark corners.

"Never mind them, dearie. They're my headache, not yours. Mind you, they hand me a good laugh, I'll give them that. Now, I'm going to slip in next door where there's a telephone, and get you a taxi, for you ought to be getting along. Never know who may come here later."

* * * * *

Charles and Henry sat in the kitchen. Charles on the table, Henry on the chair. Henry's nose was red and his eyes watery.

"You could 'ave knocked me down with a daffodil when the 'orspital rings through to say she's gone. She goes off with 'er little suitcase just as if she was off for the day. Do you s'pose she knew?"

"Of course. She fixed every damn thing with my father."

"No! An' she so set on you and all."

"That's why. She spoke to him about Miss Julie and myself, and arranged things so that some day Miss Julie would have some money of her own." He offered Henry a cigarette. "She's left you 'The Goat in Gaiters.'"

Henry's head shot up.

"That she never!"

"Truth. There's a tag to it. The Frossarts are to live there with you, for as long as they care to stay; she hoped you would make up to them for losing those sons of theirs. You have to keep the horses, and when they retire the fourteen greyhounds . . ."

"They won't never retire, not if I know Perce, they won't."

"Perhaps she thought of that one. She told my father there was no need to worry about Perce, you'd see after him."

"That's a cert, that is. What about Gamblers' Luck? Miss Julie 'avin' that?"

"Some day Miss Julie comes into the lot, but all she gets now is the lease of this place. Mrs. Gladys Smith is to live for life in number one Lipton Grove, Paddington, and she also gets the proceeds from Gamblers' Luck Limited for her lifetime, the proceeds to be used for the benefit of four ladies whose names I forget."

Henry's eyes widened.

"They aren't called Dorrie, Eunice, an' . . ."

Charles stopped him.

"That's them. Who are they?"

Henry was speechless for a moment.

"'o'd have thought it of 'er! When did she see 'em? They're Jane Shores, or was, they're gettin' on now."

Charles slid off the table.

"That's the lot. Except money for Mr. Hilton's stone and a wish to be buried near him."

Henry swallowed. He took a furious puff at his cigarette.

"Left nothin' for a stone for 'erself I s'pose. Still, I've got a nice piece what I can spend on one. Might 'ave an angel pointin' up, she'd like that."

Charles got up. He whistled to disguise the fact that he was moved.

"She could have a hell of a great stone, we'd all see to it, but she wouldn't like it. She left a wish that if there was money for a little stone, all that should be written on it was, 'She hath done what she could.'"

www.ingramcontent.com/pod-product-compliance
Ingram Content Group UK Ltd.
Pitfield, Milton Keynes, MK11 3LW, UK
UKHW040642280225
455688UK00003B/82